MW01491429

PRAISE FOR ROAD

This is a wild ride fueled by fun and faith. You may want to find your old junker, load up your pals, hit the road and hope for the best. Mario Villella and Marian Rizzo have delivered an adventure with smiles.

~Dave Schlenker
humor columnist and author of
Little Man, Big Mouth
30 Years: Newspaper and Magazine Columns
by an Average Dad in Cargo Shorts.

I have known and admired Marian Rizzo for over thirty years. She is a great mother and an incredible writer. I have enjoyed her past novels and *Road Trip*, co-written with Mario Villella, may be the best yet. Their imagery puts the reader right in the middle of the story.

~Bobby Goldsboro
entertainer, song writer, wildlife artist

novel. A truly astonishing survival tale of ministry and marriage will keep you from putting this book down.

~Pastor Wayne King
48 years of pastoral ministry and church planting

If you are looking for a spine-tingling novel that touches on the reality of spiritual warfare in the church today pick this up! Great warnings of dabbling in the darkness are arrayed against the faithful preaching of the gospel. Don't miss [Presence in the Pew].

~Art Ayris
Kingstone Studios

[In Search of Felicity] gives voice to those of us who find inspiration and insight into our own lives through great works of literature. Rizzo's work will resonate with Rawlings fans and even those who will take up her books for the first time.

~Florence M. Turcotte
literary manuscripts archivist
George A. Smathers Libraries
University of Florida, Gainesville

Truth be told, I am not a novel guy. But I have to admit, Marian Rizzo's In Search of the Beloved drew me in from the first page. I love how she weaved her characters in and out of the search for the Apostle John. Great read.

~Dr. Woodrow Kroll
Creator of The HELIOS Project
Radio host, Back to the Bible

Marian Rizzo is a gifted storyteller, whether it be for news reporting or fiction. She has a keen eye and ear for the intricacies of a story, which translates into very powerful narratives. Marian can turn the mundane into the magnificent through the masterful weaving of character, context, and scene-setting.

~Susan Smiley-Height
Longtime journalist and editor in the newspaper industry

Plague thoughtfully presents the emotional trauma and feelings of helplessness healthcare workers experience while caring for the sick and dying. Its poignancy and vivid exposition highlights how little has changed over the last 100 years of responding to pandemics.

~David Kuhn, M.D.

Faith yields courage is what strikes me most about *Plague*. Marian Rizzo skillfully takes us back a century to remind us we are not the first to pray for God's protection of America's brave doctors and nurses, or who had such a desperate need of their aid.

~Gerry Harlan Brown
author of *White Squirrels and Other Monsters*

Plague is historic fiction at its most timely! Marian Rizzo's narrative style is perfectly suited for this clinical yet intimate perspective on how the invisible threats among us tear at family and society. This family drama is wonderfully told from the perspective of a nurse and mother married to the town physician as they witness their community besieged by the deadliest flu in American history.

~Aaron Shaver
PR guide
Author of *Furious* and other works.

ROAD TRIP

Also by Marian Rizzo

Angela's Treasures
Muldovah
In Search of the Beloved
In Search of Felicity
Presence in the Pew
Plague
O Holy Night: A Christmas Gift Book
The Legacy of Mrs. Cunningham
In the Boat with Jesus
Silver Springs (with Dr. Robert Knight)

Also by Mario Villella

Working Our Way Through Life
It Takes Two to Tangle.

ROAD TRIP

a novel

Marian Rizzo *[signature]*

MARIAN RIZZO & MARIO VILLELLA

WordCrafts Press

Published by WordCrafts Press
Cody, Wyoming 82414
www.wordcrafts.net

Mario is dedicating this book to Wifey, Ocean, Bubby, Muffin, and the Triumvirate.

Marian is dedicating this book to her sisters, Theresa and Rose.

You'll travel safely, you'll neither tire nor trip ... Because God will be right there with you; he'll keep you safe and sound.
~Proverbs 3:23, 26 MSG

Prologue

Twenty-five years have passed since I joined up with two of my best buddies for a cross-country road trip from Gainesville, Florida, to the waterfront in San Francisco. Three guys—3,000 miles—on $300 apiece. It seemed impossible.

Well, we did it, and despite some near-death experiences, I'm still here to talk about it. Believe it or not, Jamal, Sean, and I have remained friends, though there were times when at least one of us wanted to strangle the other two or take off running and never look back.

Sometimes, I mentally relive our trip. I laugh over the ridiculous things we did, and I cringe as I recall the dangerous moments, most of them brought on by our own stupidity.

We were three college students on spring break, taking time off from our part-time jobs, blazing an unfamiliar trail in an older model, silver-gray Honda Accord that boasted good gas mileage and windows that still went up and down. Undaunted, we trusted the $900 we had between us to take us to the West Coast and back home to Florida. Truthfully, at times, we didn't know for certain if we'd get home in one piece, and there were other times when we didn't think we'd get home at all.

I'm a married man now, with a family and a good job. I'm comfortable, happy, and blessed beyond my wildest dreams. Sometimes, however, I look back at that road trip, inhale a breath of nostalgia, and I ask myself, if I had the chance, would I do it again?

You bet I would.

Charlie Black

Chapter One

Gainesville, Florida, Spring Break, 1998

It was 5:30 in the morning. I glanced at the clock, then rolled over and squeezed my eyes shut. Then, I remembered. The road trip! My eyelids popped open, and I sprang from my bed. Right about then, my nosy roommate let out a sleep snort on the other side of the room. I froze. Hank had been asking me what was up. No way did I want to tell him I was heading for California.

Holding my breath, I dashed around the apartment on tiptoe and gathered my stuff. Have you ever tried to dash around quietly? Let me tell you, it's possible.

With everything in hand, I tiptoed into the hall. For a split second I was tempted to slam the door, but I thought better of it. Self-discipline is the hardest thing to master, isn't it?

As planned, I entered the parking lot at 6 a.m. and found my two best friends leaning against my '85 Honda Accord, which I'd fondly dubbed the Silver Bullet. Freshly washed and waxed, she sparkled like a shiny chariot beneath the light of a streetlamp. I could almost hear the theme song from *Back to the Future* playing somewhere in the ozone layer.

We stuffed our bags in the hatchback, then each of us counted our money in front of the other two. We had $300 apiece, give or take a few bucks. I placed mine back inside the tube sock where I'd been storing it. Sean crammed his stack of $20 bills inside his leather wallet. And Jamal? His mama had given him the tiniest little safe I'd ever seen. She must have found it in the novelty shop at the mall. Sean and I shared a laugh, but Jamal, looking quite serious, slid his cash inside the safe, and, narrowing his eyes at us, he locked the door with a loud click.

3

"I'll put it in the trunk under our clothes," he said with a nod. He eyed each of us and added, "I'll keep the key on myself—at all times."

Like he couldn't trust us. His mama must have lectured him real good before he went to bed last night. I shrugged, not willing to make an issue of something that dumb.

Not that we didn't trust each other. We knew we could. But it's an unwritten law amongst twenty-year-old males that we look like we don't trust anyone, even when we do.

Before we hit the road I used some duct tape to attach an auto bra to the front of the Silver Bullet. I'd made it out of an old pillow case on which I'd inked the words, CALIFORNIA OR BUST!

As we started out with me driving, adrenaline surged through my blood. The road ahead looked inviting, like it had been waiting for three trailblazers to come along, exactly like us—fearless, undaunted, maybe even a little daft.

For the past three years, I'd been following the same routine. Classes in the morning, stocking shelves at Walmart in the afternoon, and squeezing in a few hours with my girlfriend on weekends. Except for seeing Heather, I needed a vacation from everything else, and spring break offered the perfect time to claim it.

I suspected my two best friends felt the same. There we were—Jamal Waters, Sean Murphy, and myself, Charlie Black. What an unlikely trio.

I met Jamal on the basketball court in our sophomore year. I was tall. Six feet and 160 pounds, so skinny when I looked in the mirror with my shirt off, I could count my ribs. Jamal towered over me by four inches and looked like a human string bean with dreadlocks. He played basketball better than I did and dreamed about a future in pro ball. I wanted to be an architect, if and when I grew up.

Then there was Sean Murphy, a true Irishman if I ever met one, from his flame-red hair and intense green eyes to his collection of Ireland-themed T-shirts. He sometimes hit us with expressions his father used at home, like "Don't be an eejit," instead of "idiot," and "It's all grand," whenever he was pleased about something. At five feet, six inches, and weighing 230 pounds, Sean stood out like a sore thumb whenever he walked between Jamal and me—two tall bookends and one thick, squatty book between us.

Sean wore solid green T-shirts silkscreened with the flag of Ireland and bearing slogans like, "Top o' the mornin'," and "May the road rise up to meet you."

It was that *road* T-shirt that got me thinking the three of us should take a little trip. I presented the idea to the two of them one day during a quick lunch in the college dining hall.

"How about it, guys?" I said. "Let's do something ambitious for spring break. Let's take a long-distance road trip."

"What-a ya mean, Charlie? Like to Miami?" Sean said, wrinkling his nose at me.

"No, my friend. To San Francisco. We can drive across the country and be back in school in two weeks. I've already calculated the mileage."

I raised my eyebrows and waited for a response. They looked frozen, like two Siberian icemen, Jamal's beady black eyes and Sean's two emerald lasers boring holes in me.

"C'mon, you two," I urged. "It could be fun."

Jamal was the first to awaken from his trance. "Yeah," he said, kind of slow, like he hadn't yet wrapped his mind around the idea. "I'm game."

Sean gave a shrug. "Okay. If you guys are goin', I don't want to be left behind. I'll give it a lash."

If I hadn't been hanging around him and his family for more than a year, I'd need an interpreter to figure out the little expressions he threw into our conversations now and then.

We all agreed. The road trip was a go. Fired up, I plunged into my studies like our road trip depended on my getting good grades. I also needed to spend more time with Heather—had to protect my turf. I'd be leaving the next couple of weekends open for Robby Richards to worm his way into my girlfriend's heart. I'd caught him staring at her in the library one day, like he was waiting for me to walk out so he could make his move.

Heather and I had been dating for about eighteen months. I

hadn't thought much about marriage, although, if I'd been ready at the time, I would have picked Heather. For the moment, we had a sort of understanding. I wanted Robby to *understand* that too.

I chose the perfect moment to tell Heather about the trip. It was Sunday morning, and we had just come out of church. I suggested we take a stroll in a nearby park. In the light of the midday sun, Heather's blonde hair glowed like a halo. I took her hand and gazed into her sky-blue eyes. At five feet, ten inches, she didn't have to stand on tiptoe to kiss me, unlike my last girlfriend, Bunny, a dwarf of a female with a two-second fuse.

Bunny would never have stood for me runnin' off with my buddies. I'd seen her blow her cork over lesser issues, like when I accidentally spilled a chocolate milkshake down the front of her blouse. Believe me, I didn't do it because she'd called me a stupid bore when I told her I wanted to take golf lessons. It was an accident. Honest. A vacation—like the one my friends and I were planning—would have sent her over the wall. Needless to say, our relationship didn't last long.

But Heather wasn't at all like Bunny. She had a gentler reaction to the road trip.

"I'm gonna miss you," she said, her lower lip trembling. Then, her forehead wrinkled a little, like she was waiting for me to say something equally romantic.

I shrugged. "It's a guy thing," I said. "When the spirit of adventure calls, we answer."

She gazed at me with moisture in her eyes.

"It's not like I'm going to Afghanistan," I assured her. "There's no need to tie a yellow ribbon around the old oak tree. I'll be home in two weeks."

We ended our walk in the park with an invisible wall between us. Heather didn't say anything negative. She didn't have to. She said more by the way she slipped her hand out of mine and walked two feet ahead of me. Though rivers of guilt traveled up my spine to my brain, I stood my ground, determined to go on a road trip with my two best buddies. They didn't try to control me with tears in their eyes and quiet pouting. No sir. Guys controlled each other in a different way. With muscle. With an arm lock or a half nelson. Outsmarting females presented an entirely different challenge.

We reached Heather's front porch. She turned to face me, her eyes swimming in tears. "Will you do something for me?" she murmured.

"Sure," I said, though I had concerns about what she might ask.

"Will you bring me a bottle of Pacific Ocean water?"

At first I thought, *Well, that's a silly request.* Then I looked into her imploring face, and I caved. If that's all my girlfriend wanted, I certainly could get a bottle of ocean water for her. One more reason to make it to the West Coast.

Meanwhile, keeping the road trip a secret from my roommate turned into a real challenge. Already, he'd been skulking about the apartment, passing my desk and craning his neck. Feeling much like a CIA agent, I hid the road maps and my mileage calculations inside a folder, which I slipped under my mattress, and I left useless class notes strewn across my desk. This must have thrown him off some, because he stopped skulking and took to sitting on the edge of his bed, watching my every move.

With budget being our biggest issue, the three of us needed to make a definite plan. Up until then, we'd been meeting in the school dining hall and the library, which didn't allow us much privacy. My roommate kept hanging around us, like he wanted to find out what all the whispering was about. Whenever we caught sight of Hank, the three of us clammed up and shifted our conversation to classes and the weather. We didn't want him horning in on our trip. For that reason, we couldn't meet at my apartment either.

It isn't that we hated the guy, we just didn't think of him as a real person, at least not anybody we wanted to hang out with. For one thing, he had almost no personality. He talked ad nauseam about boring court cases he'd read about in his law books. Besides, as far as I could tell, the guy rarely bathed or brushed his teeth. Who'd want to travel with him for two weeks?

I might have moved out of that apartment, except my mom had forked over nine months' rent to get me out of the house and on my own. She'd paid the landlord directly. Next semester, when

I have to foot the bill myself, you can bet I'll be out of there and living alone—if I can afford it.

Anyway, after classes ended on Friday, the three of us met at McDonald's, huddled in a corner booth over three kid's meals, and talked about our road trip, less than a week away. A family of five sat in the next booth. The parents had ordered gigantic three-story hamburgers that made my mouth water, and the kids hovered over meals that looked an awful lot like the pressed particleboard we'd settled for. If I hadn't been saving my money for the trip, I might have sprung for one of those three-story burgers.

Budgeting had presented a real problem. Not as much for me, since I'd been living on ramen noodles and whatever the college dining hall served. But my two friends still lived at home and had grown up on wholesome meals their mothers prepared.

Since math was my best subject and I believed I had this little internal accountant living inside me, I assumed leadership over the budget. One of the first things that came up involved transportation. At the time, we hadn't settled on taking the Bullet.

"We can use my dad's extra pickup truck," offered Sean. "It's an older model Ford F-150, has a comfortable backseat and a six-foot bed where we can put a mattress for sleeping."

I thought about Jamal being six-four with his feet dangling off the end, but so what? Travel across the country and sleep in the back of a pickup truck? I loved the idea.

"What about rain?" Jamal wisely said. I could depend on Mr. Killjoy to think of something like rain.

Sean was quick to answer. "My uncle has a topper. We can borrow it."

Jamal shook his head and narrowed his eyes, like he'd pictured his feet hanging out in the rain.

"What's the mileage like?" he said—another smart question.

Sean frowned and thought for a minute. "I don't know. I think about eleven miles per gallon in town and maybe fourteen on the highway."

I leaned across the table, my face mere inches from Sean's. "Fourteen miles to the gallon? That heap will use up all our cash."

Sean shrugged. "We can take turns driving, so we won't have to stop as often." He raised his eyebrows and grinned. "Think about it, guys. If we *do* have to stop, we can pull off the road, sleep three across, get a few hours of shut-eye, then keep going. We won't have to stay in motels, and we'll have more money for food and gas."

I scratched my head and tried to imagine sleeping in a narrow truck bed between two sweaty college guys.

Jamal frowned and shook his head. "What about *your* car, Charlie?"

Sure, my car, suggested by a guy who rode a moped to school.

I scrambled to think up a reasonable excuse not to use the Bullet. I needed my car to get to school and to work. A 3,000-mile round trip to the coast might end its life. Still, I couldn't think of one argument in favor of Sean's truck over my car.

In the end, I had to agree, my '85 Honda Accord made more sense—financially, at least.

"It does get pretty good gas mileage—about twenty-five in town and up to thirty-nine on the highway," I admitted. "I suppose, it could save us a couple bucks."

"Then we'll have to stay in motels," Sean whined. "Not sure that's a good idea. Remember the fleabag we stayed in at the beach? It cost us $29.99 for one night. That means, every time we stop for the night, we'll have to pitch in ten bucks apiece in order to stay in more fleabags. Factor in food and gas, and all our money will be gone in less than a week. How do you expect us to get home?"

At that, I pulled out a notebook and pen. For the next five minutes, I scribbled a bunch of figures while Jamal and Sean ate up all the French fries.

"Okay," I said, sliding my calculations in front of them. "This is how much money we can save by taking my better economy car. Certainly, every town we stop at will have a motel like the fleabag. So, which is it? A fleabag motel or the back of a pickup truck?"

Sean eyed me with uncertainty. "Anything else wrong with your car besides the sagging front bumper?"

I shrugged. "A tear on one side of the backseat. Might be a good place to hide our cash. And, sorry to say, the air conditioner is temperamental, kicks on and off at times. But the windows work, so at least we won't suffocate."

I'd been excited about the truck idea, but we had to be practical. I suggested we take a vote. The decision was unanimous. The Silver Bullet won.

We then talked about what to pack, and all three agreed clean underwear was a must. So were deodorant and toothpaste. After that, the decision went to individual choice.

We left McDonald's with a plan and a purpose. Each of us had a job to do.

Jamal needed to go home, dig through a pile of boxes in the basement, and look for an Atlas his mom had stashed down there. That woman never threw anything out.

I needed to hit an Interstate gas station that still carried road maps. A good road map could serve as a backup to the Atlas. Meanwhile, Sean agreed to sit at his computer and print out a MapQuest of our entire trip. He ended up with nine pages of routing.

Remember, this was before GPS and Google maps. It might have been overkill, but whatever happened, we didn't want to get lost somewhere in the desert and have to backtrack. Not on our budget.

I also had to service my car—you know, oil change, full tank of gas, air in tires, check the water. And I packed an emergency kit with extra spark plugs and a screw driver. I also put a bottle of distilled water in the trunk, in case the radiator overheated.

I gave the Silver Bullet a good wash and cleaned out the inside, tossed out the fast food wrappers, and vacuumed the seats. Then, I applied fresh duct tape to her sagging front bumper and I whispered a promise to have it repaired when we got home.

As far as I could see, the Bullet was ready for a cross-country road trip. All I had to do now was drive.

Chapter Two

Our next covert meeting took place at a Burger King over a kid's meal we shared in order to save money for the trip. This time, the three of us had gotten together to talk about how our respective families had received the news about our planned trip.

Jamal shook his head despondently. "Mama lost it. Know what I'm sayin'? She really lost it."

Then, raising his voice an octave and wringing his hands, he mimicked his mama's reaction. "'Oh, Lord, please, knock some sense in my boy. He's plannin' to head out to a wild and dangerous territory. Where will he lay his head at night? On a hard rock in the wilderness? At the base of a prickly, old cactus plant? What about the rattlesnakes and mountain lions? And the outlaws and cattle rustlers and gunslingers?'"

I suspected Mama Waters must have watched old westerns on TV while cooking and cleaning the house. I stifled a snicker and waited for Jamal to finish his account.

At that point, he changed his voice back to his own. "I told her, 'Mama, we're not goin' on a cattle drive. We'll be in a car most of the time. And I'm not gonna lay my head on a rock in the wilderness. The three of us are plannin' to stay in motels. We'll be warm and dry and safe. And guess what? There are no outlaws or gunslingers, these days, and no wild beasts where we're goin'. Before you know it, those two weeks will fly by, and I'll be home and back in school.'" He smiled a big smile of victory. "I think she bought it," he said.

Being twenty-one years old and the eldest of four children, Jamal didn't need anyone's permission. But he and his mama had shared a special bond since his father passed away, and out of courtesy he checked with her before doing anything out of the ordinary. Except maybe that one time the three of us climbed to the top of the Belleview water tower and left our own artwork amidst the graffiti others had already plastered up there.

Did that mean Jamal couldn't go on our trip? Not a chance. Somehow, he'd convinced his mama he'd be super careful, he'd stay out of the saloons, and he'd avoid strangers who wore a bandana and carried a gun.

Sean's mother had a different reaction. The youngest of seven children, Sean ate more than the rest of his siblings put together. His mother wasted no time helping him pack.

"You need to take this and this and this," she'd said, tossing handfuls of clean underwear and socks at him.

She even contributed fifty bucks to his road trip fund. On top of that, his brothers kicked in a few dollars each. It sounded to me like the whole family wanted to be rid of him for a while. Or maybe they simply wanted him to have fun.

Sean's father also gave a thumbs up and insisted the trip might do his son good.

"Give it a lash," Joe Murphy told Sean. "It's time you got out in the world and found out what it's like. You'll leave home a boy, and you'll come home a man. And may the road rise up to meet you." Then he tipped a Guinness to his lips and went back to his pot roast.

To Sean, it was as if his father had waved a checkered flag. He sprang from his seat at the table and raced to his room to start packing, even though our trip was still four days away.

As Sean recounted the moment, I pictured the warmth and understanding that traveled between him and his parents, and a flicker of envy overtook me. My two friends enjoyed a family connection I'd missed for most of my life. My older sister left home when I was a freshman in high school. Our dad had already walked out when I was twelve. All I had left to remember him by was a wrinkled photo of a man who looked like an older version of me. I had his same thick, black hair, hazel eyes, and broad jaw. The main difference was, my father was clean-shaven, and I had grown a goatee and a mustache, admittedly, a vain attempt to cover up any resemblance I shared with the man who'd begotten and then abandoned me. To a certain extent, it worked, but I couldn't cover up the pain that still lingered inside.

I grew up with no father to guide me. No dad to take me fishing or boating. By the time I reached my junior year in high school, my mother had remarried and shortly after divorced again. When I started college, she began taking cruises and overseas trips with a guy named Jack. I hardly saw her anymore.

It wasn't that she didn't love me. My birthday cards said she did. So did the three thousand dollars she'd paid to get me out on my own and into an apartment for nine months.

Strangely, I'd grown up thinking my home life was like everyone else's. Husbands and wives yelling at each other. Kids lying in bed at night covering their ears. Dads walking out and moms crying behind closed bedroom doors. And some of us having to grow up way too soon.

Then I met Jamal's mama. Though widowed and trying to raise four kids by herself, that big, black bundle of joy never treated Jamal like he was an inconvenience. She lavished him with love and attention, had to know everything that went on at school, and ordered him to tuck in his shirt and wash his hands for supper, like he hadn't even reached puberty yet. I might have deemed all that pampering a little embarrassing if I didn't long for some of it myself.

I experienced a similar awakening the first day I went to Sean's home for supper. His older brothers kept roughing up his mop of red hair. His older sisters teased him about one of his classmates, Erin Hagelmeyer. His face flushed a deep red, and his green eyes shot fiery darts at his siblings, but he didn't speak up and defend himself, just reveled in all the attention they poured on him.

I took it all in with a mix of envy for Sean and pity for myself. What I wouldn't give to have a family like his. A mother and father who honored their marriage vows, and brothers and sisters close to my own age, so I could banter with them, and play games with them, even share a bedroom if necessary, and borrow money from them, like Sean often did.

In a way, I lived that missing part of my life through my two buddies. Their families made me feel welcome whenever I went to their homes. They never failed to invite me to their table. "Always room for one more," they told me. And the food? To die for.

I began to feel like a member of two other families. Jamal and Sean had become like brothers to me, in more ways than one. Now, the upcoming trip promised to cement our friendship even more.

Unlike my two friends, I didn't think I needed to tell my mother about the trip, but I did it anyway. I didn't expect the kind of resistance Mama Waters gave Jamal. Didn't expect a rallying approval like Sean received. I only hoped for something in between.

But when I told my mother about the road trip, she gazed at me in disbelief.

"You? Drive that beat-up, old car of yours all the way to California?" Then she laughed. Not a, *Ha, ha, that's sweet,* kind of laugh, but one that made me want to crawl under the sofa and never come out.

So far, I hadn't done much to impress her. My grades could be better. I wasn't the best athlete in school, didn't even make the team that year. And I hadn't shown any promise of a future career, though I'd been leaning toward architecture, but she even snickered about that. After graduation, I'd have four years of graduate school in front of me—four more years of feeling like a failure.

I left my mother's house convinced she disapproved of the road trip. The smirk on her lips and the roll of her eyes said it all.

At twenty-one years old, I finally understood what leaving with your tail tucked between your legs meant. If I had a tail, that's exactly where it would have been.

To save myself from utter defeat, I'd developed a theory about life. When things don't go the way you plan, it helps to set your mind on something positive. My psych professor kept saying something like that in class, and I never forgot his message for some reason. Now I knew why. His philosophy on life had turned into a sort of mantra for me. But I couldn't go around reciting such long sentences, so I worked on an alternative and came up with, *It is what it is.*

I drove away from my mother's house with those words swirling around in my head. "It is what it is," I kept saying to myself.

I could apply that mantra to almost every part of my life—my grades; my work at Walmart; even my relationship with Heather.

As the day of our departure grew closer, I couldn't leave without visiting her one more time. While I drove to her house, I kept repeating my mantra over and over again. "It is what it is. It is what it is."

I parked out front and made a little detour to her neighbor's yard, where I picked a handful of daisies. Mrs. Green would never miss them. That woman's front yard had more flower beds than the entrance to Epcot.

When Heather opened the front door, I thrust my slapdash bouquet at her and gave her my biggest grin. Instead of making her smile with glee, my little gesture brought on an unexpected gusher. She flung her arms around my neck. I didn't know what else to do, so I patted her shoulder and waited it out. Isn't that how most guys respond to their girlfriends' emotional outbursts?

Eventually, she backed away from me, clutched the flowers to her chest, and collapsed on the front porch swing. I joined her and flung an arm around her shoulder.

"I've been trying to accept the fact that you're leaving in two days," she murmured. "I didn't think you were serious. And, Charlie, it could be dangerous." Now she was starting to sound like Jamal's mama.

I clambered for something I could say to ease her mind but came up empty, so I repeated what Jamal said to his mama.

"Heather, I'll be inside my car most of the time. And I don't expect we'll run into any outlaws or gunslingers or wild animals. I'll be home in two weeks." I held up two fingers. "Two weeks."

There. That should do it. Instead, she started weeping all over again, and I suspected it wasn't only because of the trip. I hadn't yet told her I loved her. Those three little words sometimes seeped out of my brain, but they never made it past my lips.

It's true, I'd been experiencing the onset of cold feet lately. For some reason, I couldn't bring myself to go to the next level in our relationship. With graduate school still in front of me, I needed to stay focused on my studies, needed to become an architect and bring home a good salary. Only then would I be ready for a solid commitment. I struggled to find the right words. I had no choice but to fall back on my mantra.

"It is what it is," I said, though it came out pathetically weak.

"Huh?" She frowned in puzzlement.

At least she stopped crying.

I was concerned her parents might hear all the commotion out there and wonder if I might be hurting their little girl. I didn't want to get on their bad side. Her folks had been missionaries to Brazil. They came home when Heather entered college. Now they served as counselors in their church. And me? I'd been trying to convince them their daughter had found a good, church-going guy who treated her with respect.

Heather looked down at the bouquet. "They're so beautiful," she cooed, and I couldn't help but think that she was beautiful too.

She turned her tear-filled eyes at me, and I almost gave up the road trip altogether. A lump came to my throat, and I couldn't speak, an unusual condition for me.

"You don't even have a cell phone, Charlie."

I shook my head. "No," I said, with genuine sadness. "They're too expensive."

Remember, this was 1998, and flip phones cost around $1,000 at the time. Plus, a cell phone owner had limited hours, and long-distance calls could put you in the poor house.

Heather brightened. "Daddy said he'll allow you two collect calls, but they can only be for ten minutes each."

I smiled. *What a guy,* I thought. *He must like me, after all.*

"That's nice of him," I said aloud. "I'll call on a motel phone in a couple of days. And again when we're on our way home."

She rested her head on my shoulder, and something akin to wanting the moment to last forever stirred within me.

Then she sat up straight and smiled.

"Wait here," she said, rising. "I'll be right back."

She disappeared inside the house with the flowers and two minutes later came back without the flowers but holding an empty Zephyr Hills water bottle.

I stared at it, amused. What on earth did she want me to do with an empty water bottle?

"I drank this today," she announced. And I thought, *So?* But, I didn't say anything, just stared at the bottle, dumbfounded, like a kid opening a Christmas present and finding pajamas inside.

"It's for your trip, silly." She shoved the bottle at me.

I took it, but gazed with confusion at her glowing face.

"Have you forgotten already?" she moaned. "You're supposed to get me some Pacific Ocean water."

Light bulb! I had clean forgotten my promise. More proof I wasn't ready for commitment. If I forgot a dumb little thing like a bottle of water, how could I promise anything *really* big?

"Oh, yeah," I managed. "I wasn't sure what kind of bottle might work." It was lame, I know, but I didn't want to set her off crying again. I held up the bottle and admired it. "This is perfect," I said, and Heather beamed with delight.

The rest of our evening went beautifully, and all because of an empty Zephyr Hills water bottle. Every time I thought Heather might lose it again, I held up the bottle and made some trite comment about what a nice bottle she'd given me, and how it could hold a good amount of ocean water, and I couldn't wait to bring it back to her, filled and ready for her to display somewhere in her bedroom, knowing I had been thinking about her the whole time I carried it back from the coast.

Before I left, I went inside and visited briefly with Heather's parents. Her mother gushed all over me and said what a brave young man I was to go off on such an adventure. Tears trickled down her cheeks. I turned anxious eyes on Heather and caught her wiping her cheeks, too. The two of them looked like they'd been to a funeral.

Meanwhile, Heather's nine-year-old brother, Josh, jumped up and down, begging to go with us, but his mom placed a firm hand on his shoulder and put a halt to his squealing and bouncing.

Then her dad pumped my hand and smiled. "You know," he said, and it looked like his eyes had begun to water too. "A trip like that will be good for you. That's the kind of experience that prepares a young man for missionary work."

I swallowed hard. I had never pictured myself as a missionary, but, oh well. I wasn't about to correct the guy. After all, my future with Heather depended on his acceptance.

Mrs. Mills handed me a bag of chocolate chip cookies, and Heather gave me six power bars. "To start your trip," she said. "If I know you, you'll get on the road long before the fast food restaurants open."

In the privacy of a front porch that was lit up like floodlights on a prison yard, I kissed Heather good-bye. Out of the blue she quoted a familiar verse from Proverbs: "Trust in the Lord with all your heart, and do not rely on your own understanding; think about Him in all your ways, and He will guide you on the right paths." Then she tearfully waved me off, and I sprinted away from where I'd been to where I was going.

Chapter Three

The night before our trip, I walked around inside my apartment filling my suitcase and a duffel bag with clothes and anything else I thought I might need during a two-week adventure. With a little smugness filtering into my head, I left my bags standing by the front door, right where Hank could trip over them when he came in late that night. I no longer cared if he suspected something was up. I was leaving the next morning, and he'd just have to guess where I went.

As expected, a few hours later, he came staggering in, stumbled over my bags, and grumbled. He managed to hit the light switch.

"What's this?"

I sat up in bed. "What's what?"

"This duffel bag. Why's it sittin' right here where someone can trip over it? And, what's it stuffed with?"

"Who wants to know?" I said, grinning like a Cheshire Cat.

"I do. What's goin' on, Charlie?"

"Oh, I don't know. I may have to make a quick escape. I want to be prepared."

For some reason, he bought it, didn't ask another question, just fell on his bed, and thirty seconds later he was snoring like a turbo-prop on takeoff.

I'd gotten so wired up about the trip, I expected I'd have a hard time getting to sleep that night, so I took one of Hank's sleep aids. I rarely did this, but I had agreed to be the first one driving, and I needed to get a good night's rest.

The sleep aid did its job. I slept easier, didn't have another thought about family issues or the lack of them, stopped worrying about Heather and Robby Richards moving in on her. I fell into dreamland with nothing but a cross-country road trip on my mind.

I woke with a start at 5:30 and got ready to leave. I met the guys in the parking lot at six. Since we started out before any fast food places opened, as Heather had wisely predicted, we munched on her power bars and Mrs. Mills' cookies for the first two hours of our trip. Right off, I told Sean, "No smoking in my car." He'd been chompin' on the stem of his Peterson pipe as if he wanted to light up. I glared at him in the rearview mirror.

"I know, Charlie," he groaned from the backseat. "I've ridden with you before."

Still, the guy needed reminding at times.

Jamal winked at me from the passenger seat. He didn't smoke or drink, and, as far as I knew, he'd never even tried pot. Not so much to please his mother, but he told me a couple times that he wanted to please God, a confirmation that he truly did walk the talk. His well-worn Bible sat on the dashboard right in front of him, but he rarely needed to open it. Depending on the situation, Jamal spontaneously quoted verses from memory, and I sometimes questioned whether he needed to carry a Bible at all. It appeared he knew most of it by heart. To be honest, having no male role model in my life, if I wanted to be like anyone else, I'd most likely pick Jamal.

Before starting out, we made a few additional rules besides the *no smoking* I'd levied on Sean. Whoever rode in the passenger seat maintained control of the radio, but please consider the ears of the other riders. We'd pool our money for gas whenever we stopped to fuel up, and we'd buy our own food, sharing only when the situation called for it. We needed to rotate drivers. When one got tired, one of the other two had to take over. That way we could cover more miles each day.

Since I drove first, Jamal had charge of the radio. I already knew he liked gospel, so it didn't surprise me when CeCe Winans' honey-coated voice came over the airwaves. Sean had already told us he liked country music and couldn't wait until we got out west. As for me, I kind of liked the Golden Oldies for some reason I couldn't explain. My mom used to play lots of Elvis and Pat Boone favorites while she puttered around in the kitchen, making supper or sometimes a batch of chocolate chip cookies. Maybe that's why I still held onto that music. It brought back the few pleasant memories I had.

We'd been on I-75 heading north for a while, and Jamal had run through an entire repertoire of gospel songs. I'd begun to sing along with his choices, when something rancid tickled my nose. The smell of burnt bicycle chains filtered into the car and what looked like smoke rose up from under the front hood.

I darted into the right hand lane, cutting off an old woman in a Chevy, and pulled onto the soft shoulder. After blaring her horn at me, the woman took off, swerving from one side of the road to the other, like she'd lost control of her vehicle. I flinched and mumbled, "Sorry."

I shut down the Silver Bullet and hopped out. Holding my breath, I carefully lifted the hood. Expecting flames to leap out at me, I jumped back, but only steam spewed from my radiator in a big, billowing cloud of water vapor.

As I stood there scratching my head, a sleek, black BMW pulled off the highway in front of us. An older man in a business suit got out. He was laughing heartily as he strode toward my car. When he got close, he pointed at my pillow case sign.

"So, you're heading west, young man?" he said, still chuckling.

I nodded sheepishly.

"Well, son, if you want to get there, you're gonna have to get rid of that public announcement. It's blocking the air flow to your engine."

It struck me then that my *California or Bust* sign nearly busted our entire trip. Jamal got to work pulling off the duct tape, and together we crumpled up the old pillow case and stuffed it on the floor of the back seat where Sean sat, stifling a laugh. His face was so puckered up, he couldn't talk, couldn't even call me an *eejit* for almost destroying my car's engine and leaving us stranded fifty miles from home. If he'd said anything, I would have reminded him of the time he almost trashed his father's truck by putting the wrong fuel in it.

"You got water?" the older gentleman said.

I nodded, grateful for the jug I'd placed in the trunk.

"Wait about twenty minutes and let everything cool down, then slowly remove the radiator cap and add the water," the guy said, looking like he might bust out laughing again. "You might want to wear gloves or hold a piece of cloth in your hand so you won't get burned. Otherwise, you're gonna have another problem. Like maybe a trip to the emergency room."

He walked back to his fancy car, his shoulders shaking like he was having a good laugh at my expense.

Though it meant wasting precious time, I did what the man said, knowing that *another problem* could involve second-degree burns. After dumping the entire jug of water in the radiator, we took off again, this time without letting the public know where we were heading.

A short time later, we caught I-10 westbound. By the time we got a little past Tallahassee, Sean started to complain about his empty stomach. I couldn't help but agree. The only thing all those cookies had given me was a temporary sugar high. Then, I plummeted. Now, I was afraid I might pass out.

"There! Let's stop there," Sean said, lunging from the backseat and pointing through the windshield.

Up ahead, about 500 yards, stood an old-time diner—silver with a horizontal red stripe painted across the front. A sign out front said, **What's Cookin' Diner.** The gravel parking lot was packed with cars and trucks of all makes and models, evidence that the food must be good. I pulled into the lot, looked for a spot, and managed to squeeze my Honda between two semis.

Sean leaped from the car and raced up the walk to the diner's front door. Jamal and I sauntered up behind him. As we entered, the aroma of grilled hamburgers and fried potatoes struck me. Sadly, our budget didn't allow for such an indulgence. We had to settle for the cheapest thing on the menu, maybe even share a sandwich three ways.

A juke box was playing Willie Nelson's "Always on my Mind," and for a second I traveled back to Gainesville and Heather's front porch. I let out a sigh. Jamal poked me in the arm and winked like he understood.

We had to wait a good twenty minutes for someone to clear
a booth, then we grabbed it before the waitress had a chance to
wipe the crumbs off the table. Her name tag said, **Lilly Mae**, and
she smiled, which told me she didn't mind us sitting there while
she swept away the dirty dishes and wiped down our table with a
sopping wet rag that looked like it had been used to wipe down a
hundred other tables.

At that moment I didn't care about hygiene, and apparently
neither did Sean, who was already looking over the menu.

I waited until Lilly Mae walked away, then I lowered my voice
to a whisper. "Guys," I said. "Need I remind you we're on a budget?"

Jamal frowned at me. "Killjoy," he said.

Sean acted like he hadn't heard me at all. He ogled the selections
like a kid choosing a new bike.

I elbowed his arm. "Check out the dollar menu. The all-you-can-
eat chili special looks reasonable enough. Three bucks and it comes
with crackers and coffee. And we can get refills on everything."

It wasn't until after we had enjoyed the lunch special that I realized we may have overextended. Three dollars a meal meant by the
end of the trip we each would have spent $170 on food alone. A
huge chunk out of our budget had gone for chili and coffee. If we
kept eating like that, there'd be nothing left for lodging and gas.

"I suggest we stop at grocery stores and load up on supplies," I said
after we got settled in the car, burping and rubbing our stomachs.
"That way, we can cut our meal expenses down to a few dollars a day."

Jamal gave me a nod. Sean let out a groan from the backseat.

As we continued along I-10, the car's supply of fuel dropped
below a quarter tank. First chance I got, I pulled up to a convenience
store that had two pumps. At $1.06 a gallon, it meant we'd have
to contribute $4.36 apiece, another painful cut out of our budget.

The inside of my car had been filling up with a different kind
of gas, so I suggested we all use the bathroom before taking off
again. The stop made all the difference in the world. With the air
conditioner cranked up to full force, I found I could take a deep
breath again.

At one of our meetings last week, we'd sketched out a rough

itinerary. We had all agreed that the more relatives we could visit along the way, the better for our budget. For our first overnight we needed to go a little past Pensacola and stay with Sean's distant cousin, Henry, and his family. I'd never met Henry, but the idea of free food and lodging appealed to me. With Sean calling out directions from the backseat, I made the appropriate turns, until we ended up on a dirt road leading to a double-wide mobile home nestled amongst oak trees on a rustic plot of ground.

To the right stood a clapboard garage with a tin roof, and out front loomed a big, red pickup truck with huge monster tires that had the chassis sitting about four feet off the ground. The rear window displayed an American flag and a large deer rifle.

Sean had failed to mention that Henry had seven kids and a bulldog of a wife. Clad in a housedress, Martha dominated the front porch, her arms crossed in front of her. She barked orders at two boys who were playing tug-o-war with a Frisbee and an aggressive Rottweiler. Kids were everywhere—climbing trees, tumbling on the lawn, jumping rope, and the littlest ones sat digging in a pile of sand that had fire ants crawling all over it. Immune to all the activity, Henry lounged on a log out front and tipped a bottle of beer to his lips.

As soon as we exited my car, Martha turned into a master sergeant, rounding up the kids and ordering them to line up and form a welcoming committee.

After the initial introductions, she sprang into action again, waving her catcher's mitt hands at the children and directing them into the house. They scrambled up the steps and hurried inside, like they knew what to expect if they didn't.

"And clean up your messes in there," she hollered after them.

Henry didn't budge until he finished his beer. Then he tossed the bottle on a pile of trash where other empties had ended up. Sean introduced him as Henry Crzanski.

"He's not Irish, is he?" I whispered to Sean.

My friend smirked at me. "Good guess, professor. No, he's not Irish. He married my cousin, Martha. But, he's the nicest guy you'll ever meet."

I had to believe him. After all, Henry had offered us free room and board for the night.

We visited for a while in the living room. The 12 X 12 space all but disappeared beneath a grouping of sofas and recliners. We had to walk sideways to get around it all and find a seat. A black-and-white *Gunsmoke* oldie flickered on the TV. The kids who had been everywhere outside were now everywhere inside, chasing each other in and out of the narrow walkways between the furniture and the walls, and tumbling on the floor at our feet when one of them caught one of the others.

The whole scene had me thinking about breaking up with Heather. What if we had a houseful of out-of-control children? What if I didn't have a decent income to feed and clothe them all? Worse yet, what if Heather ended up looking and sounding like Martha?

"What's for supper?" Henry called out.

"Chili," his wife yelled from the kitchen.

Jamal and I looked at each other, speechless. Not more than four hours ago the three of us had finished off six bowls of chili. Jamal shrugged. I sank deeper into my chair and didn't move until Martha called us to the table. Fortunately, Martha also had set out a huge platter of corn, along with a bowl of string beans, and a basket of cornbread, enough options to keep me from starving if I avoided the chili.

Suppertime got even busier in the Crzanski household. The older children argued over a TV show they'd seen about alligators, and the little ones shot spitballs across the table at each other and kicked the shins of those sitting closer. In between bites of food, I anxiously guarded my own shins.

Sean was in his element, having grown up with an equally large family. Jamal had a look of terror in his eyes. Supper at his house involved soft talking and polite passing of bowls. His Mama enforced the rules of proper table etiquette. And me? Well, my mom had drilled a few manners into my own head. Most of the time, I focused my attention on the food, finished whatever I put on my plate, and silently thanked God for what He had provided. It never mattered where I sat down to eat. Sean's cousins didn't intimidate me. I simply blocked out the noise. Living with Hank and his constant yammering had taught me that. And I kept reminding myself this was for only one evening, and it was all free.

That night, the three of us slept on sofas and chairs in the living room. The same noxious odor that had permeated my car after our chili lunch now hovered over the three of us.

When I got up the next morning, my neck was stiff, my back ached, and it felt like ginger ale was running inside the veins of my legs. I shook both legs to wake them up, did a couple stretches to shift my bones back in place, and reminded myself that the three of us had saved a chunk of dough by not having to pay for food and a motel.

After a breakfast of bacon and eggs, fried potatoes, and cinnamon buns, we patted our full stomachs, gave Martha a well-deserved hug, and expressed our gratitude to Henry.

As Jamal took the wheel and drove us away, I knew we'd never see the Crzanskis again, since our preplanned itinerary had us taking a different route home.

Still, in my side mirror, I caught sight of a man and his wife standing arm-in-arm, and seven kids milling about, huge smiles on their faces, and all of them waving good-bye like they hated to see us leave. I couldn't help but smile.

The scene carried me back to Gainesville and a lovely girl who'd waved a tearful good-bye to me from the top step of her front porch. I released a sigh. Perhaps a large family wasn't completely out of the question. I could make anything work if I set my mind to it.

Chapter Four

We'd been traveling along at a leisurely pace and had almost reached the main highway, when Jamal caught sight of a little country church and made a sharp turn into the parking lot. The white painted siding, pristine steeple, and stained glass windows spoke of the 1920s Bible belt in a day when prohibition prevailed and local residents went to church, or else.

I gasped in frustration. "What are you doing, Jamal? We have to stick to our schedule."

He ignored me, pulled into a parking spot, and opened his door.

"It's Sunday," he said, his voice soft but firm. "This looks like the church I attend back home—only this one's bigger."

With that, he exited the car. He'd gotten halfway up the walk when I lit out and hurried to catch up with him.

"This will cut a huge piece of time out of our schedule," I protested.

He kept on walking with the same determination in his eyes he displayed whenever he faced another center at the start of a basketball game. I knew then, there'd be no turning back.

Sean came up close behind us, huffing and puffing. He either didn't have an opinion, or he was too out of breath to say anything.

People spilled out of their cars and flooded past us toward the church. More came from the surrounding side streets and swarmed onto the sidewalk ahead of us, behind us, and beside us, their momentum forcing the three of us closer to the front door. The flow was so strong, we had no choice but to move forward.

I looked around at the crowd of church-goers. Everyone had dressed in their Sunday best—men in seersucker suits, bright colored ties, and wingtip shoes, and women in flowered dresses with lace trim, wide-brimmed hats with flowers circling the band, and spike heels that clicked on the sidewalk. Even the children wore their good clothes as they marched up to the church behind their parents, not a single bit of soil on their pastel pinks and blues, the boys' hair gelled and combed, the girls with bright ribbons decorating their locks and curls.

I looked down at my distressed shorts and wrinkled T-shirt and stopped short of the door. Jamal pranced ahead of us, like his cut-offs and sandals didn't matter. Sean stopped beside me and tried to smooth the creases out of his bright green T-shirt with the Irish flag emblazoned on the front.

"What-a ya think?" he whispered. "Do we go inside or wait out here until it's over?"

I shook my head. "I don't know what to do. Look at how we're dressed. I don't want to offend anyb—"

Before I could finish, a big man in a starched shirt and black suit, thrust his right hand at me. "Welcome, brother." His voice had a mellow depth to it that got me picturing Moses. "I'm Isaiah Baker, pastor of New Harvest African American Fellowship. Please, join us in worship of our Great God and Savior, Jesus Christ."

My fingers as limp as wet noodles, I made an effort to grasp his outstretched paw. Sean did the same, but I caught him shrinking under the minister's steady gaze.

As though hypnotized by the big man-of-God's shiny brown eyes, the two of us followed him inside the church, like two lost sheep trotting after their shepherd. The music had already started. I say, music, but it didn't sound anything like the orderly worship songs I'd grown up hearing. This was more like a celebration. People leaped about in their pews, and some of them spilled into the aisles, waving their hands in the air and shouting. The organ rattled the windows, and the piano nearly bounced off the stage.

A blue-robed choir stood on risers, bobbing and weaving in unison, and I almost expected Kirk Franklin to spring from their midst, stomping and shouting, and lighting even more fire under an already frenzied gathering. Without warning, the music settled to a hush, and the Rev. Isaiah Baker mounted the steps to the pulpit. After pointing out the three visitors in their group—which caused me to cringe a little in my seat—he delivered a high-spirited sermon, drawing shouts of "Amen!" and "Tell it, brother!" from the audience.

Jamal appeared to be in his element. He joined the rest of the congregation with his own zealous cries of "Yes!" and "Praise Jesus!" He raised his hands high in the air and clapped along with the rest of them. While Sean and I sat like two lumps of granite, unmoving and without looking around, Jamal looked like he fit right in.

I ventured a look at Sean, and he stared back at me, his green eyes big and round, his face flushed, an anxious wrinkle on his brow. My round little Irish friend had grown up within the solemn rituals of the Catholic church, where everyone whispered. They knew when to kneel, when to stand, and when to utter a programmed response to the priest's recitations.

I had visited his church on occasion. It was like entering a mausoleum. The front of the sanctuary glimmered with votive candles lined up like tiny luminaries on three rows of a metal rack. Ceiling fixtures cast muted lighting on the pews. And a hint of sunlight streamed through the stained glass windows, creating an even more ethereal aura. I wouldn't have been surprised if a host of heavenly angels descended on the sanctuary.

The entire mass, from beginning to end, held a sacred ambiance, further emphasized by the nostril-stinging incense wafting from a silver thingamajig in the priest's hand and the spray of holy water that struck my cheek. No one—absolutely no one—shouted. The choir stood rigid, barely moving their mouths to hymns performed in Latin. I came away feeling like I'd been taken to heaven and back. The whole experience left me wanting to clean up my act as soon as possible.

As for me, I attended a non-denominational church—that is, when I went. The service fell somewhere between the solemnity of Sean's church and the exuberance of Jamal's form of worship. The building I entered on Sunday mornings didn't look like a real church. It hadn't been built in the traditional crucifix shape, didn't even have a spire. No stained glass windows. No statues in niches up front. Not even a cross displaying the suffering Savior.

If Sean ever entered my church he would have been appalled.

Before the service started, people milled about chatting, shaking hands, even hugging each other and laughing out loud. Everyone dressed however they wanted, from suits and dresses to sportswear. Kids chased each other up and down the aisles, kind of like Henry's children did in their home, squealing and chattering like squirrels and having a grand, old time, even in church.

Our music involved a worship team, with guitars and drums and singers, each of them standing in front of a microphone. A big screen on the wall displayed the Bible verses, and our pastor didn't stand behind a pulpit, but strode about the stage, speaking to us in a conversational tone. I imagine both Jamal and Sean might have been shocked if they'd attended church with me.

In any case, on that Sunday morning during our road trip, I felt super self-conscious about being a white man in a building full of black people. I didn't know how we'd be received. As soon as the service ended, I planned to slip out the door and head for the safety of the Bullet.

But I didn't get very far, because a colorfully clothed tsunami of smiling church-goers swarmed around us, genuinely thrilled that we had joined them in worship. I reeled beneath all the handshakes, hugs, and pats on the back.

Sean gawked like he'd awakened from a coma in the middle of a black revival meeting. A couple of the women peppered us with questions. What were our names? Where did we come from? Where were we going? Sean smiled and nervously gave them our entire itinerary.

Several people invited us to join them in the church hall for a time of food and fellowship. How could we refuse? After sitting through a three-hour service, we were ready for lunch. I followed the others into a side building decked out with tables laden with every kind of soul food that existed.

Except for what I'd dined on at Mama Waters' house, I tasted some of the most fantastic barbecued ribs and fried chicken I'd ever eaten. Without shame, I filled my plate with gobs of coleslaw, macaroni and cheese, and something rich and flavorful they called Hoppin' John.

No one appeared to notice our scruffy traveling attire. In fact, the subject never came up. People wanted to know all about us. I no sooner shoved something in my mouth when someone asked me another question.

In the end, stuffed and ready for a nap, I left New Harvest African American Fellowship with a whole new perspective on the different ways people worship and honor God. I envisioned the Father looking down on Sunday mornings, enjoying the various celebrations of faith. Perhaps, he even summoned the angels and said, "Come here. Look at all this."

For the moment, Sean and I had gotten caught up in Jamal's style of worship and the overwhelming attention we received from the New Harvest congregation. As we walked out to the parking lot, several smiling church-goers followed us to our car and called out blessings for the road. We piled in the Silver Bullet, with Jamal grinning from ear to ear as he resumed his place at the wheel. I settled into the passenger seat, and, once again, Sean seemed content to have the entire backseat to himself. As we drove away, several people spilled into the road behind us, still waving and smiling. I shook my head in awe and smiled.

During the next few hours, we passed from Florida to Mobile, Alabama, and then through a section of Mississippi where we refueled the Bullet.

We hadn't gone more than fifty miles, when Sean perked up and offered a suggestion.

"We'll be in New Orleans in a few hours," he said. "Let's spend some time in the French Quarter. It might be fun."

The French Quarter? I thought it over and shrugged. *Oh well,* I figured. *We'd already used up the morning at church, might as well use up the afternoon in the French Quarter.* Besides, the famous landmark promised to be a good place to stop and stretch our legs. We couldn't just drive and eat and sleep. We needed to do a little sightseeing, too.

We made up some of the time we'd lost while attending church that morning, perhaps because we'd been so well fed we didn't have to stop for food. By mid-afternoon, we reached St. Tammany Parish and the town of Slidell on the north shore of Lake Pontchartrain.

A few minutes later, we drove onto the five-mile bridge. Right then, I went into a state of shock. Instead of meandering along at a snail's pace, the traffic whizzed by us at top speed. People drove like maniacs. They wove in and out of traffic and cut each other off without using their turn signals.

"Don't those people know how to signal when they want to switch lanes?" I griped.

Jamal gripped the steering wheel with both hands. "It's like driving in the Indy 500," he said, scowling.

I peered out my side window and wondered how many older model cars like mine had been forced off the bridge and now lay rusting at the bottom of the lake.

Somehow, we made it to the end of the bridge without incident, and I began to relax as the death-defying speed slowed to an instant crawl. We came upon a broad marshland similar to the Florida Everglades, but without the proliferation of scrub pines and palm trees. Except for tall reeds along both sides of the road, the endless swamp appeared far more desolate.

Eventually, we passed a strip mall, a Walmart store, and several low income apartment buildings that appeared to rise up out of the swamp.

Then came a welcome sign that bore the words, *"Vieux Carre."*

Sean nearly leaped over the front seat. *"Vieux Carre!* That's French for *Old Square*," he shouted. He leaned past me to look out the front window. "Fellas," he yelled. "We're about to step foot in another world. Bourbon Street. The French Market. Jazz music. Street performers. Too bad it isn't Mardi Gras time."

I smiled at Sean's enthusiasm.

As we entered the French Quarter, the Mississippi River paralleled our road on the left. A passenger-laden steamboat drifted past and emitted what sounded like a train whistle accompanied by a big puff of steam.

To our right loomed the glaring white, triple-spired St. Louis Cathedral, its loud gongs reverberating through the air. A large clock in the center of its facade indicated 4 p.m. *Almost time for supper,* I thought.

As the person who'd assumed the role of budget keeper, I immediately laid down the law.

"No meals in this place," I said, glancing first at Jamal and then at Sean. "Not with the high cost of food here. And don't expect to spend the night in New Orleans. We'll have to find a cheap motel somewhere else outside of town."

Neither of them acknowledged what I'd just said. Jamal turned his head from side to side, hardly paying attention to the traffic ahead of us. And Sean bounced back and forth from one side of the backseat to the other, looking out this window and then that window. Both of them were obviously interested in the scene outside the car and could care less if I wanted to hold a budget meeting.

"Hey, you two," I said, keeping my voice calm and controlled. "We're three guys on a road trip. We don't have much cash, and we can't stay long. That means keeping an eye on where we're going, Jamal, and maintaining a firm check on our spending, Sean."

"Come on, Charlie," Jamal chided me. "We didn't come this far to talk only about budget. And our one goal can't be merely a turnaround in San Francisco. This trip needs to be fun."

His words struck me like a cold shower. I'd been behaving like a penny-pinching Scrooge. I shook my head at myself. We were on a vacation. That meant we should be having fun. We should be sightseeing and relaxing and soaking up the ambiance of an unfamiliar place. For the time being, I had to become a tourist.

As Jamal maneuvered the Silver Bullet into the district, I, too, forgot the budget and was captivated by the ambiance. This place was a budding architect's dream. On both sides of the road loomed three-story buildings steeped in French and Spanish culture, with wrought iron railings running along the balconies of upstairs apartments and hotel rooms, and quaint shops and restaurants linked together in an unending chain along the sidewalks below.

I felt Sean's breath on my neck, turned, and caught a glimpse of his face lit up like a kid with a new puppy.

We didn't get far, when, in unison, Jamal and Sean voted to park the Silver Bullet so we could get out and walk around. There were no parking spaces on the main drag which teemed with people strolling amidst bicycles, horse-drawn carriages, and clanging trolley cars. Jamal made a turn down a couple of side streets and caught sight of a spot someone else was just leaving.

"We can walk around a little, stretch our legs, maybe get something to drink," he said.

After being scrunched up in the front seat for several hours, I needed to unfold my legs and shake off the sleep bubbles from my right foot. But something to drink? In a place like New Orleans we might use up our entire day's food money just to quench our thirst. There I was, thinking about the budget again. I couldn't help myself.

"Let's take a little stroll and then get back on the road," I said, still trying to be the sensible one. "We don't need to buy anything. There are plenty of water bottles in the trunk."

Once again, they outnumbered me. I looked at my buddies standing firm with their arms crossed and their feet planted in the direction of the nearest watering hole. I began to cave. My taste buds wanted something more flavorful than water too. I figured we could cut our spending somewhere else.

As we walked away from my car, I happened to glance back. Not far from the Silver Bullet stood a lopsided sign bearing the words, **No Parking**. I didn't know if it meant our spot or the one in front of it. The sign looked like it pointed in the opposite direction from where my car was.

It occurred to me we may have broken the law. Though we'd walked a good four or five yards away from the Bullet, I decided to go back and move it.

I grabbed the keys from Jamal. "I'll catch up with you guys," I said, and sprinted away.

But I soon learned that in New Orleans things don't always go as planned. Before I could reach my car, a meter maid had descended like a phantom from out of nowhere and was already writing out a ticket. She must have been lurking in a nearby alley, quietly waiting for some numbskull out-of-towner to come along and park on that very spot.

"Wait," I called out. "I just now noticed the sign, and I was coming back to move my car."

"Too late," she quipped, grinning.

The meter maid looked to be a little too big for her uniform and a little too old for me to flirt with. So I tried common sense.

"That sign isn't visible from the parking spot," I reasoned. "Stand over there and look. There's no way my friends and I could have seen it until we walked away and turned around."

"Sorry," she said with feigned sympathy. "Once I start to write out a ticket, I have to serve it. I can't tear it up."

With a smug grin on her face, she pulled a sheet off the pad and held it out to me. "Payable in thirty days," she said.

I looked at the ticket. *Twelve bucks.* I heaved a sigh. Thankfully, it didn't have to come out of my travel budget. I could mail it in after I got back home, and I assumed the guys would chip in. Four dollars sounded a whole lot better than twelve bucks to a starving college student.

I looked at the ticket and shrugged. "It is what it is," I said, recalling my mantra. The meter maid stared bullets at me.

Needless to say, I drove away angry and started looking for my friends. I found them on a street corner sipping lemonade from tall plastic cups of ice. At that moment, a car vacated a spot around the corner. I grabbed it without the threat of Miss Meter Maid lurking somewhere. Feeling like I'd outsmarted the law, I joined my friends.

"I got a parking ticket," I told them. "Twelve bucks."

"That's a shame," said Jamal.

"Yeah, too bad," said Sean, and he sipped his lemonade.

I was stunned. Neither of them had offered to help pay for the ticket. I stopped walking and gave them my wounded puppy look. They both burst out laughing.

Jamal patted my shoulder. "Of course, we'll share the fine," he said, smiling.

"Yeah," said Sean. "Did you think we'd stick you with the whole thing?"

I breathed a sigh of relief, not so much because of the money, but I didn't want anything to spoil our friendship and ruin the rest of the trip, which is what might have happened if they hadn't offered to help pay for that ticket. After all, Jamal had been driving, and Sean had pointed out the parking spot. I was the innocent victim here.

I nodded toward their drinks. "Where'd ya get those?"

They gestured toward a street vendor who'd set up shop on the next block. I hurried toward him and waited while he served someone in front of me. I looked him over, fascinated. He had a sun-bronzed, square face, dark-as-coal eyes, and a graying pony tail at the back of his neck. He had a stocky build, was about as short as Sean but lots bigger in the shoulders. He wore a bright red linen shirt and a New Orleans Saints baseball cap.

I approached his kiosk, still holding my car keys, like I didn't plan to stay long. Upon spotting them, he said, "Wha dat in yo hand? You gonna leave us, yeah?" The soft, nasal dialect rolled easily off his tongue and reminded me we'd arrived in Cajun country.

His look of disappointment convicted me. I tucked the keys in my pocket, smiled at the guy, and said, "No, we're not leaving yet." I nodded toward a row of plastic cups. "I'll have one of those lemonades."

"Three dolla," he said, handing me a frosty drink.

Then, as we walked away, he called after us, "Y'all have fun, yeah?"

Right, have fun. By spending $3 for a lemonade I had used up my entire day's meal ration.

"Sure," I huffed aloud. "Three lousy bucks for a drink."

"Look," Jamal reasoned. "When we leave here, we can find a grocery store and buy enough sandwich fixin's and snacks to last us for two days."

He'd made so much sense, I was able to relax and walk the streets in the French Quarter of New Orleans like I deserved to be there as much as those other rich tourists. Knowing I might never get to do this again, I handed my pocket Minolta to passers-by and asked them to take pictures of the three of us clowns in front of one establishment or another.

I shot additional pictures of the quaint historic buildings and the crowds of people milling about, and I even took one of the memorable street vendor.

As a future architect, I had stumbled on an awesome opportunity for research. Handing the camera to Sean, I pulled out my little budgeting notebook, flipped past the pages with dollar signs and decimal points, and started writing down the unique architectural features of the buildings. I must have filled five or six pages before we got to the next block.

One thing I hadn't expected to see was the number of homeless people lying around in dark alleys. Apparently, the homeless population had become part of the fabric—a mix of old world charm and modern day poverty, the same kind that prevailed in every big city.

While the homeless lay in squalor a few yards away, well-dressed tourists sat at little round tables at outdoor cafes, drinking wine and beer and dark roast coffee, and dining on jambalaya and po boy sandwiches. Pleasant aromas wafted from open doors—chicken roasting on a fire pit, pulled pork sizzling on a grill, fresh baked bread and beignets coming out of the fryer—masking the filthy odors confined to the nearby alleys. More camouflage existed in the jazz rhythms and laughter that poured from open doorways as happy hour descended on the square. Street musicians strummed banjos and mandolins and sang in French and Creole tongues, creating more of a diversion from the lost and needy souls who remained hidden from view.

A rush of discomfort swept over me. How often had I walked past a similar scene in the section of town where I lived? Had the homeless population become so much a part of the city's tapestry, I no longer saw them—or cared? I frowned at my own insensitivity. For a moment, I'd looked at another part of life I hadn't paid much attention to before. I succumbed to a prick of empathy. It was like that saying, "There but by the grace of God..."

As though reading my mind, Jamal grabbed my arm and ushered me along the street. "Wake up," he said. "We're in the French Quarter. You may never get this opportunity again."

I nodded and breathed a sigh. "Just trying to commit this place to memory," I said, more to myself than to Jamal.

We continued to stroll about the French Quarter for a while. I breathed deeply of the old world atmosphere.

Giving in to another bout of hunger, we agreed to go back to the car so we could find a grocery store. For some reason, a sadness tugged at my heart, and I realized I wasn't ready to leave after all.

Chapter Five

J amal again took the wheel, and I remained in the passenger seat. Sean grabbed the back, having the shortest legs and therefore able to fit more comfortably back there than either of us long-legged dudes.

We left the French Quarter, made a few turns, got back on I-10, and kept our eyes open for a grocery. We found one on a side street not far from the main highway. The three of us agreed to pool our funds.

Leaving the Bullet in the parking lot, we grabbed a grocery cart and filled it with enough lunch meats and cheeses, bread, and peanut butter and jelly to last us through Tuesday. We added a jar of mustard, bags of potato chips and pretzels, and a six-pack of Gatorade. That's right. Florida's hit energy beverage had traveled across the U.S. before we did.

Our order came to $16.38, or $5.46 apiece. We were finally back on track—financially at least.

We sat in the car and fixed our sandwiches, and eating as we drove along, we returned to I-10 and agreed not to stop for the night until after we crossed the Texas border and found a cheap motel.

Our conversation turned to school. We started comparing grades and our plans for after graduation. Jamal had mostly A's and B's, I had a mix of A's, B's, and C's, and Sean accepted his two B's and four C's without complaint, but he bragged endlessly about his one A in science, his best subject.

Jamal dreamed of a pro basketball contract, but even if it never happened, his grades could get him a scholarship to grad school, and he could pursue any course of study he chose. I needed to bring up my two C's if I wanted to go for a master's in architecture. As for Sean, he could always fall back on his dad's plumbing business.

It was called Murphy & Sons for a reason. After working alongside his brothers on weekends, Sean already knew the trade and said it paid well enough to suit him.

Eventually, we got bored talking about school—one of the things we'd escaped from, besides our part-time jobs. We settled into a lengthy quiet, with each of us staring out our respective windows as the landscape continued to fall away.

The sun dropped closer to the horizon. I changed stations on the radio and caught Bobby Goldsboro singing one of his hits, of all things, "I'm a Drifter."

"Hey! That's us!" shouted Sean from the backseat. "We're *drifters*."

Jamal broke out in song, and before too long, Sean and I had joined him in singing the chorus. There was a poignancy that enveloped us as Bobby sang, and a bit of heartache. Hadn't we all experienced our share of loneliness, rain, and pain? Weren't we all looking for answers and wondering if they were waiting for us at home in the arms of that certain someone?

I couldn't help but imagine Heather waiting for me to come back home. Sean may have had Erin on his mind. When I looked at Jamal, tossing his head and belting out the lyrics, I figured he may have been thinking about Caroline. He'd been dating her for six months, yet he rarely mentioned her name anymore.

Even after the song ended, we kept on singing, and while immersed in the chorus for the fourth time, I spotted a lone figure a short distance down the road with his thumb out. Like the song said, we'd come across a real live drifter. I stopped singing and said a really dumb thing.

"Do you think we should pick him up?"

Jamal frowned at me as if to say, "Are you nuts?"

But, Sean leaned over the front seat. "Let's," he said. "It'll break the monotony."

Since every decision depended on majority vote, Jamal gave in and eased the Silver Bullet to the side of the road a few yards beyond the guy, who set off running after us.

He wore torn jeans and a wrinkled shirt, and he carried a backpack and a guitar. He climbed into the backseat beside Sean, unaware that my hard-earned cash lay inside the seat cushion directly under him.

I asked him his name.

"Dusty," he said.

I turned in my seat and made the introductions, then asked him the most obvious question, "Where you headin'?"

"Lubbock, Texas."

"We can take you as far as Beaumont," Jamal told him.

He grunted but said nothing more. Now, with the guy sitting in my car, I got a better look at him. He appeared to be in his late twenties, had a scar on his left cheek, and looked like he hadn't washed his hair in a month. He slowly removed his dark sunglasses and stared back at me, his eyes narrowing like he didn't trust me.

That's a joke, I thought to myself. *He doesn't trust me, when he's the one who looks like a criminal.*

Jamal must have read my thoughts, because he asked Dusty what he did for a living.

"I play country music," he said.

Sean perked up. "Anything we might have heard on the radio?"

"Doubt it. I write my own."

"Do you have a band?" Sean asked, a ring of interest in his voice.

"Nah, I'm a loner. Still lookin' for a gig."

"Will you play something now?" Sean begged.

"What? Here? In the car?"

"Sure, I love country music."

Dusty gave a shrug. He slid his guitar out of the case and strummed a few chords. "There. Happy now?" He glared at Sean. Then, he put the guitar back inside the case and snapped the latch with a loud click.

He settled down then, pulled out one of those thin, brown cigarettes and was about to light up.

"No smoking in my car," I told him, wishing we hadn't stopped to pick him up.

He tucked the cigarette in his shirt pocket and puffed out a disgruntled sigh. He leaned back and fell asleep, or let us think he had.

We rode along in uncomfortable silence for at least an hour, then Jamal said, "There's a truck stop up ahead. What do you say we stop and eat?"

I nodded in agreement, hoping our new friend might catch another ride with one of the truckers who'd parked there.

Sean sat upright. "It'd be nice if Dusty shared a little more than two or three chords," he said. "We could eat while listening to music."

Dusty let out an annoyed grunt.

Jamal found a parking spot. We spilled out of the Bullet and grabbed a picnic table.

Dusty remained in the backseat. I suggested one of us go over and offer him a sandwich and a bag of chips. I was a little nervous about the guy sitting on the seat cushion where my money was buried.

"I'll do it," Jamal offered.

He ambled over to the Bullet, opened the back door, and stuck his head in. I was in the middle of spreading mustard on a slice of bread, when Jamal came flying out of the car, fell flat on his back on the gravel drive, and wailed like a banshee. Seconds later, the Silver Bullet rumbled to life, peeled out of the parking lot, and headed off down the road.

I dropped the plastic knife and ran over to where Jamal lay writhing on the ground.

"What happened?" I screamed in his face. "Why did you let that guy take my car?"

"Hey, man!" he yelled back at me. "When I got to the car I found him cleaning his fingernails with a switchblade. He stuck the blade in my face and demanded the keys. What was I supposed to do?"

"Great! We've been carjacked!" I screamed.

Sean flew off the bench and came running toward us. I extended a hand and helped Jamal to his feet. The three of us raced after the Bullet. We didn't get very far, just ended up standing helpless by the side of the road as the taillights grew smaller in the distance.

A semi loaded with dairy peeled out of the parking lot, kicking up gravel. The driver was talking into his CB handset.

Please call the police, I mouthed. I didn't know if mental telepathy worked, but I had to try *something*.

A terrible panic squeezed my gut. The guy had taken more than our means of transportation. He'd taken our clothes, the rest of our food and water, our Atlas and our road maps, Jamal's miniature safe in the back, and all my cash in the sock inside the torn seat cushion where the guy had been sitting. Only Sean had escaped with his bulging wallet, stuffed full of twenties and safely tucked away in his pocket.

As the trucker's taillights also diminished in the distance, another big semi carrying pigs for the market rumbled past us at top speed. We waved frantically. He blew his air horn and sped on by. I caught a glimpse of the driver, also talking on his CB. I frowned. Was that all those guys did for entertainment?

Next thing that happened, two highway patrol cars appeared out of nowhere, sirens blaring and lights flashing. They whizzed by in the same direction as the Silver Bullet and the two semis.

The three of us started running down the highway after them. Several minutes later, we caught up with the blue and red lights and the big semis parked by the side of the road, one of them a few feet in front of the Silver Bullet, blocking our carjacker's exit, and the other behind my car, boxing the guy in like two hulking prison guards. The Bullet sat there, rescued and waiting for us to reclaim her. I got a lump in my throat and came embarrassingly close to shedding a few tears.

When we approached them, the cops already had the carjacker sitting in one of their cruisers. One of the semi drivers dropped down from his cab and strode toward us, his boots crunching against the gravel soft shoulder.

"I saw the whole thing," he said, his John Wayne voice matching the bulk of his muscular frame. "You kids oughta be careful who you pick up on the highway. You coulda been robbed or even *killed!*"

We all nodded and mumbled excuses. As for me, twenty-one years old and supposed to be the most mature of the three of us, I bowed my head in shame. Not only had I done a foolish thing suggesting we pick the guy up, but I hated that it made me look like a stupid kid.

As it turned out, the carjacker never knew we'd stored hundreds of dollars in our car, right under his nose, as well as another major part of his body. He just wanted our car. Why he'd chosen a beat up old '85 Honda Accord, I'll never know. He could have held out for a Mercedes or at least a Lincoln Town Car.

The three of us settled back in the Silver Bullet. Fortunately, Dusty had left the keys in the ignition. It was my only set.

With Jamal again at the wheel and me in the front passenger seat, an unearthly silence fell on us. I had a million *what if's* running around in my head. What if the guy had stabbed Jamal? What if he'd killed all three of us? Best of all, what if I hadn't suggested we pick him up in the first place?

All of a sudden, seismic activity took hold of my entire body, and I couldn't stop shaking. I guess it was a delayed reaction.

I glanced at Jamal. Though he appeared calm, he had a death grip on the steering wheel, and he kept clenching his teeth and flexing his jaw muscles.

I turned to look in the back seat. Sean had doubled over, trembling so violently he shook the whole car.

"That was a close one, wasn't it?" he squealed.

Jamal nodded. "I got bad vibes from the guy the minute he stepped up to the car, but then he climbed in and it was too late."

"Who knew Dusty had a switchblade?" I said.

"What?" Sean screamed. "He coulda killed us."

"No way, Sean. He wanted my car."

"Right, he wanted this piece of junk. Get real."

I bristled but held my tongue.

"So what do we do now?" Sean said. "Should we drive back and finish eating our sandwiches?"

I shook my head. "Forget it, the ants have them by now." I looked at Jamal, who was frowning at nothing in particular. "Just keep going, Jamal. We'll get something later."

He nodded. "I can't eat right now, anyway. I'm too shook up."

I leaned toward the radio and turned the knob. For some reason, I found one country music station after another. And why not? We'd just crossed the state line into Texas. For the time being, I figured there'd be no gospel and no golden oldies. I settled on Glen

Campbell in the middle of "By the Time I Get to Phoenix," an appropriate song for the way we were heading.

Sadly, the lyrics also reminded me of Heather, safe at home and believing I was safe too. A part of me wished we'd never come on this stupid trip. I thought about the guy with the switchblade. Little did Heather know I'd almost made her a widow before she got to be a bride.

I vowed, at that moment, no more hitchhikers. No shady-looking characters in the back of my car. Not with all my cash stashed inside the torn seat cushion.

I turned around. "Hey, Sean, check the seat cushion and see if my money is still there."

He did and gave me a nod. "Stupid guy, he didn't know he'd been sitting on a small fortune," Sean quipped, then laughed. "Yeah, a fortune. Right. What do you have left, Charlie? A couple hundred? And we haven't made it halfway yet. How do you think you're gonna get home?"

"I don't know, Sean," I said with a good amount of sarcasm. "I have a car and a credit card. So, how are *you* gonna get home? Oh, I guess you'll have to stand on the side of the road with your thumb out—kind of like our carjacker did." I glared at him, impatience filtering into my voice. "Meanwhile, pass me my sock of money. I'm gonna put what's left in my wallet."

He did, and I did. Jamal said, "Wow, Charlie, got enough room in your wallet for all that cash?" Then he also burst out laughing, and Sean quickly joined him.

I swallowed their ribbing. Somehow, their joking took the edge off. The tension inside the car eased, and I started to laugh, too. I had to admit, as tense as things became now and then, we always managed to find comic relief in nearly every situation—even this. After a reasonable amount of tittering and friendly banter, the air cleared enough for me to relax.

I turned my attention to the radio and caught, "I Will Always Love You," with Whitney Houston belting out lyrics that could get every female in the country singing along and weeping.

Of course, I didn't need much of an excuse to start thinking about

Heather again. I must have looked like a lovesick fool, because Jamal turned toward me and raised his eyebrows.

"You missin' her?" he said, like he already knew.

I shrugged. "Sure, when a song reminds me."

He chuckled. "Yeah, music can have that kind of effect."

I stared at him with appreciation. Jamal knew when to end the joking and when to empathize with a friend.

Hoping to find a song that might get my mind off of Heather and back on the road trip, I turned the knob again. This time I picked up Elvis singing "Can't Help Falling in Love."

With that, I gave up and shut the darn thing off.

Chapter Six

Daylight was dwindling. I gazed out the window and gawked at the junipers and rolling green landscape, not far removed from what we'd left behind in Central Florida, but so much bigger. It seemed the land went on forever. I'd heard that everything was bigger in Texas. Now I was beginning to believe it. From all the old movies I've watched, I always thought Texas was one vast desert with tumbleweeds, tall saguaro cactus, and longhorn cattle everywhere, but at least this part of the state looked an awful lot like the lush, green landscape where I'd grown up near the Ocala National Forest, where a guy could get lost amidst the scrub pines, giant oaks, and grass as high as your armpits. That sudden reflection of home brought on a sense of nostalgia.

I pulled out my wallet and snuck a quick look at Heather's picture. I missed her something awful, and we'd only made it halfway to our destination.

Somehow, even with his eyes trained on the road ahead, Jamal flashed a quick look. "She's a pretty girl," he said, smiling. "I always thought so."

I turned toward him and asked the question I'd been pondering for a while. "What about you, Jamal? When did you go out with Caroline last?"

"It's been a few weeks," he said. Then, his smile faded. "Trouble is, I can hang around her for just so long. The girl talks in question marks. Know what I'm sayin'? Every sentence leaves you hanging, as if she hasn't finished talking, or she's dangling a question out there for no one to answer."

"How's that?"

"Even when she's not askin' anything, the last few words go up, like a question. She sounds like a three-year-old beggin' for cookies."

"Question marks, huh?" I said. "Come to think of it, my roommate, Hank, talks in question marks. He sounds like a teenage girl. Says things like, 'I'm goin' out *for a while? Be back about midnight? Don't wait up.*' He also over-uses the word, totally. Like, 'That's *totally* gross,' or 'That's a *totally* cool car.' I want to shut the guy up. *Totally.*"

"Here's what Caroline sounds like," Jamal said, stifling a chuckle. "'I was walkin' downtown where *all the shops are?* And, I met Melanie coming out of *a hair salon?* It looked like someone had combed her hair with *an egg beater?* And, so on, blah, blah, blah.'"

At that moment, Sean rose up from the backseat and joined the fun. "Here's one. My father wants me to work for him *during summer break? He's in the plumbing business?* He should know I might want to *do something else?*"

"How about this?" I said. "I've been in school *all my life?* If not for all the studying and tests, *I might like it?* But, if I stick it out, I might *become an architect?*"

By this time, Sean and I were holding our sides laughing, and Jamal was falling over the steering wheel, delirious. Still, we managed to keep the joke going.

"That carjacker *ruined my day?*" Jamal said. "I thought I'd never *stop shaking?*" Then, he quit laughing and frowned at the memory. "You know," he said, turning serious. "That stupid jerk picked the wrong car. We only had about a quarter of a tank of gas left. How far did he expect to get on fumes?"

Stunned, I sat up straight. "A quarter of a tank! We need to stop, pal, and soon."

"Why? You said this thing gets good mileage. I figured we'd catch an off-ramp somewhere down the road."

"No, Jamal. I failed to tell you that sometimes the gauge reads a tad higher than what's in there. That's why every time the fuel drops to a quarter tank, I stop and fuel up."

"Thanks for waiting until now to mention it," Jamal sneered. Then, he nodded toward a sign by the side of the road. "Houston, Texas, is still seventy miles away. Can we make it?"

"That's a great question," I said. "It'll be dark soon. Let's turn off the highway first chance we get and find a gas station, and maybe some food and lodging for the night."

Jamal nodded and pressed his foot to the floor, as if going faster might keep us from running out of fuel.

Thankfully, a right turn did come up a few miles down the road. We pulled onto the exit ramp and immediately came upon a gas station and the Countryside Inn, a literal stone's throw from I-10. After fueling up, we checked into the motel, paying twelve bucks apiece for a room with two queen beds, a TV, and a countertop refrigerator. To our relief, the motel also offered a complimentary breakfast.

"Look," said Sean. "We lost our meat and cheese at the truck stop. We still have another loaf of bread and the peanut butter and jelly, which we can save for lunch. And we can load up on the complimentary breakfast foods before we leave tomorrow. Why don't we splurge a little and hit that McDonald's sitting right next door? After what happened today on the highway, I'd say we deserve a treat."

I could depend on Sean to suggest something like that. But, this time, he made sense. I was hungering for a burger or chicken sandwich, anything but peanut butter and jelly.

"Sounds like a good idea," I said.

Off the three of us went to McDonald's where we spent a pre-arranged $3 apiece and ended up with a to-go order of three one-dollar bacon burgers, one large order of fries to share, and three chocolate milkshakes. We settled on the two beds and ate the best meal ever while watching a rerun of *Columbo* on a little black-and-white TV.

Sean grabbed one bed for himself. Jamal and I—both of us skinny as a rail—bunked together, with Jamal all the way on one side of the bed and me all the way on the other, leaving a huge gap between us.

Before I fell asleep, I heard Jamal whispering a prayer. I listened intently, caught a little of it, and mouthed my own "Amen." How could I have thought anything bad might happen to us with a true prayer warrior in our midst? Had my friend been praying for God's intervention the whole time while we'd been carjacked? We hadn't lost anything except our sandwiches and a little time.

If I could get more serious about my walk with God, maybe I could pray like Jamal did. Maybe, together, God and I could figure out a better plan for my life.

Privately, I thanked the Lord for my two friends—Jamal, for his strength of spirit and unwavering faith, and Sean, for his innocent but quizzical mind, almost always open to whatever we wanted to do. Though Jamal and I hadn't succeeded in convincing him to take a step of faith or even to come to church with either one of us, he never told us to shut up when we discussed spiritual things, just nodded, like he was taking it all in and maybe storing it up for later.

Though he'd grown up in the Catholic faith, Sean had strayed from whatever he'd been taught in the church his parents attended. I needed to be more of a listener, maybe find out exactly what my friend believed. How cool if the three of us could talk about our faith and maybe even pray together.

As it was, my mom rarely went to church, and she didn't push me to go. I went because I knew that's where Heather went on Sunday mornings. Meanwhile, Jamal had the support of a godly mother who loved to sing gospel and went to church on Sunday dressed like she belonged in a wedding party. The rare times I went with them, I forced myself to wear the one suit in my closet. Of course, I enjoyed a huge lunch afterward, kind of like we'd experienced at the Reverend Baker's church, but on a smaller scale. While New Harvest Fellowship had about 300 attending, Jamal's Glory Chapel numbered less than half of that.

Still, like New Harvest, their service lasted for three hours, with a lot of singing and shouts of "Amen!" And, like the Reverend Baker, Jamal's preacher gave a powerful message that left me feeling like I needed to take a closer look at my walk. For one thing, I'd been way too self-serving. My mother said I was, and if I wanted to be honest, I had to agree with her. No wonder she'd wanted me out of the house.

There was no doubt hanging around Jamal and his mama had a soul-cleansing effect on me. I didn't mind it at all, but welcomed it—*needed* it even. I believed in Jesus and prayed a lot, but they had something else, something beyond simple faith, beyond family ties and closer to what bonded them together spiritually. I wanted something like that with my own mother.

Meanwhile, Heather's parents treated her and her little brother with respect. They prayed together, played together, and gave them a say in decisions. They behaved like a TV family—*Ozzie and Harriet* or *The Brady Bunch*—except with Heather's family, it was real life. Though I wanted that, too, I didn't know if I had the ability to create it for myself.

If I could clean up my act, perhaps at some point, I might feel worthy of a girl like Heather. I had to admit, the main reason I hadn't taken our relationship to the next level had a lot to do with my own lack of self-worth. Such thoughts had troubled me for a long time. I held onto way too many doubts about my own ability to live out my faith as I should. Now, during that long-distance trip, when conversations fell away, I had lots of time to think.

I drifted off to sleep that night with Jamal still whispering a couple of feet away from me and Sean snoring like a dog fight had erupted in the other bed.

Our trip the next morning was uneventful. We got up at 7:30, ate breakfast at the motel's free cereal bar, then stuffed apples, bananas, muffins, and donuts in a plastic laundry bag we found in our room. We left the motel with three paper cups of coffee and a handful of mints from a bowl on the front desk.

I took over the driving again. I'd heard Houston traffic was a nightmare, and Sean said he wanted no part of that job. I suspected he hadn't gotten over the carjacking yet, or maybe he liked having the backseat all to himself.

We made it to the other side of Houston by 10 a.m. and discovered a rest stop where the highway crossed the Brazos River. Jamal sat up straight in the passenger seat and eyed the water below, his eyebrows raised with interest.

"Let's stop for a while and explore that river," he suggested. "I'd like to stretch my legs, and we can make time for a mid-morning snack."

"Yes, let's give it a lash," the Irishman in the backseat said. He rolled down his window and craned his head out to get a better look.

Always up for a little adventure, I agreed. We parked in the shade of a massive live oak, then took the opportunity to avail ourselves of the reststop's facilities. Refreshed and relieved, the three of us removed our shirts, flexed our muscles, and tumbled down the grassy hillside toward the river's edge. We skipped stones across the water, took off our shoes, and stepped into the coolness of the river. The rush of water took my breath away. I didn't dare go any deeper.

"Hey," I called out to the other two. "We ought to try a white water rafting trip somewhere."

"Yeah, man, that sounds cool," said Jamal.

"No way," Sean erupted, his face looking panic-stricken.

I eyed him with skepticism. Twenty years old and he didn't have an adventurous bone in his whole body. But I had to admit, Sean had been the equalizer in our little threesome. Jamal and I needed someone to tone down our impulsiveness—someone a lot like his mother, only male and closer to our age.

I backed off for the moment, but I kept the raft trip in the back of my mind. We couldn't just drive a car and sleep in motels. At some point we had to do *something* fun. If Sean didn't want to go, he could just wait in the car.

We spent the next half-hour hiking along the riverside, dodging rocks and keeping an eye out for snakes. Each of us picked up a long stick to keep our balance as we navigated the uneven terrain, but also as a defensive weapon in case one of those critters happened to cross our path.

By the time we got back to the car, we'd developed a taste for some of the snacks we'd packed, compliments of the Countryside Inn.

We sat in the car with the doors open and munched away. Fortunately, we'd also packed a cooler full of water bottles when we left Gainesville, so we had plenty to drink. We just needed to add a fifty-cent bag of ice now and then.

Eventually, we started back on the road. I drove, and, as expected, Jamal took our musical entertainment to a gospel station. The click of our tires on the highway blended well with the tempo of "Open

Up the Heavens." Jamal clapped his hands and tapped his foot. I found myself bouncing a little in my seat. Even Sean got into it. I looked in the rearview mirror and caught him smiling and bobbing his head in time to the beat.

As we journeyed farther west, the landscape went through a metamorphosis of sorts. More dirt and sand appeared along both sides of the road. Deep purple hills and craggy mountains rose up in the distance. I shook my head in awe, and thought, *What might Jamal's mother say if she could see this?* Perhaps her fear of gunslinging outlaws wasn't unfounded after all. With almost no traffic on that part of the highway, I began to take her warning more seriously.

This particular stretch of road went on for a long, long time. Nothing but sand spread out on either side of the road. Occasionally, a dust devil stirred up a good bit of sand. I started to see a lot of cacti too, some of them as tall as Jamal. I tried not to let the desolate landscape unnerve me. We'd get through it soon, I kept reminding myself. Best to turn my attention to something more pleasant, like the rousing gospel music pouring from the radio.

By now, Jamal's hand-clapping music had given way to more mild forms of gospel. "Rock of Ages" resounded over the airwaves, like a tribute to the brown hills in the distance. The hot sun painted streaks of gold on the mountains, and the road sizzled beneath the harsh glare. It was noon in the desert, the hottest time of the day, and we'd reached the driest part of Texas. My eyes drifted toward the gas gauge, and I silently prayed we wouldn't run out before we got to a place where we could refuel.

Chapter Seven

Even with the air conditioner blasting full force, the inside of my car absorbed the heat like an overworked pizza oven. I downed another bottle of water, and prepared myself for a long drive into the wilderness. Jamal turned off the radio and fell asleep with his head resting on the passenger side window. I thought about Heather standing on her front porch, weeping and waving, and me, riding off into the sunset like one of those western heroes who'd left the beautiful saloon girl behind.

Of course, I didn't know for sure if Heather had been weeping. By now, she might have given up on me, and with good reason. I'd been less attentive lately, hadn't staked my claim. Maybe Robby Richards was knocking on her door at that very minute. Or he might be ringing her phone off the hook and maybe chumming up to her father, pretending to be a God-fearing, church-going young man, when I knew the truth about that player. A jealous prickle traveled up the back of my neck, and my face grew hot. I fiddled with the air conditioner knob, but couldn't generate more air. I had a good mind to turn the Silver Bullet around, head for home, and claim what was rightfully mine.

After more than twenty minutes of self-torture, I came back to reality when Sean piped up from the back, "Hey, Charlie. Did I ever tell you about the funny conversation I had with Erin Hagelmeyer?"

"No, you never did," I said, annoyed by the interruption. While I needed to resolve my fear of losing Heather, my friend needed to talk about his own issues. I gave up, and, for the time being, I pretended to be genuinely interested in Sean's love life—or lack of it.

Jamal and I both knew Sean had had a crush on Erin for several months. And why not? She had a cute, little turned-up nose, long brown hair that she often wore in a French braid, and she fit the right height for Sean, five-feet, three-inches of bubbly wholesomeness.

"I think she's pretty hot," I offered. "Don't tell me you had a real conversation with her, Mr. Shyness personified." I couldn't help but snicker.

"Very funny," Sean snorted. "Of course, we talk. Have you forgotten Erin and I have been working on a project together in geology class? We don't just sit there and stare at the wall."

"Come on, Sean. I don't know about *every* project you work on. Nor have you told me much about your personal encounters with the great Erin Hagelmeyer."

Sean leaned over the seatback between me and Jamal, who, by the way, remained in La-La Land with his head resting against the passenger window. The spastic shifting of his shoulders told me he was probably dreaming of jump shots and free throws.

Sean continued his tale. "Professor Conrad must have thought we'd make a good team. At the beginning of the year, he assigned us as partners, but if I'd had a choice, I would have picked Erin anyway." He released a long sigh. "Except for study issues, we had never spoken much about personal matters, until last month when I showed up in the lab wearin' this same shirt I'm wearin' now and my favorite pair of plaid shorts."

Sean's bright green psychedelic T-shirt had a silk-screened, glow-in-the-dark Irish flag in the middle. I pictured the plaid shorts and groaned.

"Are you talking about the pair of shorts that didn't match this shirt or any other shirt in your closet? The pink and purple ones without a trace of green in them?"

"The very ones," Sean said, chuckling. "Erin walked in and made an even snottier comment about my outfit than you're doing right now." He shook his head. "She looked me up and down and said, 'Plaid shorts?' Then, she made a face like she'd smelled something rotten."

I pictured Erin's reaction and couldn't help but laugh out loud. My own troubles fading like dust, I found Sean's story entertaining. There was a certain innocence in his telling of it—a real godsend when you're on the road—mile after lonely mile—with nothing but flat plains all around you.

"Go on," I said.

Sean cleared his throat. "Well, I don't know what came over me, but I suddenly got this weird shot of confidence. I looked Erin dead in the eyes and said, 'Listen, when I want your opinion, I'll give it to you.'"

"No way! You didn't really say that."

"Yes, I did."

"And what did she say back?"

"Get this," he said, straightening. "Her whole demeanor changed after I stood up to her. She smiled and said, 'Hmm, you're all right, Sean.'"

"She did not."

Sean leaned closer to me, glanced at Jamal, still appearing to be asleep, and lowered his voice. "I couldn't believe it," he whispered. "From that point on, she acted as though she *liked* me. I don't mean that she *like*-liked me. But she's been more respectful ever since. While we worked on the project together, she kept asking my opinion about different things not even related to our schoolwork, like what did I think of the color they painted the library and how did I like the movie, *Men in Black*. She never did that before. And, guess what? If we disagreed about something, she almost always gave in."

I gave him a thumbs up. "Man, that's interesting how some people respond to self-confidence in someone else. Think about it, Sean. In the beginning, she might have been testing you. It's a girl thing. You know, they have to find out how confident you are in your own skin before they can trust you with their feelings. You need to hold your ground, let her know who's boss."

Things got quiet for a few minutes. I figured he needed to mull over the bit of wisdom I'd tossed his way. He stared off at the distant hills, maybe thinking about how he could use my insightful comments to win Erin's approval. Of course, I'd forgotten that I hadn't done well in the courtship arena, myself. I'd nearly driven Heather away from me with my self-centered nonchalance.

Jamal stirred from his sleeping spot against the side window.

He sat up and stretched as much as a tall and lanky guy can in the front seat of a Honda Accord.

He turned and faced the two of us. "Men are liars," he said, adding his own observation to our discussion. It occurred to me that he hadn't been sleeping at all. Maybe he'd been listening to every word and chuckling to himself.

"What do you mean, *liars?*" I raised my pitch and my eyebrows at the same time.

"That's right," Jamal insisted with a nod. "Think about it, Charlie. Most of the time, we clam up, 'cause we don't want to let people know what we're *really* thinking. Know what I'm sayin'? Sometimes, our girlfriends have to catch us off guard to get to the truth. Girls tend to be more straight-forward. Either they like you or they don't. It's as simple as that. But we hide our feelings, until somebody— usually a female—pries them out of us."

So, Jamal had been listening all along. I had thought it might be more helpful to Sean if we could talk one-on-one, you know, like two buddies sharing their deepest secrets in private. With Jamal in on the act, our little talk wasn't much of a secret anymore.

While Sean had been somewhat private about his personal life, I had nothing to hide from either one of them.

"Okay," I said. "Do you think Heather is testing *me?*"

Jamal shrugged. "I don't know. Tell us more."

I took a deep breath. "Well," I said, "last week, Heather told me she misses me all the time. When we're in separate classes, when she's at home and I'm in my apartment. Sometimes she misses me when I'm sitting right next to her. She said she feels like I've mentally gone off somewhere else."

I looked at Jamal and waited for him to assure me that I never did that. I guess I needed some sort of confirmation from someone I trusted. Sadly, that assurance didn't come.

"What did you say to her?" he asked me, instead.

I turned my eyes back on the road. "I told her, *It is what it is.*"

A numbing silence settled inside the car.

"That's the dumbest thing I ever heard," Sean said at last. "To use that phrase in that kind of situation sounds cruel."

Jamal scowled and shook his head. "I'm afraid I have to agree with Sean."

I managed an awkward shrug. "I didn't know what else to say. I mean, I like Heather a lot. Maybe even *love* her."

The word, *love*, kind of stuck in my throat, but I said it anyway. I'm certain I turned three shades of red.

"The problem is, I don't want a long-distance relationship," I insisted. "Did you know, Heather applied for a position at a Christian school in Chicago? She wants to teach first grade. Guys, I'm not about to move to Chicago. It's a thousand miles from Gainesville."

"Sounds like there could be another road trip in the works," Sean said, snickering. "But only for you, Charlie."

I was stunned. "Forget it. One road trip is enough. If Heather gets that job, it'll be decision time. I don't want to move there. I want to pursue my master's right where I'm at. And I can't ask her to give up *her* dream. The sad thing is, we may have to break up."

Sean placed a hand on my shoulder. "Don't you see, Charlie? That was definitely a test. Heather wants you to make a decision. And she wants you to make it *now*."

"A decision? Like what? M-m-marriage?"

"Bingo. You've been dating since the beginning of your junior year. That's eighteen months, Charlie. She wants to know if you love her enough to move across the country for her. Or maybe she wants you to ask her not to go, because you can't live without her."

"Really?" I now was the D student in the car, and Sean had miraculously turned into a genius. What he'd said made a lot of sense.

Even Jamal nodded his agreement.

This brief conversation may have been exactly what I needed to get me back on track. No more fretting over some guy who may or may not move in on Heather. This was strictly between her and me.

"I'll think about it," I told my two friends. I said it firmly, making it clear I wanted to drop the subject for the present.

Sean flopped back in his seat. Jamal started fiddling with the radio knob. And me? I set my eyes on the road ahead and tried to stop dwelling on something I couldn't change at the moment. I needed a break, anything to shift our thoughts back on the road trip.

We'd been driving along for a while with nothing but flat earth in front of us when we came upon a side road and a sign bearing the word "Gas" with a red arrow pointing to the right.

"Anybody need a bathroom break?" I said, grateful for the distraction.

They both said they did, and I turned right. We went a couple of miles and came upon a ramshackle service station with only one gas pump and what looked to be a hole-in-the-wall convenience store. Outside on the gravel drive stood two wooden picnic tables and benches. After using the station's box of a bathroom, we grabbed one of the picnic tables and laid out the remaining food from our traveling pantry, which amounted to half a loaf of Wonder Bread, jars of peanut butter and jelly, and the remainder of the goodies in the motel laundry bag.

The hot sun had turned the peanut butter and jelly to liquid, and the bread had bits of mold around the edges. We pulled off the mold, tossed it to the birds, and slathered oozing peanut butter and jelly on the slices. I grabbed a muffin from the laundry bag, and Jamal started munching on an apple. Meanwhile, Sean juggled two handfuls of muffins and mints.

We'd reached a place where food was food, and we didn't expect to go grocery shopping again until Wednesday. You'd think being in Texas we'd be dining on thick steaks grilled over hot coals instead of what kindergarten children eat for a snack. Right then, I made up my mind that when this trip ended I'd head right for the nearest Outback.

During this part of our trip, we relied on Jamal's cumbersome Atlas. He spread it open, and it took up a good half of the picnic table. We leaned our heads over the map of Texas, dripping peanut butter and jelly on parts of Dallas and Houston.

Jamal traced our route along I-10.

"We're about right here," he said, pointing with confidence. The distance on the map looked distressingly short, like we hadn't traveled very far from Houston.

Sean and I nodded in ignorance. After all, what did *we* know?

The truth was, West Texas consisted of miles and miles of wilderness, and the distance between cities looked huge compared to what us Florida boys were used to. It looked like it could take a whole tank of gas to get from one town to the next. Of course, we didn't know that for certain, nor had we bothered to ask anyone.

We finished eating and dragged ourselves back to the Bullet. Now rested up, Jamal took the wheel, and Sean leaped into the backseat again. It was his domain now and neither of us wanted to uproot him. In my place by the passenger window I could keep an eye out for road signs, play whatever I wanted on the radio, and fall asleep if I chose to. I cued in a golden oldies station. I can't explain why I liked those old songs, except they took me back to happier times and reminded me of my mom standing over the kitchen stove, stirring up a pot of macaroni and cheese for just the two of us. She knew all the lyrics and often sang along. She had a beautiful voice. Too bad it turned harsh when I became a teenager, and she kept saying she didn't know what to do with me. At the time, I couldn't decide if our squabbles were my fault or hers. Now I know the truth and wish I didn't.

Jamal had been driving for a few hours when he told me the gas needle had dropped to the quarter tank level. A cold sweat came over me. We were in the middle of nowhere, coming up on six o'clock, and darkness was about to settle over the plains.

"We need to fill 'er up," I said, aware of the panic in my voice. "Like, *now*."

"Hey, Sean," Jamal called out. "Check the Atlas, and see if there's a town anywhere out here." The nervous ring in his voice did nothing to ease my own anxiety.

Sean spread the Atlas open on his lap, and I gazed out the window, my eyes searching the wilderness for any sign of life.

"I don't see any cities or buildings or civilization of any kind," I informed them.

"Nothing on this map either," Sean moaned.

Jamal glanced at me. "Did you bring a gas can?"

"Yeah, but it's empty. Anyway, the next gas station could be ninty miles away."

"You brought a gas can with no gas in it?" Jamal was livid. "Who does such a stupid thing?"

I shrugged sheepishly. "I didn't want to travel with gasoline fumes in the car."

With little else to do, all three of us leaned toward the gas gauge and held our collective breath as mile after mile, the needle continued to drop toward Empty.

Chapter Eight

As we continued along that lonely desert road, Jamal commented on how we hadn't seen another vehicle in almost an hour. Before us stretched a vast wasteland of sand dunes and clumps of dried sage grass, and not far away, a row of slate-colored mountains and rolling foothills. Sickly trees and shrubs popped up amidst giant cacti and olive colored bushes with red, probably poisonous, berries all over them.

Sean checked the Atlas again. No doubt about it. We'd entered the Trans-Pecos, the driest, most under-populated part of Texas.

"It looks like a whole other country," I said, marveling at the huge wasteland that went on as far as the eye could see.

"Like we landed on the moon," added Jamal.

"I don't suppose they get much rainfall around here," Sean groaned from the backseat.

"Well, it ain't Florida," I noted.

Jamal shook his head. "This doesn't look good. It doesn't look good at all." He pointed at the gas gauge.

The needle had dropped down to a fraction above empty.

Sean snorted. "You'd think somebody would have put a few gas stations out here."

I didn't say a word. I owned the car and the empty gas can. My heart began to pound with anxiety. What if we all perished out there? Once we drank all the water, we'd wither away like most of the vegetation had done. What about the people we'd left behind? Jamal had a mother who cherished him. Sean lived with a whole family of huggers. And me? I had Heather. My eyes stung as I pictured her sobbing over the news that my skeleton had been found inside the Silver Bullet in the middle of a vast desert, with the skulls of longhorn cattle strewn across the sand and no watering hole for miles.

I kept watching for another vehicle. Anything. A semi maybe, or the miracle of a tow truck. I began to pray, quietly, in my head, pledging all kinds of good deeds to convince God to help us out. I could make peace with my mother. I could finally put a ring on Heather's finger. I could buckle down in my school work, raise my grades, and set better goals for the future. Of course, I only *considered* those promises, just let them dangle there in case we got rescued.

While I prayed silently, Jamal started talking to God out loud. That guy sure had the words. He didn't promise anything, but while asking God to bring us safely through our trouble, he committed to whatever our Heavenly Father wanted. By the time he finished speaking, an amazing peace had settled inside my car. I began to relax. I think Sean did too.

But besides praying, we still needed to come up with a plan, to do our best and let God do the rest, as the saying goes.

This all happened before GPS and the ability to Google *gas stations near me*. None of us had a cell phone, so we couldn't even call AAA, not that any of us could afford the membership fee. Anyway, cell phones cost too much back then, especially for college students who could barely afford a movie ticket.

I kept thinking about the people we'd left behind. Jamal's mama, who'd probably been on her knees most of the time since we left. Heather, moving on with her own life, having applied for a job more than a thousand miles away from home. And, Sean's ongoing saga with Erin, plus a large family who would grieve for months, if he didn't make it home.

Right about then, Jamal interrupted my thoughts.

"Uh, oh!"

I followed his gaze to the low fuel light. "Uh, oh," I said.

Sean leaned over the front seat. "Uh, oh."

Sean and I looked at each other, wide-eyed. Then, I turned my attention to the wilderness that stretched before us. I remained frozen that way, watching the miles tick by until the Silver Bullet lost her get-up-and-go and crept to a crawl. Jamal eased her over to the side of the road, where she gave one final shudder and died.

Everything went still with the Silver Bullet's engine silenced. There wasn't a bird or a plane or anything else outside to break the unearthly quiet. The only sound inside the car was our steady breathing, now more pronounced than ever. No one spoke. It was as if we had become part of the dried up and desolate landscape— struck dumb and hanging in the balance.

Sean slumped back against the rear seat. Jamal dropped his forehead to the steering wheel. And I pressed my fingers to my temples, hoping to stir up an idea and get us out of that mess.

Finally, Sean spoke up. "Maybe another car will come along. You never know."

"Keep an eye out for one and get ready to jump out and flag him down," I told him.

"I say we set out walking," said Jamal. "I spotted a sign a while back that said *Pine Spring Ahead*, but I didn't catch how far."

"You should have said something," I lashed out. "That's crucial information. It could make the difference between life and death for us."

"Sorry, man," Jamal said, his voice soft and apologetic. "Things look different out here. We'd have to go miles and miles before we see any signs of life."

"So, what do we do now? Did you say, *walk?*" I said, still irritated.

"I'm not walkin' anywhere," whined Sean.

Jamal stepped out of the car and motioned for us to follow. We did, not knowing what else to do.

"Let's pray," Jamal said. He extended his hands, and we formed a little prayer circle, right there in the middle of the Texas desert.

Sean squeezed my hand. "Yeah. Pray Jamal. Pray hard."

It surprised me that Sean had reacted with such intensity. If nothing else positive came out of this tragedy, maybe my Irish friend might draw closer to God. Maybe he'd even make a profession of faith. Perhaps, if this were our last day on earth, all three of us might go straight to heaven, together.

Still, I wanted to live, and as Jamal prayed, a surge of adrenaline began to build up inside me, and I formulated a plan. Though walking anywhere in that hot, desolate wasteland bordered on the insane, that's exactly what we needed to do. I couldn't just sit there and wait for help to come. I had to *do* something, and walking was the only thing that made sense.

The thing was, Jamal and I were both athletes. We'd trained for years and had built up our endurance. Sure, we played basketball. But we also lifted weights, and, in recent months, we'd entered a couple 5-K races.

Meanwhile, Sean avoided all manner of exercise, was at least sixty pounds overweight, and played no sports whatsoever. There was no way he could walk more than a mile on a sizzling highway in the middle of nowhere.

After adding my "Amen" to theirs, I raised my head and turned to Sean. "Jamal and I can walk. We'll head west and look for a town, a gas pump, a hermit's cabin, a tepee, anything that might have life in it. You should stay with the car. If someone comes along and can siphon some gas into our tank, then go ahead and drive after us. Or, hitch a ride and come find us. If no one comes along, you can just sit here and wait for us to return."

Sean's face screwed up like he was about to cry.

"I promise, we're gonna be all right," I said with even less confidence than I'd had during the carjacking.

Jamal handed Sean the car keys. Their eyes met in what looked like a final goodbye. I loaded a backpack with six bottles of water, a few snacks, a pack of Sean's matches, and a flashlight. Then Jamal and I donned baseball caps and sunglasses. Jamal slipped into the backpack. I grabbed the empty gas can, and we started out on what promised to be a long, hot journey.

I looked back once to see Sean in the driver's seat with the window down, a bottle of water in his hand. Then the two of us took off in the direction of the sinking sun.

As we strode along the deserted highway, Jamal and I talked about our two favorite subjects—sports and girls, and you can guess who talked about which.

"Wasn't that close between Duke and Kentucky in the NCAA Championship game?" my friend said. "I rooted for the Blue Devils right to the end."

"Of course, you did," I noted.

Jamal had set his heart on playing for Duke when he got into grad school. He had yet to hear from the scout that came to see him play several weeks ago. By now, I suspected Jamal had pretty much given up.

"There's still lots of time." I offered. "Those coaches don't make a decision overnight."

"I know, but if I don't hear something soon, I doubt I ever will."

I paused on the road for a moment, and turned to look at him. My friend needed a word of encouragement.

"Tell me, Jamal," I said. "What was your favorite basketball moment? Was it that time you shot four three-pointers in one game?"

He'd stopped walking too, and he stared past me, like he was remembering. "Yeah, that was the moment, the best I've ever done. But as far as *watching* a game, my favorite moment had to be Duke versus Kentucky seven years ago. I was fourteen years old at the time, and it was a defining moment for me."

He'd started walking again. I stepped up beside him. "Yeah," I said, nodding. "I read about that game. Never saw it though."

"It was incredible. I watched it on television with Mama and my cousins. It literally changed my life."

"Life-changing, huh?"

"Yeah. That game sealed my desire to play for Duke. The score was 103 to 102, with Kentucky up by one. Only two seconds remained and everyone figured Duke lost. But Grant Hill had the ball at Kentucky's goal, and I suppose everyone figured he'd try to get it to half court and then they'd call a time out and go from there. But, like I said, only two seconds remained on the clock."

Jamal was breathing heavy, either from the heat of the day or from the excitement of rehashing the game. With a burst of new-found energy, he launched into a blow-by-blow account of those last two seconds.

"The clock started back up and Grant Hill chucked the ball, overhand, in a 79-foot pass to Christian Laettner at the opposite foul line. Christian did a turnaround jump shot, sinking the ball during the last second of the game and making the final score 103 to 104."

Jamal's voice had turned more excited, and he'd started shouting. "On the TV, Christian's teammates crowded around him, hugging him, screaming, and celebrating. But you know what? Grant Hill just stood there on the other side of the court crying tears of joy. And the same thing happened at my house. All my cousins went crazy, hugging each other and yelling and jumping around. But like Grant Hill, I just stood there in front of the TV, my eyes watering, my heart in my throat."

I chanced another look at Jamal. Even now, his eyes had glazed over.

"That was the moment I went from *liking* basketball to *loving* basketball," he said, choking up a little. "It struck me that although the win depended on Laettner making the final shot, Hill had to throw an impossibly long pass with less than a second to spare. They had to work together to make it happen."

I gave him a minute to collect himself. We kept walking, two buddies sharing an emotional moment in the life of one of them.

"You know," I said at last. "Even if you never play for Duke or any other team, I'd say you have a great future as a sports announcer."

We laughed together over that one, then turned our attention to the road ahead and our smiles faded. There was no sign of a town of any size—only stark wilderness, and a ribbon of road that seemed to go on forever. Even more crucial, the sun had dropped closer to the horizon.

For a long time, it looked like a puddle of water had collected on top of the highway ahead of us, but every time we got closer, the puddle moved farther down the road. We'd been walking for about two hours when we spotted what must have been another one of those mirages. This time, however, the mirage grew larger and had a sign that said, *Pine Spring*.

At last. We'd found Pine Spring. We started running. My lips were parched. My breath came in short gasps. Jamal raced ahead of me, like always. Even so, I could see his shoulders heaving, like he'd started panting for air.

He got to the sign first and slumped to the ground. I staggered up beside him, my lungs feeling like someone had kindled a fire in there. I looked past the sign to more nothingness.

"Do you see a town?" I said, scanning the landscape.

Jamal shook his head, then buried his face in his hands.

"Do you see any springs?"

"No, Charlie. There's no town. No springs. Just a place called Pine Spring."

He staggered to his feet. "Look around, Charlie. "There's no gas station, no store, no houses, not even a real spring." He stared at me, his eyes big and round like he was in shock. "It's like a big highway bait-n-switch. There's nothing except more sage brush, more rocks, and more sand."

I looked behind us at the road we'd traveled. I figured we'd gone at least ten miles since we left the car. We couldn't go back. Then, I looked ahead. Before us stretched another expanse of nothingness. It was decision time.

"We need to go on," I conceded.

Jamal squeezed his eyes shut and nodded. Then, he gave the sign post a solid kick and walked away, limping.

Sighing and mumbling, we trudged on, drained two more bottles of water, and kept our eyes trained on the highway ahead. The mountains to our right now loomed closer. They looked to be steel gray, like someone had carved them out of pure metal. The entire scene had taken on a dismal, foreboding appearance. It was like all of Texas was telling us to go home, but now we couldn't.

"Please God," I pleaded. "Send a car. Send a semi. Send a *mule*. Anything."

The sun arced a little to the south, then slowly sank behind the hills. Streaks of orange and gold rippled across the purple sky. It would have been a beautiful scene if not for our trouble. I swallowed my heart. Night was falling on the desert.

"We'd better find something soon," Jamal said. "Before it gets so dark we can't see the road anymore."

"I have a flashlight," I reminded him, but he gave me one of his screwed up looks that said, *Really? A flashlight out here? You've got to be kidding.*

"So, what do we do when it's too dark to keep going? I figure the flashlight can light up the road, and nighttime will be cooler for walking."

Jamal shook his head. "We need to rest. We'll find a rock for a place to lay our head, like my mama feared we'd have to do. And we'll burn some sagebrush to keep the critters away."

My skin began to crawl. "Critters?" I said.

Desert wildlife differed from what lurked in the back woods of Florida. Back home, we knew how to stay clear of bears and snakes while trekking through the national forest. But this unfamiliar territory had me looking over my shoulder about every five minutes. Weren't there cougars out there? And Gila monsters? And prairie dogs with big teeth? Not to mention rattlesnakes. I swallowed hard and started to tremble.

Jamal, a former Boy Scout, gazed at me with his chin up and his shoulders back. Either he'd learned to be a true man of the wild or he had a knack for pretending he was. He gestured toward a flat piece of ground. He gathered some sagebrush and started a fire, then made a rock pile for himself to lean on.

"You can use the backpack for a pillow," he said, and I took him up on his offer. I wasn't proud. In my weary condition, I wasn't about to get magnanimous—not in no man's land.

Chapter Nine

With the departure of the sun, a bitter chill settled on the desert. Fortunately, Jamal and I had brought jackets along. Though lightweight, they gave us a reasonable amount of shelter from the cold. Jamal's small fire also helped. I gazed into the flames and thought about Sean, huddled alone inside the Silver Bullet.

"Do you think Sean's okay?" I said.

Jamal snickered. "Don't worry about Sean. He's safe inside the Bullet. And don't forget, he's got whatever's left of our food and water."

Sighing, I reclined against the backpack with my hands behind my head, and I pictured Heather, sitting on her front porch, perhaps looking up at the same star-filled sky I was looking at. The time difference was one hour, maybe two depending on whether we had already crossed into the Mountain Time zone, so it already had to be dark in Gainesville, too.

The blackness above extended far beyond anything we could have imagined. Even the broad desert appeared miniscule compared to the diamond-studded expanse above. My comfort came from knowing the same One who'd created it all was looking down on Jamal and me. He knew our plight, and He could rescue us.

I listened as Jamal sent a prayer into the star-filled heavens above. When he finished, I thought I heard him whisper, "Know what I'm sayin'?" even to God, and I had to smile.

Moments later, I found myself tubing down the Rainbow River, floating along without a care in the world. Moss covered oaks passed overhead, and I lay back and let the Central Florida forest swallow me up. A sense of peace settled over me as I drifted along. I had no problems, no decisions to make, no desert monsters to trouble me.

Suddenly, an unexpected violence disturbed my tranquil setting, and a vigorous shaking threatened to send me flying off the inner tube and into the dark water.

"Charlie! Charlie! Wake up!" Jamal's voice broke through my serenity.

I opened my eyes, blinked, and found my friend leaning over me shaking my arm. In the light of the flashlight he held, his face glowed with excitement.

"Headlights!" he shouted. "Get up! Headlights are coming down the highway."

I don't know if Jamal yanked me upright or if I flew to my feet under my own power, but seconds later I was standing by the side of the road next to him.

I frowned with confusion. A desolate highway stretched ahead of us to the west. Jamal turned me around, and, sure enough, two headlights had broken through the darkness and were barreling down on us.

We started waving frantically. Jamal signaled with the flashlight. The vehicle drew closer and larger. A semi was coming toward us at top speed. We continued waving our arms, then started yelling. The driver didn't stop, just blew his air horn and sailed on by. I suppressed a curse word on the tip of my tongue and started to slump to the ground, when I spotted another set of headlights about a half-mile behind the semi.

As this second vehicle drew closer, I joined Jamal's leaping and shouting. The silver gray car with a sagging bumper glistened in the light of the moon. It looked like a beautiful chariot from heaven. And in the driver's seat sat a smiling Irishman.

Jamal tossed sand on the fire. Then, he and I gathered up our belongings and reached for the door handles mere seconds before the Silver Bullet came to a complete stop. Sean greeted us with a laugh and a beckoning hand. "Come on, guys. We've been rescued."

We piled in with backpack and empty gas can. I grabbed the passenger seat, and Jamal folded himself up in the backseat with his knees bent and his feet pressed against the opposite door.

"That semi—" Sean began. "The driver had several gas cans—every one of them full of precious fuel. Said he never traveled across

Texas without 'em and could spare a little to help out a stranded vehicle. Do you believe it? He poured a can in our gas tank. Then he handed me this religious tract, and said, 'God be with you.' He took off before I could thank him."

Sean handed me the tract, titled, "Truth for Travelers." It bore a series of drawings and a text that gave the plan of salvation in simple terms.

"Do you think he was an angel?" Sean said, his face aglow.

I shrugged. "Maybe. I'm sure such things happen, though I've never had the experience, as far as I know."

"It had to be," Jamal hailed from the backseat. "Think about it. We don't see another vehicle all night, then one comes along with free gas, and then he disappears down the road—just vanishes into oblivion. What else could he have been but an angel?"

I handed the tract back to Sean, and he slipped it in his pocket. "I'll read it later," he promised with a nod. "So, we're all set, guys. Angel or no angel, God must have answered our prayers, right?"

I loved that Sean had acknowledged God's help in our troubles. Perhaps our rotten luck had opened up more doors for us to talk to him about spiritual matters. Like the Bible said, God could work good out of the worst circumstances.

The three of us made quite a balanced trio. Jamal with his spirit of adventure mixed with memorized quotes from the Bible. Me, ready and willing to try the next big dare, no matter how risky. And, Sean, so cautious he often put a damper on even the safest activities. I had to laugh. Not long ago, I'd suggested a safari ride at Busch Gardens. Sean nearly had a breakdown.

"Don't they have wild animals in those open air pens?" he'd said, his face flushed with fear. "I mean, they could get loose, right?"

I have to admit, I used to play it safe like Sean. It was Jamal who got me to try things I'd never done before, like zip-lining and skydiving. I almost lost my breakfast after jumping out of a plane, but looking back I deemed it one of the greatest thrills of my life. I still bragged about that one jump to anyone who showed the slightest interest, probably bored some of my friends to tears by repeating the story ad nauseam.

Sean was driving slower than what Jamal and I would do, but then, he wasn't the most confident behind the wheel. It would probably take forever to get to the next town. It didn't matter. We'd cheated death. We were together again and back on our road trip. I sat comfortably in the passenger seat, content that Sean was doing a fair job of keeping my car on the road. While Jamal had been my *best* friend for a couple of years, Sean had moved into a close second. After all, I'd learned to trust him enough to let him drive my car.

We three didn't have the usual, run-of-the-mill friendships that die off after graduation. It looked like our relationship could last a lifetime, despite our differences, which, believe it or not, made up the glue that held us together. We balanced each other. We kept each other in check.

I was smiling at the thought, when I caught sight of a beautiful sign that said *Dell City, gas and lodging.* The arrow pointed to a side road sixteen miles north on highway 180. I hated to lose time by getting off on a rabbit trail, but, I feared if we didn't turn now, we might end up on another stretch of highway with an empty gas tank.

"Do you think it's another trick?" Jamal piped up from the back seat.

I shook my head. "At least it has the word *city* in its name. Not like Pine Spring where there was no city, no pine trees, and not even a real spring."

By this time, our supply of gas had dropped below the quarter mark again. It amazed me that the semi driver had known exactly how much gas we needed to get to the next stop.

Miracle of miracles, one of the first structures we came to after entering the city limits was a gas station. Okay, it had only one pump. Nevertheless, the three of us let out a resounding cheer.

"We'll fill up the Silver Bullet and then move on," Sean said, and I kind of liked the tone of authority in his voice. So out of character for him.

To my disappointment, however, everything in town had closed down for the night, including the gas station. Jamal suggested we park next to the pump and sleep in the car until morning when the station opened.

I started to nod my agreement, then I did a double-take at the "Pay at the Pump" sign. I pulled out my one credit card and filled the tank to the top. For a second, I thought I heard the Silver Bullet sigh with satisfaction.

We couldn't see hanging around a town where everything had closed for the night. El Paso was less than two hours away, so we hopped back on U.S. 180 South and then picked up U.S. 62 going west. We arrived in El Paso around midnight and started looking for a motel, though, at that hour, I doubted any of them would be open.

We bypassed the more ritzy looking places we couldn't afford and drove deeper into the city, finding ourselves in a rundown section of town. Except for a wino staggering along the street, we didn't see anyone who could recommend a motel. The one we ended up staying in looked an awful lot like the fleabag we'd slept in at the beach. We didn't have much choice. It was the only place that still had a **Vacancy** light on out front. While the fleabag cost us $29.99, this one came to $54. That meant $18 apiece had to come out of our budget, leaving almost nothing for food for the next two days.

We thought about the cost for only one minute. We were exhausted, bummed out over the trek in the desert, and we didn't want to leave El Paso in the middle of the night.

We agreed to take the room and make up the finances somewhere else along the way.

It wasn't easy forking over $18 of my hard-earned cash to the seedy looking motel clerk with the horn-rimmed glasses and five-o'clock shadow. He handed us two room keys—plastic cards with an arrow indicating which end goes in the lock.

We trudged around the outside of the motel until we found our room in the back on the second floor. The entire motel looked like it needed a good pressure washing, and the walk past the down-stairs row of rooms was littered with empty beer bottles and fast food wrappers. I approached the lopsided metal stairway to the second floor and thought about going back to the front desk and demanding the clerk give me my money back. I had a bad feeling about this place. The Silver Bullet's cramped backseat suddenly seemed more inviting.

Right about the time I needed to make a decision, the outside lights went dark, and the *Vacancy* sign changed to *No Vacancy*. Up the stairs I went, my duffel bag in one hand and in the other hand, the motel laundry bag containing our few remaining snacks. Red paint covered the door to our room and I had a hard time getting inside, had to jiggle the card in the lock several times before something sprang and the door popped open with a groan.

I entered the room to the odor of dirty socks and the clicking of a struggling air conditioner. I hit the wall switch, illuminating the room in a pale shade of yellow. The three of us unloaded our bags on a little side table. I swallowed hard. Even my apartment with Hank's junk strewn all over was ten times cleaner than this.

Things went slightly uphill from there. To my surprise, clean towels hung in the bathroom, which reeked of a heavy dose of bleach. Tiny one-inch tiles covered the bathroom floor, and the fixtures glistened. At least housekeeping had done its job.

The two full-size beds had freshly laundered sheets, thank the Lord. But, the shag carpet was a sick shade of green and had matted strands I didn't want to walk across barefoot.

I grabbed the shower first. The pounding hot spray almost redeemed the place. But as I exited the shower and crossed over to the door, several of those tiny tiles stuck to the bottoms of my damp feet. I took a moment to peel them off and press them back into the webbing where they belonged. Then I slipped into my sandals, wrapped a towel around my waist and relinquished the shower to Jamal, who'd been waiting outside the bathroom door.

Twenty minutes later, he came out sputtering and complaining about the loose tiles.

Sadly for Sean, by the time he got to use the shower, there was no hot water left. He let out a shriek that should have awakened the snoring drunk in the room next door. The paper thin wall did little to muffle the guy's nasal eruptions. He sputtered a little, then went back to a steady snore. I knew then that I should have slept in my car.

Worse yet, the full-size bed meant Jamal and I didn't have as much space between us as we had when we slept on the queen size mattress at the other place. I lay rigid all night, like a stick of dynamite in a bed full of matches. Jamal must have done the same, because not once did he bump or kick me.

Around 2 a.m. I lurched out of bed to a loud popping sound somewhere outside. In that part of town it could have been anything from a car backfiring to a gunshot. Then, someone screamed at the other end of the motel. I checked to make sure our door was chained, and I made up my mind right then and there that from now on we needed to stay in nicer parts of town, preferably areas that attracted tourists instead of local druggies.

We took no delay packing up the next morning, left the key cards in the room, and raced down the metal stairway. No surprise, the motel offered no continental breakfast, no coffee, and no friendly, "Goodbye, come again." Only one thought cheered us as we made our departure. We were on our way to the Grand Canyon, which promised to be one of the main highlights of our road trip.

It was still dark when we departed, so we munched on stale muffins and water. Sean used our flashlight to look over the pile of highway routes he'd printed up on his computer. The steady snapping of paper as he flipped through the pages began to irritate me. After a night of little sleep, trying to keep my distance from Jamal, and then flying out of bed every time I heard a popping sound, I wasn't in my best humor.

"Can you please hurry up and find the route and stop flipping those darn pages?" I snapped.

"Cool it, Charlie. I'm almost there—ah, here it is. Okay, the next town is Alamogordo, New Mexico, located about 80 miles to the north. We should be able to find a grocery store there. All I know is, I'm tired of these muffins. They're beginning to taste like sawdust."

"Oh, yeah?" piped up Jamal. "And how do you know what sawdust tastes like? We need to thank the Lord for whatever He gives us. So, we have muffins. Or maybe you'd like to scrape some peanut butter off the bottom of the jar, 'cause there ain't no bread or nothin' else in our little make-believe food pantry."

"Just shut up, Jamal," Sean barked from the backseat.

"You stink, Sean," Jamal shot back. "Didn't you brush your teeth this morning?"

"Yeah, I'm breathin' out your hot air."

Our fourth day on the road and tension had started to build. How could we expect to get through another ten days? Jamal was driving, and I needed to keep him calm and handling my car safely. I figured we could use a lift of some kind, so I started singing one of my favorite Roger Miller songs, "King of the Road," a perfect accompaniment to our travels.

My vocal offering was met with groans from the other two guys. But by the time I got to the line about "old stogies," raucous laughter filled the car, and seconds later, all three of us belted out the resounding chorus.

As we continued north, we must have sung that song nine times. About then, we entered the city limits of Alamogordo. At 9:15 a.m., the city had already come to life. First thing, we started searching for a grocery store, but before we found one, Sean came up with a super idea.

"Hey, guys. I know how we can get a free lunch."

I perked up and I'm pretty sure Jamal did, too.

"How's that, Einstein?" I said, a slice of sarcasm entering my voice.

"Did you know if you take a tour of a college, they sometimes give you a free cafeteria pass?"

"And where do you expect to accomplish this?" Jamal said, his tone skeptical.

"We're in Alamogordo, right?"

"Right," we both said, like a male duet.

"Alamogordo has a community college, a branch of New Mexico State University."

Aside from raving about the genius in the back seat, nothing more needed to be said. We followed the signs to the college and went straight to the administration building. It turned out most of the classrooms were locked. Students and teachers had left on spring break. The receptionist informed us the school had no one who could take us on a tour, however, we could walk around the campus and check out the layout of the buildings. To our relief, the cafeteria was one of the buildings that had remained open so the working staff and maintenance people could eat lunch.

We left the office with three meal tickets in our hands and big smiles on our faces. We found the cafeteria, disappointed to find there were no hot foods. So, we loaded up on two sandwiches apiece, along with chips, cookies, and six cans of soda.

Chapter Ten

We strolled about the campus, found a park bench in a shady spot, and while eating lunch, we agreed to take stock of our budget. Between the three of us we still had $610, two-thirds of what we'd started with, but we hadn't reached San Francisco yet. It was Tuesday, day four of a fourteen-day trip.

"What should we do, guys?" I shook my head and puffed out a sigh. "We can't keep freeloading off college cafeterias."

"Why don't we find work somewhere," suggested Sean. "I can wash dishes, maybe get us a meal in a decent restaurant for a change."

Jamal frowned. "That'll slow us down. We have to make California within the next three days or we're cooked."

"What? You can't show up a day or two late for classes?" Sean said in disbelief.

"We're already taking an extra week for this trip," Jamal countered. "I don't know about you, Sean, but I'm buckin' for a scholarship."

Sean let out a snicker. "Yeah," he sneered. "In basketball."

"My grades have to be up, too."

Sean backed off then and scowled.

"We'll figure something out," I said, but the tension remained.

When we got back to the car, the two of them still hadn't spoken, just cast annoyed glances at each other. Jamal settled into the driver's seat and checked out our routing pages.

"The Grand Canyon is almost nine hours away," he announced. "If we leave now, it'll be dark by the time we get there."

I leaned close to him to get a better look at the page. "Anyplace we can stop for the night?" I said.

He scanned the route again. "We can take I-10 to Phoenix and spend the night there, then leave for the Grand Canyon in the morning."

Sean started singing "By the Time I Get to Phoenix," but he substituted *Heather will be risin'* instead of the original lyrics.

"Shut up, Sean," I growled. "You're no Glen Campbell."

He clammed up then and slumped down in his seat.

"Sorry," I said with feigned remorse. "I'm just tired of eatin' the same ol' thing, day after day. And I'm afraid we're gonna run out of cash long before we start for home."

"We should have planned our budget better," said Jamal. "But who knew the prices changed from place to place?" He glared at me. "It's your fault, Charlie. You took charge of our budget. You should have come up with better calculations."

I glared back at him, certain he'd turned into Mr. Burnside, the fifth-grade teacher who'd made my life a living hell. Then, I turned to look in the back and pictured Satan himself sitting there, red-faced and wearing an Irish T-shirt. We'd been on the road for four days and already I wished I'd never thought up the insanity of a 3,000-mile road trip with the two of them.

If I could have caught a bus or a plane, I might have headed back to Florida. But we were driving *my* car. I suppose I could have dumped the two of them without feeling a single thread of remorse for doing it. But could I live with my conscience after that?

Fuming, I mulled over all the bad stuff we'd experienced over the past four days.

So far, I'd nearly destroyed my car by taping that *California or Bust* sign on the front. Okay, that was my fault, not theirs. Then, we'd suffered through a real carjacking, My fault, too. I was the one who'd suggested we pick the guy up. Then, Jamal and I had to walk for several hours on blistering pavement with the sun beating down on us. Again, my fault. I hadn't told the guys about the fuel problem. I crumbled under the realization that every disaster, so far, had been my fault.

Not only had I made a mess of our road trip, I'd driven away from my girlfriend, maybe left her to the clutches of wolves like Robby Richards. The dream of a road trip had become a nightmare, and we still had a long way to go.

Overwhelmed with regrets, I pulled my wallet out and flipped to

Heather's picture. I stared at her trusting blue eyes and her sweet smile. If I went home now, I'd be telling her I'd failed to complete a simple thing like a 3,000-mile trip across the entire United States. What did that say about my ability to complete a marriage?

I might find it easy to disappoint Jamal and Sean. Guys don't care what you do. But Heather? I didn't want to let her down, didn't want her to see me as a failure, not even at this.

I put my wallet away, then glanced at Jamal and then at Sean. The truth was, I didn't want to disappoint them, either. Nor did I want to ruin a friendship that had given me so much stability while I suffered through classes and a thankless part-time job. At that moment, conviction settled into my heart.

"Look, guys," I said, turning to face them. "I've been a little short with you, and I want to apologize. Why don't we forget all the nasty remarks and set our eyes on Phoenix? The rest of our trip should be a piece o' cake. Let's take each day as it comes and cut expenses wherever we can."

Still, a stirring inside my gut got me hoping nothing else bad lay somewhere down the road. It didn't help that during our journey to Phoenix, more yammering started up again. Our hoard of snack foods had almost run out, leaving us hungry and irritated. I had Sean check the laundry bag. He found a stale muffin and a dried-up piece of bread. I'd had my fill of leftovers. By now, I was famished enough to eat the stuffing out of the backseat.

Along I-10, between Tucson and Phoenix, several small towns literally sprang up out of the desert. Most of them had little to offer, so we kept on going. In one village, however, we spotted a little grocery store. By this time, my stomach had started churning, and Sean moaned something about starvation.

We agreed to stop and fill up our *pantry*.

We couldn't get inside fast enough. All three stomachs had started growling so loud, we sounded like a chorus of hyenas in *The Lion King* movie. Other patrons turned to stare at us. It didn't matter what they thought. Sean looked pale and weak, like he might pass out at any moment. I determined to save his life. And my own.

We charged up and down the aisles with Jamal pushing the grocery cart. Sean and I tossed in whatever we could find under a dollar or with a two-for-one price on it. We lined up at the checkout counter with a box of six protein bars, two cans of tuna fish, day-old bread, a bag of pretzels, a large bunch of bananas, and a six-pack of Gatorade. Funny how that UF sports beverage had gained popularity all the way across the nation, but there it was again, big as life, in a little ghost town grocery store in Arizona. Our total purchase came to $10.59, so we put back the pretzels and all but three bananas, bringing the cost down to $8.98. Terrific. We'd come within two cents of our nine dollar budget.

The second we piled back in my car—this time with me at the wheel—we tore into those grocery bags like three starving college students, which is what we were. When we finished eating, one can of tuna and three granola bars remained in the bag, plus several bottles of water in the cooler.

Satisfied that we'd been fed, but miserable because lunch had cost our entire day's allotment of cash, we continued along I-10 for the next three hours.

By the time we entered the Phoenix city limits, our appetites had returned, or maybe had never left. Jamal pitched an idea that sounded terrific.

"Guys," he said, pointing. "Look at that sign. It says, *Down Home Diner and Truck Stop. Authentic Southwestern Cuisine. Half-Price on Tuesdays.*" He paused and checked our reactions. "C'mon, you two. Today is Tuesday. The canned tuna and granola bars will be just as fresh tomorrow. Let's eat a real meal."

Sean nearly leaped over the seat. "Let's do it."

I hesitated. "We need to stretch our dollars," I said, the nervous accountant inside me clenching his little fists.

I had to admit, though, after living on sandwiches and rations for four days, I also wanted a hot meal, something I could sink my teeth into, something to warm my stomach until we got to the next grocery store, at least.

I looked again at the sign, and my mouth began to water. "You know," I said. "Half-price Tuesday might be the best deal we'll find in a long while. Maybe we should take advantage of it and cut back somewhere else."

I found a parking space, and the three of us bounded inside. A beautiful señorita with shiny black hair and flashing eyes seated us in a booth, then returned with menus and glasses of water. We gulped the water down, then perused the menus.

Other than something called "Add Guacamole for $1," the cheese quesadillas were the cheapest thing on the menu. We ordered three plates and a basket of nachos to share.

While waiting for our order to arrive, we visited the bathroom. We weren't back in our booth more than five minutes when Señorita returned balancing three sizzling platters on a tray. The aroma alone sent me reeling. I'd been eating what had begun to taste like particle board for four days and had almost forgotten what real food tasted like. It turned out the quesadilla was the most delicious thing I'd eaten in a long time. The melted cheese. The chunks of chicken. The peppers and salsa and sour cream. I cleaned my plate and smiled with satisfaction.

"I could eat another plateful," I commented, rubbing my stomach.

"So, order another one," Jamal challenged.

"Dude, I can't afford another one."

"C'mon, Charlie. This is a once-in-a-lifetime opportunity. Get yourself another quesadilla."

I shook my head. "No," I said, but my voice was weak. "My budget—"

"You have a credit card, don't you?" Jamal goaded, his eyes twinkling.

"I brought it for emergencies."

"Well," Jamal reasoned. "Isn't this an emergency?"

Then, like Satan in disguise, Sean joined the temptation. "If you can't finish it, I'll be glad to help," he said, mopping up the leftover puddle of salsa on his own plate.

I kept shaking my head, but my resistance already had begun to wane.

"Don't be such a tightwad, Charlie," Jamal prodded, "It's half-price Tuesday. You will pay the same price as if you waited until tomorrow, but you'll get two for the price of one right now."

His outrageous reasoning made sense to me. "Man, you guys are relentless."

Our server happened to walk by at that moment. She paused and looked down at my empty plate. "Did you want another quesadilla, sir?"

Sir? She'd called me *Sir*, and I wasn't much older than she was. I found myself nodding my head and smiling.

As Señorita walked off, I looked at my two buddies and shook my head. "Maybe you two should work here."

Jamal winked at me. "Oh, Sean and I know exactly how to tempt you, Charlie. Especially when you've been starving yourself and now there's real food available."

"Right. Like I'm Adam and the two of you are Eve and the snake in the garden. And instead of a piece of fruit, you're dangling a quesadilla in front of me."

When my second plate arrived, I plunged in with enthusiasm, without another thought about the budget.

Sean chose that moment to lean across the table, his eyes intense. "You mentioned Adam and Eve," he began. "Tell me. Do you guys believe they really existed, or are their names simply a metaphor for the earliest humans?"

I looked up from my plate. "Yes, Sean, I believe they really existed." Then I scooped another forkful into my mouth.

Jamal nodded his agreement, "Same here."

Sean snickered. "Yeah, well, that's what I thought you'd say. You guys always act like the stuff in the Bible is for real. But, come on. The Bible has a lot of hard-to-believe stories in it." He fidgeted with his fork, and serious wrinkles creased his brow. "For one thing, I don't get how we all descended from two people. I mean, doesn't that make us all related?"

He stared at Jamal, who didn't hesitate. "Yeah, Sean. We're all distant cousins. It's one of the reasons racism is so stupid."

Sean pointed at the Irish-themed logo on his shirt. "So you believe if we go back far enough, I'm related to some Chinese guy?"

I swallowed another glorious bite of cheese-dripping tortilla, while Jamal took over.

"Not only a Chinese guy, but even to me," Jamal said with a snicker.

Sean chuckled, "Does that mean I have to call you *Bro?*"

"Yeah," said Jamal. "But say it with respect."

We shared a laugh, then I went back to my quesadilla, and Jamal continued his monologue.

"Let's face it, Sean," he said. "It isn't so much about where everything started and what people are related as it is about where we'll all end up. Heaven and hell are for real, and you need to start thinking about where you want to go."

He went on to explain the importance of believing in a Savior, rather than trusting in oneself for the outcome.

Maybe it was the jalapenos, but Jamal's mini sermon had me feeling a little flushed and tingly inside, like we'd stumbled on a tent revival meeting and Sean was about to be filled with the Holy Spirit.

But, our Irish friend didn't leap from the booth and shout, "Hallelujah!" Instead, he appeared to be relieved when Señorita came back with our check.

I looked at Jamal for a response. With a blink of his eyes, he sent me a message to let the subject drop for the time being.

That night, we settled down with full stomachs, contented that the next day we'd be coming up on one of the most scenic parts of our journey. The Grand Canyon National Park—about four hours away, and I couldn't wait to get there.

We lucked out with a fantastic motel room for $23.99, which saved each of us a few of the dollars we'd lost by overeating. *Every little bit helps,* I told myself.

Jamal and I crashed on a spacious queen-size bed. As usual, Sean used the bathroom last, and he stayed in there for a long time. At one point, a loud kerplunk resounded from behind the closed door, followed by Sean's self-incriminating "Eejit!"

Jamal and I looked at each other.

"Did he have that much to eat?" Jamal said, snickering.

"I don't think so. But, why did he just call himself an idiot?"

"Don't know," said Jamal, and he rolled to his other side.

Sean mumbled a string of curses.

The two of us rose up on our elbows and stared at the bathroom door.

"What's going on in there?" I said to Jamal. "Do you think we should check?"

My bed-mate shook his head and flopped back against his pillow. "You go, if you want to. I'm not budging."

Then, on the other side of the bathroom door arose a whirring sound.

"At this hour he's blow-drying his hair?" Jamal said.

I frowned and got out of bed. "I've got to find out what's going on in there."

I knocked on the bathroom door, then I opened it and froze. Sean had spread all of his money on the floor, like a great big picture puzzle of cash. He knelt over the array of sopping wet greenery and moved the hair dryer back and forth in a slow sweeping motion.

He turned to look up at me, a sheepish grin on his face. "My wallet fell in the john," he explained, then went back to sweeping the hair dryer back and forth, back and forth.

I burst out laughing, then leaned out the door. "Get over here, Jamal. You gotta see this."

Seconds later, he was at my side.

The three of us had a good laugh over that one, so side-splitting in fact, we didn't get to sleep for a long time after. Nobody had to say a word. Every five minutes or so, one of us started laughing and then the other two joined in. Finally, Jamal said, "Enough! We have to get some sleep, guys."

All went quiet. My side stopped aching from all the laughing, and I was able to catch my breath. But, about fifteen minutes later, a noise erupted from my side of the bed that must have awakened people in Cleveland.

"Sorry, fellas," I said. "But, two quesadillas were a little much."

And the howling started all over again.

Chapter Eleven

At 6 a.m. we were ready to hit the road. A little after ten o'clock, we made it to our most anticipated stop of the whole trip. The Grand Canyon!

The visitor's center on the south rim had already opened its doors. We stood in line with a bunch of other tourists, then strolled along a wire-fenced walking trail that led to a lookout point. We stood there, wide-eyed, on the brink of a huge abyss, and stared out at the most incredible layers of multi-colored rock and slate, plunging below and towering above. I stood speechless, an unusual condition for me. It looked like someone had taken a giant chisel and a humongous paintbrush and created the most spectacular work of art I'd ever seen.

A nearby rock face at Lookout Studio contained a large plaque bearing Psalm 104:24, *O Lord, how manifold are thy works! in wisdom hast thou made them all; the earth is full of thy riches.*

Jamal read the words aloud.

I couldn't agree more. Here we were, on the edge of a deep rainbow-streaked abyss with a copper colored river trailing into the distance below. Steep walls loomed on all sides in shades of pink and gray, brown and mauve, purple and blue, with stark, black shadows in the crevices between them. It truly was *Grand!*

As I stood there, taking it all in, the murmurings of the people faded amidst the grandeur of the scene before me. I was gazing at of one of the most awesome wonders of the world, and I could hardly breathe.

I pulled my eyes away long enough to look at my two friends.

"God's artistry is so much better than man's," Jamal crooned.

And Sean? Well, his reaction was expectantly different. While Jamal and I were clearly awestruck, Sean shook his head and invoked a little boring wisdom from his geology class.

"What you're looking at resulted from a huge tectonic uplift that started sixty million years ago," he spouted.

I gawked at him, like I couldn't believe he hadn't caught the grandeur of that place. I gave him one of my best frowns, the kind I usually reserved for my opponents on the basketball court.

Oblivious to my reaction, Sean continued with his monologue. "Over the centuries, the top layers eroded away, and the Colorado River cut through the area and left behind these magnificent walls of stone. We read all about it in our geology class."

So much for the grandeur of that place. Why didn't Sean see what *I* saw?

"Look, pal," I snarled. "You can't tell me all of this beauty happened by chance." I waved my arm toward the abyss. "How can you look at the size and grandeur of this place and not believe a great Creator did it all?"

"It's called education," he shot back. "Something you obviously know little about."

"Oh, really, Mr. D in math?"

He smirked at me. "Need I remind you that my one A is in science?"

"Enough, guys," Jamal interrupted. "Let's put our differences aside and just enjoy the view. We have a lot to be thankful for, know what I'm sayin'? Beautiful weather. Clear skies. Not a drop of rain to spoil our day."

I had to agree. We had come there during spring break, the area's driest time of the year. But, although the hot, dry climate should have turned the canyon into a fiery furnace, the altitude made up for the lack of moisture and brought a steady flow of breathable air to our lungs. With it came the unmistakable scents of pine needles and rich clay. And except for the soft murmurs rising from the crowd of awestruck people, I could imagine myself standing there alone, just soaking it all up.

"What do you say, guys, do you want to take a hike?" Jamal said, breaking through my trance.

My spirit of adventure awakened. "Sure," I said. Then, I checked out the gathering crowd. "But, let's find another place, somewhere more private."

We left the mob of tourists and drove along a side road that took us to a more secluded part of the canyon. Along the way, Sean cleared his throat and treated us to more bits of wisdom.

"Listen to this guys," he said, flipping through a notebook he'd brought along.

"The average depth of the Grand Canyon is one mile, and the gorge is more than 2,000 feet deep. The average width is ten miles from rim to rim. *Ten miles*, guys! but in most places it's a lot narrower. Over millions of years, the river carved out its path through the canyon. Each layer formed when sediment eroded away and more deposits filled in the gaps."

I let Sean ramble on, chose not to shut him down. Something I heard a preacher say once made a lot of sense right then. "You can't change a person's convictions until you find out what they believe," the preacher had said.

If I wanted Sean to listen to me when I had something important to tell him, I also needed to listen to what he had to say. I grew politely quiet.

But, millions of years? I scoffed internally. Sean had never been outside the classroom—not to an archaeological dig in the Middle East, and not even to one of those organized surveys of the wetlands south of Gainesville. He'd had no hands-on contact with any kind of geological excavations. Nor had he visited the Grand Canyon before. Yet, he claimed to be an expert.

I could have dismissed everything Sean said. I did that in class all the time, without my professors knowing. It's what my mother referred to as, *going in one ear and out the other*. But, did I want to play that game with Sean? After all, he'd been studying geology for three years. Certainly, a lot of what he'd learned had substance. Didn't the natural course of things often play a role in God's plan? Hadn't He allowed His Son to grow in the womb for nine months? Since none of us know God's ways and thoughts, I had to concede, anything was possible.

After a short drive, we found a secluded spot, left the Bullet by the side of the road, and wandered onto a path that wove between pine trees and thick, flowering shrubs. Sean had left his Cliff notes in the car. Get it? *Cliff* notes?

We could now go on a hike without our friend filling our ears with more questionable data. I wondered if Jamal felt like I did about all those numbers Sean had spilled out. I tried to catch his attention. He turned to look at me and responded to my smirk with a roll of his eyes. Then, he smiled and shrugged as if to say, *Let it be.*

Jamal and I had developed a silent communication system that took little more than a slight movement—a smile, a sneer, a raising of the eyebrows, a frown, or a surprised widening of our eyes. We talked to each other like that almost as much as we used words. We'd done the same on the basketball court. For example, I only had to look at Jamal's face to know when he was about to pass me the ball. And he knew where I'd be standing when he passed it. Our silent communication went beyond a preplanned play. It was spontaneous.

At that moment, without another word, Jamal beckoned me with a bob of his head and started walking along a dirt path that meandered uphill. I followed him.

The canyon remained on our left and a copse of tall pines spread out on our right. Sean came up behind me, and the three of us went single file until we reached a widening of the path. Then, leaving Sean, I caught up with Jamal, and the two of us began to jog, side-by-side, up the hill. Jamal picked up his step, and so did I. He kicked up a little dust. I did too. Before I knew it, our leisurely stroll had turned into a footrace. Jamal sprinted ahead. I passed him. Then, he passed me.

Within seconds, we'd put a great distance between ourselves and Sean, who was lumbering up the hill behind us. I turned once to see how far he'd gotten, then Jamal and I plunged into a full-out race to the top of the grade. I sucked in the crisp air, puffed out my chest, and lengthened my stride. So did Jamal. We were neck-and-neck, then nose-to-nose, gasping and straining for that one last burst of energy. I could almost hear Vangelis' "Chariots of Fire" echoing off the canyon walls. Then, Jamal asked the question that stopped everything.

"Where's Sean?"

I stopped running mere feet from our imaginary finish line. We both turned and caught sight of our red-faced friend struggling to catch us.

As usual, Jamal was the first to show compassion. "Do you think we should wait for him?" he said.

I shook my head. "Nah, he needs to lose a few pounds. Let's make him work for it." I took off like a bat and beat Jamal to the top. Gasping, I pressed my hand against the rock wall, warmed by the midday sun, and I turned around to claim my victory. I'd beaten the great Jamal.

To my surprise, *the great Jamal* had stopped running and had started back down the hill toward Sean. When he reached him, he placed his arm around our exhausted friend and helped him make the climb to the top.

For some reason, I didn't feel quite as cocky anymore. The imagined laurel crown and silver trophy vanished from my brain, and the truth struck me. The real winner of our footrace was the guy with compassion, the one who most likely would hear God say, "Well, done, good and faithful servant."

I bowed my head in shame. If I could have chosen to do the last half-hour over, I'd have done it the way Jamal had.

As they drew close to me, I extended my right hand to Sean.

"Good job, buddy," I said, and I meant it.

We stood together on the cliff and looked out at the vast expanse of sheer walls and narrow gorges. Again, I found the magnitude of the canyon overwhelming. So huge and yet so hushed you could hear a cricket in the bushes. A hawk circled overhead. Its piercing cry shattered the stillness, then all went quiet again.

We had reached a point where the nearby cliffs must have been 1,000 feet or higher, and the drop-offs just as deep. In most places, fencing prevented us from going closer to the edge. We reached one area, however, where the fence consisted of fragile pieces of wood strung together with a clothesline, kind of like an afterthought. It stood a mere three feet high.

I sneered at the makeshift construction. I figured if danger lay on the other side, they would have made the barricade eight feet tall and looped razor wire around the top, kind of like what closes off a prison yard.

But they'd erected no such barrier, so I hopped the fence. As expected, Jamal followed me. Then, Sean, unable to hop, pushed it to the ground and stumbled over it, snagging his foot three times between the slats and pieces of rope. I could hear his frustrated grunts behind me.

With nothing between us and the great abyss, we followed the dirt path but kept a good four feet away from the edge. Eventually, we reached a huge tower of rock that looked to be about two stories high.

"Let's climb to the top," Jamal said, and, without waiting for a response, he started out.

How strange that a guy who claimed to pray about everything had plunged ahead without asking if it might be God's will. That tower of rock didn't look like something a person might want to tackle without a word of prayer.

"We can take pictures of ourselves with the Grand Canyon in the background," Jamal shouted over his shoulder.

That sounded like such a good idea, I dropped the pray-before you-leap plan, stepped up to the base, and followed my friend up the side.

Jamal and I had scaled enough indoor rock walls to have us believing we could tackle Everest. But Sean was an armchair athlete. He got his thrills sitting in front of a TV while other people performed such feats in action movies and documentaries.

"You sure about this?" Sean called from below.

"Piece o' cake," I said, though uncertain.

Prompted by the thought of having his picture taken in a death-defying pose with the Grand Canyon as a backdrop, he started up after me.

There we were—Jamal and me, driven by our overconfident egos—and Sean not wanting to be left out.

The problem was, we had no rock-climbing gear—no carabiners, no ropes to stop our fall, no friendly guide to belay us. *But*, I figured, *it's only twenty feet tall. No need for life-saving equipment.*

We edged our way up, single file, with Jamal leading the way. The jagged rock face caused me to shudder. This didn't look anything like the prefabricated climbing wall we'd mastered at the gym. Nobody had gone up ahead of us and put handholds and footholds in strategic places for us to grab onto. This was God's masterpiece, and we were mere ants attempting to conquer something far bigger than ourselves.

About ten feet up, Jamal stopped climbing.

"It's too steep to go any farther," he called down to me. He craned his neck to the right. "I can see plenty of handholds on the north side. I'm gonna start edging over that way."

He started crawling to his right and disappeared from view. I blindly followed, placing my hands and feet where Jamal had. Sad to say, the route we'd taken posed a real challenge for Sean. He couldn't stretch his arms and legs far enough and had to find his own handholds and footholds. Still, he appeared to be keeping up.

A few minutes later, and a few more feet up the side, Jamal stopped climbing again.

"Nothin' to grab onto here," he shouted, his voice echoing eerily throughout the canyon. *"Grab onto here...grab onto here...grab onto here."*

He began to crawl farther around to the west side, the complete opposite from where we had started. While the east side, where we had begun our climb, rose up about two stories from the ground, the west side hovered precariously over forty or fifty stories of sheer rock face with no net to catch us if we should fall. We'd stopped climbing a twenty-foot pillar. Now we hovered over a great abyss with jagged rocks at the bottom.

My hands had begun to perspire. I feared I might lose my grip. The journey had begun as something a little risky. Now, it had turned into something completely insane. We must have been a sight. Three novice climbers clinging to a pillar of rock many thousands of feet in the air. I thought about going back, but I couldn't, not with someone in front of me and someone else behind me. I held on, literally stuck in the most precarious spot of my life.

I surveyed the route Jamal had taken, and a chill ran through me. My fearless friend either hadn't calculated the extreme height, or he didn't care. Inch-by-inch, he'd kept on going.

What if his mama could see him now? I could almost hear her shriek, "Jamal, you get down from there!"

Like an idiot, I followed him. Stuck between them, I didn't know what else to do.

Then I did the unthinkable. I looked down.

About fifty yards below me, a hawk dipped and circled over the canyon. If I had been standing on the ground, I would have been looking *up* at a bird in the sky. But, now I was looking *down* at it. I was looking down at a bird while it was flying through the sky.

I shuddered. I'd gotten myself trapped between my two buddies—Jamal above me and Sean barely hanging on below me.

"Sean," I called out, aware that my voice squeaked.

My friend clung to the rock like he'd been super glued to it.

"What?" His voice echoed off the stone wall. "What do you want, Charlie?"

"Do you think you can back down?"

"No way. I only know how to go up. Can't see past my stomach to find a foothold."

That settled it. I had nowhere to go but up. I thought about Sean clinging to the rock wall a couple of feet below my shoes. One slip on my part could send both of us hurtling to the bottom of the canyon.

We were alone out there, just the three of us. The sensible tourists had stayed near the visitors center. They didn't drive off on their own. They didn't pass over a broken down fence. They didn't climb any pillars. No, those wise people had gathered on safe ground and, with the canyon walls as a backdrop, they took their pictures there. I regretted we hadn't done the same.

Still, I kept going, determined to stay with Jamal but having less faith in the handholds he left me. They looked nothing like the rigid grips on an indoor climbing wall. These were age-old sedimentary rocks. They could crumble beneath my touch.

Through some miracle, the three of us made it to the top. We gathered close together on a broad ledge and took in the view.

Then, as we relaxed and became more confident, we stepped away from each other and, passing the camera from one to the other, we began taking those ever-important pictures with the Grand Canyon behind us.

Jamal took pictures of Sean and me looking sweaty and worn out. I caught Jamal standing tall and proud, without a drop of perspiration on his entire body. We captured each other in a variety of animated poses, then, exhilarated by our successful climb, we began our descent, this time down the safer east side of the pillar. Still, I didn't breathe normally again until I had both feet planted firmly on solid ground.

Chapter Twelve

In retrospect, I have to admit, climbing a pillar in the Grand Canyon has to be the dumbest thing I've ever done, but—*chuckle, chuckle*—it was also the most exhilarating.

Though the adventure had left me with lots of bragging rights, I learned how foolish we'd been, when, one year later, in April 1999, I read a magazine article that said five tourists had plunged to their death in the Grand Canyon so far that year. Delayed relief washed over me. We also could have been a statistic back in 1998, when the three of us risked our lives for a picture-taking escapade on a pillar of stone over a vast abyss.

Needless to say, my arms and legs turned to jelly as we made our way back to the Silver Bullet and dropped into our respective seats, this time with Jamal at the wheel. We rode in silence for a while. I figured each of us still hovered on the brink of a cliff, at least in our minds. It could take hours for us to come down to earth.

Sean sat on the edge of his seat and stared at nothing in particular, lines of anxiety frozen on his face. I looked at Jamal. He appeared cool as a block of ice, his wrist dangling over the steering wheel, his eyes trained on the road ahead. What unseen force drove that guy? I'd seen him under pressure before, like the time he faced the last few seconds of a game with his team losing by one point. He was surrounded by opposing players with no teammate to guard him. He held onto the ball, spun this way and that, then broke out of the mold, headed straight for the basket, leaped high in the air, and did a perfect slam dunk for the win.

How I wished I had his nerves of steel. My friend remained calm in the most trying circumstances. In fact, the more stressful the situation, the more fired up he became, often relying on an extra boost of adrenaline to keep him going.

While he kept on driving without any sign of nerve damage, Sean and I engaged in an emotional account of our near death experience.

"You maggot," Sean chided me. "You should have figured out where Jamal was heading and stopped climbing."

"And you should have backed down when I told you to," I countered.

"I trusted you, Charlie."

"Let's face it, Sean. I couldn't go anywhere, up or down, until one of you moved."

"What a bunch of lunatics," Sean said. "We could have gotten ourselves killed."

"But we didn't," Jamal said, grinning. "We took a huge risk, and we lived to tell about it."

"Yeah," said Sean, patting me on the back. "You can tell Heather about that once-in-a-lifetime experience. She'll look at you like you're this big hero." He chuckled. "Little does she know, you almost lost your breakfast up there."

I shrugged. "That's okay. By the time I finish embellishing the story, she'll think I broke some kind of record."

We continued to banter back and forth. Having surfaced from the terror, we now started bragging about our daring feat over the Grand Canyon. The way we carried on, you would have thought we'd climbed Mount Everest.

As the miles ticked by, and we got farther away from the canyon, I began to breathe a lot easier. I picked up one of the maps and turned my attention to our next pre-selected location, Las Vegas. From that moment, I made up my mind, there'd be no more rock climbing, no more death-defying hovers over any cliffs, and no heroics of any kind. Now, we were just gonna have fun.

About that time, I came up with what I thought was a bright idea.

"Since we're going to Las Vegas anyway, why don't we spend the night there?" I said. "I've heard the hotels and casinos give out free drinks and food to visitors so they'll do more gambling and leave all their hard-earned cash on the tables."

"Yeah, but we don't have to gamble," cautioned Jamal. "We can do lots of other things. Las Vegas is a literal playground. Cool sights and shows, and the food is affordable, because, like you said, Charlie, they want people to play."

Sean bobbed his head with enthusiasm. "I've heard some of the casinos have buffets where people can pig out for mere pennies."

At last, we had visions of a decent hotel room, reasonably priced food and drink, and we could walk around, see a couple of shows, and maybe pull the handle on a slot machine.

The miles flew by. We pulled off the road once to make quick work of the hoard of food in the laundry sack. Then, satisfied for the time being, we headed out again, yammering about Las Vegas, and since none of us had ever been there, we came up with several theories of what it might be like. Sean saw it as a kind of Shangri-La, with nearly everything free for the taking.

"You're dreaming," I said. "Everything has a price, even in Vegas."

"We'll just have to look for the bargains," reasoned Jamal, and Sean and I both nodded in agreement.

The sun dipped lower in the west. A couple of hours later, old Sol had disappeared, leaving a trickle of spun gold on the horizon.

I tried to read our maps in the beam of the flashlight. I figured we were not far from Vegas, maybe an hour away now, when something unexpected appeared in the distance.

Right there, in the middle of the desert, huge cliffs towered off to our right, and a massive wall curved around in a half-circle, encasing a dark abyss. The entire scene was illuminated with orange and blue lights and was surrounded by what looked to be rock formations and pillars.

Jamal choked out his surprise. "What in the world is *that*?"

"It looks like a space station!" Sean blurted out.

"Yeah," I said, drawing out the word in one breath. "Doesn't it look like a scene from *Star Wars*?" The whole scene left me thinking we'd left earth by some weird osmosis—maybe Scottie beaming us up or something equally fantastic.

Jamal slowed the car and inched closer to the side of the road. "Come on you guys. It has to be manmade."

Though at first sight the setting *had* resembled a star base, I had to agree with Jamal. There were no flickering lights, no people in space suits, no movement of any kind. I rolled down my window to get a better look. Sean did the same. Except for the hushed sound of the wind rushing down the sides of the cliffs, the entire setting had fallen eerily silent. The image of a space station continued to fade. There were no antigravity land speeders, no all-terrain transports, not even a flagship or star cruiser taking off or landing.

Okay. So, I'd seen way too many sci-fi films back then, but what else did we have to do with our free time before gaming became popular? I spent the next few minutes trying to make sense of the whole thing and trying to curb my imagination.

No other vehicles had pulled up in front of us, and none had come up behind us. We'd encountered this strange nighttime spectacle on a stretch of deserted highway. And we were alone.

Jamal parked the Silver Bullet, and we hopped out and sprinted over to the outer ledge. Below lay a huge vat of water, like a big mirror reflecting all the colored lights.

Now, the spaceship began to look more like a city or maybe like a fortress. One wall shot straight up from the abyss about 200 feet with four separate towers jutting out from the base. The impressive construction had an assortment of other buildings positioned around the rim, each one illuminated by otherworldly lights in shades of green, blue, and purple, brightening that isolated dark corner of the desert.

"Awesome," I whispered. "We're alone on Tatooine, the desert planet from *Star Wars*."

For some reason, I'd gotten stuck in the movie, and with good reason. Everything in front of me looked like it belonged on the big screen. I stood stock still, gazing, and acting like I'd gotten hit with a laser.

"No," said Jamal. "It's like John's description of heaven in the book of Revelation. Lots of brilliant gemstones with an emerald glow in the middle. All that's missing is the throne of God."

"Get real, you guys," said Sean. "Don't you know what this is? It's Hoover Dam."

Jamal narrowed his eyes at Sean. "What makes you say that?"

Sean pointed at a lighted, gold-plated plaque affixed to one of the walls. *Hoover Dam*, it said. Then, turning toward another sign, he read it aloud, "*Lake Mead was created by the Hoover Dam in the year 1936 and is the largest artificial lake in the United States.*"

My sci-fi movie fizzled. The fortress had turned into a dam, and all the little outposts I had assumed housed aliens contained nothing but maintenance buildings and power supply equipment.

Still, I couldn't help but gawk. Hoover Dam made an absolutely breathtaking sight in the middle of the desert at night. How lucky for us to have experienced God's creation, the Grand Canyon, during the day, and then a man-made splendor called Hoover Dam at night.

Except for Rodman Reservoir where my high school friends and I used to leap off the bridge to go swimming, I'd never seen a really big dam before, and I'd never imagined one could look this awesome and glow at night with every color of the rainbow.

"Do you believe it?" Sean said. "Ninety-six workers died during the construction of this dam."

I shook my head, stunned silent, which opened the door for Sean to cite more statistics.

"The dam is 1,244 feet long and 726 feet high," he said, straightening to his full five feet, six inches. "The wall measures 660 feet thick at the bottom and tapers to forty-five feet at the top."

"How do you *know* all that?" Jamal challenged him. "There aren't anymore signs. Is this more textbook fodder from your geology class?"

"Neither." Sean snickered, and he held up a brochure, "I found this on the ground over there." He cast a sideways glance at Jamal. "Why don't you try climbing up the side of *this* monster?" Then, he turned toward me. "How about you, Charlie. I dare you to walk around that rim."

I scowled. "Why should I even try something like that? Anyway, Jamal's the one who keeps coming up with stunts that could get us killed."

Jamal started chuckling. "Come on, Charlie. I had my moment of fame. It's your turn to try something wild and dangerous. Go ahead and take a walk-around. Know what I'm sayin'?"

Ignoring the two of them, I walked away to another viewing

spot where I could focus my attention on the structure. The tiny, invisible architect inside me calculated the various dimensions. What if I could design something like that one day? A museum of art or maybe a palace for some rich guy to live in.

After a while, Sean and Jamal started pacing back and forth, a sure sign they wanted to leave. I tried to ignore them, but the pacing got louder. And closer to where I was standing.

"Let's go," Sean snarled with impatience.

"Yeah," Jamal said with a grunt. "I'd like to get to Vegas before midnight. Otherwise, we might not get a room."

I stood my ground. "Guys, if you don't mind, I'm not done taking it all in. We're staying for another few minutes, got it?"

I turned away from them, stuck out my chin, and continued to stare at the amazing construction. For some reason, we hadn't marked Hoover Dam on our itinerary. What an incredible scene to come upon by accident.

Moments later, out of nowhere, God's quiet voice of conviction descended upon me. I'd been treating my buddies like their opinion didn't matter. I tried to shake the thought out of my head, but the voice remained. Hadn't I had uproariously good fun risking my life with Jamal? And hadn't I come away from different places with a little more knowledge than when I'd arrived, mainly because of Sean? Whether I liked it or not, I'd entered a schoolroom of sorts, and my two friends had been my teachers. I could never have done all this by myself. They were helping to create the memories I'd take home with me for a lifetime.

I chewed my bottom lip for a second, then turned around and faced them. "Hey, I'm sorry, guys. I didn't mean to sound so harsh."

"Yeah," they both said, like a duet. Since neither of them corrected me, I figured they'd been thinking the same thing.

"All right then, on to Vegas," I said, elevating my voice. I started toward the car. They flew past me and got in ahead of me.

"Las Vegas, here we come!" shouted Sean from his favorite spot in the backseat.

An hour later, we cruised the main drag of Las Vegas, flanked on either side by illuminated casinos, restaurants, and hotels. Huge neon signs in a variety of shapes and sizes turned the black of night to midday, and live music blared from many an open door, creating the feel that the night had just begun.

People walked along the sidewalks, crossing streets at random, their strides purposeful, like they knew where they were going and couldn't wait to get there. They smiled and laughed, didn't appear to have a care in the world. I concluded that Las Vegas lived up to its reputation as the place to forget your troubles. Just go there, relax, and have fun.

Conscious of the way the three of us looked after the Grand Canyon climbing event—our shorts and shirts stained with dirt and sweat, I began to pay attention to how the Vegas crowd dressed. Except for a few divas in spangled gowns, the women wore casual dresses, skirts, and slacks. The men wore trendy jeans and cotton shirts. I figured we'd fit in once we cleaned up and put on the less wrinkled items in our suitcases.

We kept driving and searched for a hotel that looked like it fit our budget, which meant we had to leave the strip and meander up and down the side streets.

For our first night there, we settled on a little motel two blocks from the strip. The sign on the roof said, "The Good Luck Inn," but just how lucky might it be? I got my answer the minute I stepped inside the little smoke-filled box they called a "lobby." We must have awakened the desk clerk. His hair needed a good combing, he hadn't shaved, and he'd just popped a cigarette between his teeth. I almost walked out, coughing, when he gave us the price—$19 a night.

We all three signed the check-in sheet and paid cash up front, then we hurried outside and escaped the swirl of toxic fumes. None of us smoked, except Sean who sometimes puffed on his Peterson Pipe. Knowing I didn't allow smoking in the Bullet, he'd put the thing away.

First thing that happened when I opened the door to our little suite, I came face-to-face with a cockroach the size of a hamster. At the sound of my gasp, the thing scurried off into the bathroom. I made up my mind not to bathe or use the toilet in that place and to wait until we found a restroom in one of the casinos.

Sleeping posed a different problem. Hopefully, the family of roaches holed up in our bathroom didn't have the strength to lift their huge bodies onto the beds. But there might be other critters. To be safe, I lifted the blanket and checked the sheets for bedbug droppings.

Jamal came up behind me. "What on earth are you doing, Charlie?"

"Just checking," I said, rising. "We're good. Let's go and get something to eat."

We had no choice but to stay in another fleabag. We'd already paid for the room and could not get a refund. But, I reasoned, it cost $19 a night. For that price I could sleep with bugs crawling around—as long as they stayed on the floor.

When we returned to the strip, we discovered multiple hotels and casinos had big, well-lit signs that boasted free entertainment and low-priced smorgasbords. With fresh confidence, we strolled inside a brightly lit casino and checked out the display of food, our main interest at the moment. The small spread included mostly salad fixings, which satisfied Jamal but had Sean and me setting our teeth for something more substantial.

"Let's go someplace else," Jamal said. "After all, we're in Las Vegas, guys!"

We agreed on Caesar's Palace. And why not? Nintendo had named a game after it.

Chapter Thirteen

Entering Caesar's Palace was like walking onto a Cecil B. DeMille movie set. The lavish decorations reminded me of the traveling entourage in the *Cleopatra* movie. At one side of the room lurked a huge, Viking-style barge. Statues of Roman soldiers stood guard in every corner, and busts of Caesar himself graced various places around the room, giving the feel of an authentic Roman forum.

Acting like three seasoned gamblers, we sauntered into the casino and strode about with our heads held high, like we belonged there. In the center of the huge domed ceiling hung a crystal chandelier that bounced prisms of light in every direction. The gaming tables were built of solid wood, and tuxedo-clad workers dealt cards, spun wheels, rolled dice, and pulled long-handled rakes across felt tables.

The place reminded me of a video game I used to play. How awesome to play a video game using that identical setting, and then to actually walk inside it.

Toga-clad beauties roamed about with trays of free drinks. Jamal and I passed on the alcohol and asked for Cokes, but Sean reached for a glass that looked like it contained vodka. He downed it in thirty seconds, then reached for another.

Jamal and I looked at each other. A sad exchange hung in the air between us, and I knew then that we had a new mission—to keep an eye on Sean.

Speaking of Sean, when we turned around, we discovered he'd disappeared. We spent the next half-hour searching for him and found him at the roulette table, a drink in one hand and a fistful of bills in the other.

I grabbed one arm and Jamal grabbed the other and we half-guided and half-dragged our buddy away from the tables.

"Come on," I insisted. "You're coming with us. You wanted to get something to eat, right?"

Sean gave a half-hearted nod.

"Well, that's what we're gonna do," I said firmly.

Our Irish friend raised his glass to take another sip. With the speed of a rattlesnake, Jamal wrenched the glass from his hand and set it on a nearby table. Stunned, Sean screwed up his face into a pout. Together, Jamal and I shook our heads at him, like two angry parents. Sean released a sigh and grinned like a kid caught with his hand in the cookie jar.

"I was just having a little fun," he said.

With Jamal pushing Sean from behind and me tugging his arm, the three of us went looking for the buffet. Inside the dining area we spotted a ten-foot counter laden with a mouth-watering spread of chicken wings, ham, roast beef, and a colorful array of vegetables and salads.

We paid what amounted to a reasonable fee, considering where we were, then we headed for the buffet.

Forgetting about the drink he'd left behind, Sean lunged ahead of us and grabbed a tray. We loaded up our plates and found a table. The food tasted as good as it looked. The chicken wings were crisp, the ham was salty, and the salad fixin's balanced the meal nicely with a colorful assortment of veggies and fruit. I was halfway through my food when Sean went back to the buffet for seconds. Though I was concerned about his weight, I was relieved to see he'd gotten interested in something other than the roulette table or another glass of who-knows-what.

Jamal leaned toward me. "Hey, Charlie, do you believe this brochure?" He slid a pamphlet across the table to me. "The room prices in this place are not that much higher than the dump we're staying in."

"Are you sure?" I said, frowning with skepticism. "Look at the decor of this place." I waved my hand at the walls. "This has to be way outside our budget."

"I'm serious," Jamal said between bites. "I had to look twice, but there's no mistake."

It turned out the rooms at Caesar's Palace cost about double the accommodations at the Good Luck Inn, but we figured, what the heck? This was a once-in-a-lifetime opportunity. The problem was, however, we couldn't just check out of one place and pay for another. We would have to stick it out in the fleabag for one night and then spend a second night at Caesar's Palace.

Two nights in Vegas. We'd talked about doing that from the start. We could simply kick back, stretch our weary legs, and load up on food. Then, the road ahead didn't seem quite as challenging.

After dinner, we strolled through the casino, while Jamal and I kept a solid grip on Sean's arms. We paused behind a jewel-encrusted woman, fascinated by her as she attacked the handle of a slot machine. Her pulling hand was covered in black stains, and her other hand held a bulging bag of coins. At one point, the poor, abused one-armed bandit spit out a few tokens, which the woman promptly re-inserted. I looked around at the crowd of gamblers and shook my head. Some of them looked like zombies, roaming about mindlessly and pausing at tables where they likely would empty their bank accounts.

I found the whole scene both intriguing and sad. What a relief when Jamal checked the time and suggested we go back to the motel. "We've had a long day," he said. "Let's get a good night's sleep and enjoy our time here tomorrow."

I agreed. Sean puffed out a heavy sigh, but he tagged along.

And so, I tolerated one night at The Good Luck Inn but may never have closed my eyes for fear the giant roach might wander into the bedroom hungry for a taste of human blood.

Early the next morning, we grabbed our bags, which we hadn't bothered to unpack, and we tore out of there like a whole army of bugs was chasing after us. I never did see the little fellow again, which was probably for the best, for his sake anyway.

We stashed our luggage in the Silver Bullet, with plans to take it out again at 4 p.m., check-in time at Caesar's Palace. In the meantime, we wandered around town and marveled that last night's rush of activity had continued into broad daylight. The town was still lit up like—well, I normally would have said *like Las Vegas*, but now

I had nothing else to compare it to, except maybe Paris. I'd never visited the City of Lights, so I didn't know for sure if Paris glowed that bright. We passed the Silver Slipper with it's huge diamond studded high-heeled shoe hovering above the sidewalk, then several smaller casinos with signs bigger than their buildings, and a tour agency offering trips to the Grand Canyon and Hoover Dam.

"Been there, done that," Jamal quipped.

For a diversion from the casinos and shows, we pulled our swim shorts from our bags and got permission from the front desk clerk to use the pool. We splashed around for a while, then we grabbed three lounge chairs and soaked up some rays. Our time in the sun didn't last long. Not even a half-hour later, my suit had dried and I was feeling a burn.

We changed back into our street clothes and strolled inside the hotel like we belonged there. Our room reservation allowed us to sample a continental breakfast bar. Afterward, we went back to the casino, surprised to see an equal number of patrons had ventured inside in the middle of the day. Or maybe they'd never left.

Something else I noticed—there wasn't a single window or clock in the whole place. I figured the gamblers never knew or cared what time it was, like the casino owners probably wanted.

We no sooner walked in, when a gorgeous, uniformed attendant approached us.

"Are you staying at Caesar's Palace?" she asked in a honey-coated voice. We nodded, like three bashful sixth-graders responding to a hot looking teacher.

She handed us three meal tickets. "Here you go. Enjoy your supper on us," she said. Then she winked and walked away.

"It must be some kind of promotional deal," Jamal reasoned.

"Who cares?" said Sean. "We get free food."

We pocketed our tickets for later and continued through the casino. I found the noise overwhelming. Tinkling music poured from the slot machines, bells sounded off, and showers of tokens dropped into metal trays. Everyone talked at once, and now and then, a shout of triumph rose up from somewhere across the room. Every inch of the place swarmed with casual tourists downing alcohol while placing chips on the table. Meanwhile, the more serious gamblers refused to drink or eat anything. They waved the servers away without looking at them and concentrated only on the cards in their hands. The situation was even more intense at the baccarat table, where the card players wore evening gowns and tuxedoes, and their diamond studded fingers flung hundred dollar bills in the center. I couldn't help but puff up my chest a little. For the moment, I'd taken my place among the elite. For the most part, no one cared how we were dressed, just that we were having a good time.

As planned, when four o'clock rolled around, we checked into the Palace. Unlike the roach motel we'd stayed in the night before, this place was spectacular! Carpeted lobby with huge, illuminated prisms hanging from the ceiling, thick leather furniture, and a well-groomed desk clerk that wore a tailored suit and didn't reek of burned out cigarettes.

Our room exceeded everything we'd expected. Not queen-size beds. *King*-size! And a large sofa for Sean. On the desk stood a bowl of fresh fruit and a city map, which included attractions, tours, shows, and tiny chapels, in case we wanted to get married.

I flopped on my choice of the king-size beds and sprawled there, staring up at the ceiling. "Yes!" I hollered. "We've finally made it!"

Jamal chose the other huge bed. "Yeah," he cried. "A bed of my own. No Charlie grabbing all the covers. No cold feet working their way to my side. Tonight, I'm a king."

Sean shrugged and took over the sofa. "This'll do me just fine," he said, patting the plump cushions.

I lay there for a while, not wanting to fall asleep, just enjoying the moment, but my growling stomach broke my trance. I reached in my pocket and pulled out the slip of paper the attendant had given me.

"Let's use our meal tickets," I suggested.

I leaped from the bed and charged into the bathroom to clean up. Afterward, while I waited for the other two, I opened the drapes at our bedroom window and stood there, gazing out over the city where lights flickered and flashed and defied anyone from ever sleeping in this glorious, adult playground.

I thought of Heather, sitting at home with a good book or playing a board game with her little brother. Suddenly, all the lights and the music and the sounds of people having fun didn't mean as much to me. A flicker of nostalgia wormed its way into my heart, and for an instant I wanted to be back home playing Candyland.

My two buddies grabbed my arms and jolted me back to reality.

"Wake up, pal," Jamal said with a laugh. "We're in Las Vegas, and we're supposed to be having a good time."

"Come on," said Sean. "Let's not waste another minute."

I joined them in the hall, and we headed for the elevator and an evening on the town. We went straight to the open-kitchen buffet to use our free meal tickets.

After filling our stomachs, at Sean's prompting we moseyed into the casino.

"We can't leave Vegas without playing a little," he said. "We can use some of our food money."

I stared him down. "We already sank our food money into the cost of a second night in Vegas. Anyway, didn't you already play roulette last night?"

He shrugged. "I made a couple of bucks. C'mon. Let's grab a drink from one of these waitresses."

The way Sean slurred the word, *drink*, had me thinking he wanted something other than a Coke, which alerted me to one major problem. While Jamal and I had already turned twenty-one, Sean wouldn't see his twenty-first birthday until after Christmas, which meant he was underage. Though nobody had carded him for drinks and games, if someone did, he could get all three of us kicked out.

While I was still pondering this dilemma, Jamal sauntered over to a slot machine and dropped a couple quarters in. He pulled the handle, lost his change, then backed off. Grinning, he got behind me and gave me a nudge.

"Your turn, Charlie. Go on. Spend a dollar."

I didn't have the means to play blackjack or poker, but I *had* set aside some loose change to play the slot machines. I figured I could play until I lost that little bit of money, so I stepped up and gave the handle a pull.

What a surprise when three identical cherries popped up, sirens went off, and a bunch of tokens spilled into the tray. I won thirty dollars! A windfall to a guy whose bankroll was dwindling. I chose to quit while I was ahead.

"You're gonna share that, aren't you?" Jamal ventured to ask.

"Maybe," I said with a sly smile.

"What do you mean, maybe? We came on this trip agreeing to share everything."

I stared at him and narrowed my eyes. He simply shrugged and walked away, but every now and then, I caught him glaring at me. Of course, I planned to share. I just didn't want to tell *him* that.

Meanwhile, Sean couldn't understand why I didn't just have fun and gamble away my winnings.

"I'd probably lose it," I told him. "Do you think this place stays in business to make the customers rich?"

We left the casino, pretty much dragging Sean behind us. We agreed to take in a couple of shows. One featured Gladys Night and the Pips, a group my mom played on the radio in her kitchen, years ago. But Sean said, "What's a Pip?" so, we moved on.

The other show featured Wayne Newton. We didn't have the admission fee, so we stood in an open doorway until one of the ushers shooed us away.

We ended up in a small nightclub that had an outdoor sign bigger than the building. We shared a bowl of chips and each of us bought a soft drink. A jazz trio played something soft and relaxing. Four patrons sat at the bar and a few couples huddled around tables at different places throughout the room. I settled back in a lounge chair and enjoyed the quiet. No tinkling machines. No loud talking. No crowd milling about. No dinging and blaring and people screaming that they had won.

That night, we bedded down in a sparkling clean room with no roaches, as far as I could see. My watch said ten o'clock, but I couldn't sleep. Though it was late, I figured I could use one of my two collect phone calls. I plopped down on the edge of my bed and, using the hotel phone, I made a collect call to Heather, even though the East Coast was three hours of ahead of us.

She picked up on the ninth ring and whispered something unintelligible into the phone, then agreed to pay the charges.

"Charlie? Is that you?" Her voice sounded like a breath of fresh air after I'd been cooped up with two smelly guys for five days. "It's past midnight," she said, keeping her voice low.

"Yeah," I agreed. "I thought I'd give you a call. So far, we've seen the Grand Canyon and Hoover Dam—two awesome sights. Tomorrow, we'll head for Death Valley, and then San Francisco, our turn-around point. Until today, we ate like paupers but we're making up for it now. We're staying in a swanky hotel in Las Vegas—Caesar's Palace—do you believe it? I feel like a king. Nearly everything's fr—"

"Las Vegas?" There was a creaking and crumpling noise that sounded like she'd sat up in bed. Was that all she'd gotten out of the rambling account I'd just given her?

"Yeah, Las Vegas," I said. "Why?"

"Isn't that place called Sin City? Isn't that where people go to gamble? Isn't that where a lot of skimpily clad girls flirt with lonely young men?"

"I don't know. I guess so. I haven't noticed." *Although there was that one cocktail waitress*, I thought.

"We're not chasing girls," I said. "And they're not chasing us. As for gambling, I won thirty bucks off a slot machine. Just for fun, mind you. I'm not addicted or anything like that."

Why did I feel like I had to explain myself? She didn't own me. I hadn't put a ring on her finger. Not yet, anyway.

A wasted thirty seconds of silence passed, then she kind of regrouped.

"I got a response from that Christian school in Chicago. They want me to come for an interview."

My heart leaped to my throat. I took a breath. "It sounds pretty definite," I said.

"Maybe not. They have other candidates."

A kind of panic rushed through me, leaving me hot and shaky. Was I about to lose my girlfriend to a job in Chicago? Or was she getting even for the Las Vegas remark?

"If you take the job, I guess that means you'll be leaving Gainesville for good, right?"

"Right." She kept her voice soft. Maybe she hoped I'd talk her out of going.

I didn't even try. Who was I to interfere with her career plans?

I looked at my watch. Our ten minutes were almost up, and I hadn't said everything I'd planned to say. Yesterday, while Jamal was driving, I sat back, shut my eyes, and thought of all sorts of sweet-sounding words girls like to hear—things I could say to Heather when we talked. Seconds later, they'd slipped out of my mind. Now I couldn't retrieve them if my life depended on it.

"Don't forget my Pacific Ocean water," Heather reminded me.

"Oh, yeah. I still have the bottle you gave me."

"Well, our time's up," she mumbled, a distressing sadness in her voice.

She said a tearful goodbye. Tearful on her part, not on mine. Being the macho male I am, I held it together pretty well. But, looking back, I have to admit, a huge lump had found its way into my throat. On the surface, I held it together, but inside I was falling apart.

Up until then, Jamal and Sean had each made two phone calls home. They'd talked for at least a half-hour each time. That night, Jamal's mother kept him on the phone, even when they ran out of things to say. Jamal worked overtime to soothe her worries. No, he hadn't come across any gunmen. It was probably best that he didn't mention the knife-wielding carjacker or running out of gas in the middle of an endless desert. No, he hadn't gambled away his college tuition. Yes, he had plenty to eat, hadn't lost an ounce of weight, maybe even put on a couple of pounds, or so he told his mama.

Sean had to speak to each and every one of his siblings, and then his father and mother. Each person wanted the details of our trip, so he kept repeating everything. His call took almost an hour.

I wished my own mother cared about me like their folks did. I hadn't received so much as a phone call from her for months, so why did I expect her to call me now? The road trip had given her one more reason to ignore me. I tried to console myself with Heather's phone call, but even that had left me feeling down. She might be moving to Chicago, more than a thousand miles from home, and I needed to stay right there and work on my master's degree. Then, who knows? We might never see each other again.

That night, with the lights turned off and the room-darkening drapes drawn across our window to block out all the neon brilliance on the streets below, I wrestled with my pillow. Did I care that my mother didn't worry about me like my friends' mothers did? Maybe. Did I miss Heather? Most definitely. At that moment, I had to face the truth. I was falling in love with her, and I didn't know how to stop the momentum. I once heard a preacher say, people don't *fall* in love, they *choose* to love. If that were true, then I guess I'd made the most important choice of my life. The problem was, I had no idea how to hang onto Heather without also giving up my freedom.

Unlike some of our other overnights, this swanky hotel room had promised me a good night's sleep. No roaches. No fleas. No gunshots or screaming. Yet, I had a hard time shutting my eyes and keeping them shut. I don't know when I finally fell asleep. Maybe it happened while I was reciting The Lord's Prayer. In any case, I think I got about six hours of uninterrupted rest.

I came fully to when Jamal opened the drapes and our room filled with sunlight and the additional lights of a city that never slept. After being well-fed at the hotel breakfast bar, it was time for us to move on. If I wanted to enjoy the rest of my trip, I needed to shed my mind of any romantic complications. To help myself regroup, I mentally recited my motto, *it is what it is,* and I began to look forward to our next stop—Death Valley—another triple-starred location on our itinerary.

Chapter Fourteen

As usual, that Thursday morning we stuffed our bags with pastries and fruit from the breakfast bar and lugged it all out to the Bullet. First stop had to be a gas station. The needle hovered a little above a quarter tank, and since I hadn't checked the oil and water for a while, I took care of that too.

While there, Jamal and I agreed to pitch in for a large-size Gatorade for three dollars. We'd been drinking water most of the time and refilling our bottles whenever we stopped somewhere that had a fountain. Plus, we had a reserve in the cooler, so we had to keep adding ice whenever possible. If we wanted to survive the trip, we needed to skimp all the way down to pennies. At $1.50 apiece, sharing a bottle of Gatorade made sense.

I reached in my pocket and found the thirty dollars I'd won in the casino and some loose change. I started for the register to ask the clerk to break one of my tens, when Jamal grabbed my arm.

"Don't bother," he said, smiling. "How about I buy the Gatorade. We can split it, and you can pay me your buck-fifty later, okay?"

The guy never failed to surprise me with his acts of generosity. We'd moved beyond being mere friends. We were traveling companions, sharing everything. Even a Gatorade.

I took the wheel and headed west on NV-160. after we crossed into the Golden State, we picked up CA-190 West, recommended by the gas station clerk as the most scenic route to Death Valley. He hadn't lied. As we approached the expansive desert, I caught sight of a range of the most awe-inspiring, purple mountains majesties, like the anthem says. The foothills flowed from the base of the mountains, their multi-colored sides rippling downward in shades of beige and green and blue.

"Let's stop and walk around," Jamal suggested.

Reluctantly, I slid out of the coolness of my air-conditioned car into the blazing sunlight, shaded my eyes against the harsh glare, and stepped with caution into the blinding desert. All three of us donned sunglasses and baseball caps.

One minute, we strolled on hard-packed soil with cracks and fissures trailing through it, and the next, we stumbled over eroded salt rocks while trying to keep our balance. All of a sudden, we reached a place that resembled a vast sandy beach.

"Wow," Jamal cried out. "Will you look at all that sand!" He started to take his shoes off.

"It's not sand," Sean corrected him. "It's salt crystals. And they're blazing hot."

"Huh?" Jamal said, and he retied his sneaks.

"Salt crystals?" I said. I gazed out at what appeared to be acres and acres of the stuff.

Sean dropped to his knees and bent low, holding his ear close to the ground. He beckoned Jamal and me to do the same.

"Get down and listen," he told us. "You'll hear millions of salt particles bursting and popping. They're contracting from the intensity of the extreme heat."

Dropping down on one knee, I listened to the popping sounds for several minutes, so fascinated I couldn't pull away. Then, I stood and faced Sean, who also had risen to his feet. "How did you know they're salt crystals?"

It occurred to me that our A-plus science student must have spent the last two weeks doing research on every one of our proposed stops. Now, he was going to fill us in on salt crystals.

My suspicion was confirmed when he said, "Erin and I were able to duplicate this sand activity through an experiment in the lab."

He went into another geological monologue, which I was able to tune out, except for a few snippets of information—something about three million years of volcanic erosion, giant craters, and the resulting salt crystals.

Unaware of the smirk on my face, Sean went on to talk about the fifty-one species of wildlife that lived in Death Valley, and he began to list them all—one by tedious one. So far, I hadn't seen one sign of wildlife since we'd arrived in Death Valley. As far as I could see, the place deserved its name, because everything had obviously died.

As we walked on, a few signs of life did begin to appear. First, we came upon a whole array of pink and white flowers, broad patches of grass, and in the distance, yellow wildflowers and an abundance of green low-lying shrubbery that trailed off to the base of the mountains. It seemed like a magical garden had popped up out of nowhere.

With the appearance of flora, we also caught sight of a few critters. A lizard scooted between the clumps of vegetation. There were several little crawly things, and at one point, a brown-and-white speckled roadrunner scooted across our path, and I found myself on the lookout for Wile E. Coyote.

We followed a wooden footbridge bearing a sign that said, *Bad Water Basin.* But there was no basin. And no water. Why was I not surprised? In that part of the U.S., signs didn't seem to matter. Like Pine Spring—we'd found no pine trees and no spring. Now, we'd found no water; not even *bad* water.

Maybe it was the word, *water.* Maybe the hot sun. Maybe both. All I knew was, I needed a drink.

It was almost 11 a.m. and coming up on the hottest part of the day. I guessed the temperature had reached 110 degrees or more. Despite the boiling sun, the three of us had sauntered a great distance onto the hard-packed salt. Moments later, things started to get really heated, and it had nothing to do with the sun.

I was extremely thirsty.

Jamal had been carrying our bottle of Gatorade. Sean had purchased a can of Coke at the gas station. And me? Well, I had nothing but my half of the Gatorade in Jamal's hand.

The sun beat down mercilessly. Our sunglasses and baseball caps did little to protect us from the hot rays. Still, like idiots, we kept walking farther from the Bullet in sweltering heat, trudged over sand dunes and vast stretches of hard, cracked soil. After a while, I believed the burning salt crystals had started to penetrate the soles of my shoes. I wanted to go back to the shelter of the Bullet.

The heat in that place was unlike anything I'd ever experienced in Florida, where heat came with a ton of humidity. Despite the dryness of the air, I began to sweat like I'd run a marathon when I'd only walked about a tenth of a mile. Moisture dripped from my forehead, and my T-shirt began to stick to my back. I came up beside Jamal.

"I'm thirsty," I told him. "Let me have our Gatorade, so I can take a sip."

He stared at me, stunned. "What do you mean *our* Gatorade? It's *my* Gatorade. Why should I give it to *you*?"

"It's *not* your Gatorade. It's both of ours. Have you forgotten, we agreed to share?"

He gave me a sick smile. "You mean, like you're gonna share that thirty dollars you won last night?"

I couldn't believe he'd brought *that* up. "Of course, I'm gonna share it."

"Sure," Jamal said. Then he took a sip of Gatorade and walked on.

"Jamal," I called after him. "My throat is really dry, and I feel a little sick. Let me have a sip, and I'll give it right back."

He shook his head, his facial features rigid. "You never paid me your half of the money, so until you do, I guess it's *my* Gatorade, and I can do whatever I want with it. And right now, I'm gonna take a drink. *I'm* thirsty too."

He tipped the bottle to his lips again and guzzled about a quarter of the liquid. I stared at the declining level with a mix of disbelief and panic. My buddy, who a few hours ago had bonded with me, now had become my enemy.

Fuming, I turned away from him and stomped back toward my car, which, at that distance, looked like a tiny, sizzling Hot Wheels toy. It appeared to be so far away I didn't expect to reach it in time. I pictured myself like one of those skin-and-bones cartoon skeletons with torn clothing, crawling across the desert toward a watering hole and discovering it was only a mirage.

I grabbed my throat and looked back at my two *friends*. They had also turned around and were heading back to the car. Jamal strolled along behind me, as casual as can be. Every time I looked back, he took another sip. The level of Gatorade had dropped to less than half.

"Jamal," I cried out, although it wasn't a cry at all but a pathetic squeak. "Give me that Gatorade. It belongs to both of us. Are you aware we're in Death Valley? The first word is Death! I don't want to die."

"Sorry. It's all mine." He grimaced, and for an instant his face had turned red, and knobby horns stuck out of his head. I imagined he had a tail and was holding a pitchfork, too.

Near exhaustion, I stumbled along, seething. "You're an insensitive rat!" I squeaked, then added, "Know what I'm sayin'?"

He sneered and took another drink.

I was certain my organs had started to shut down. I was dying. I knew I was. And nobody cared—not even Sean, who guzzled his Coke and eyed the two of us with amusement.

Though dizzy from the overwhelming heat, I somehow made it to my car. I fumbled with the keys and searched inside the hatchback for a water bottle. I opened the cooler and found the ice had melted. I grabbed a bottle anyway, fumbled with the cap, and took a long drag. The water was lukewarm, but I didn't care. It was wet, and that was all that mattered at the time. I downed the whole thing.

Although it was Jamal's turn to drive, I grabbed the driver's seat and gripped the wheel, so angry I could have ripped it from the steering column. The whole inside of the car sizzled. I already knew how hot a car could get, because one time in Florida, I sat inside the Bullet for only ten minutes outside of a Walmart. The temperature inside my car must have reached 110 degrees, and it was still climbing.

But this was worse. This was Death Valley, and I'd left the Silver Bullet sweltering by the side of the road for more than a half-hour. The inside of my car felt like a cremation oven. Jamal settled in the passenger seat and started fiddling with the air conditioner knob. I swatted his hand away and turned the unit off.

"It's *my* car and *my* air-conditioner," I snapped. "Keep your hands off of it."

Jamal's eyes grew wide. "What? We're in the middle of Death Valley, and it's hot as you-know-what in here."

"That's right," I shouted in his face.

He reached for the button to roll down his window.

"And, don't touch *my* windows!" I yelled.

I must have looked like a maniac, because he didn't fight me. He sat there, sipping what remained of *our* Gatorade.

We drove down a highway in unbearable heat, with no air-conditioner and no window air. I gritted my teeth and kept going. Jamal had to pay for what he did with the Gatorade. The problem was, Sean and I were suffering, too.

Our poor, fair-skinned Irishman collapsed in the backseat, his Coke can drained, and him sweating like a sumo wrestler. He peeled off his shirt, picked up one of the maps and began to fan himself.

Several minutes later, his voice came sailing over the front, pathetic and whiny. "Hey, guys. Do I have to suffer for whatever's goin' on between the two of you? Come on. It's like an oven in here. Gimme some air."

I glared at Jamal, hoping for an apology. Smiling sheepishly, he lifted the bottle of Gatorade and offered it to me. It was now down to about an inch of liquid.

I snickered and shook my head. "Forget it, man. I don't want your spit."

"Suit yourself, *man.*"

Our little spat had gotten out of hand and threatened to ruin the rest of our trip. I glared at Jamal, then something inside me snapped. Did I really want to end a friendship over a Gatorade? Was Jamal's little snit in the desert any worse than the time I hid his clothes in the men's locker room, and he had to go home in 30-degree weather in his sweaty gym clothes?

"What are we doing?" I said, shaking my head. "Are we both nuts?"

He puffed out a sigh, and his frown melted into a smile. "We must be. I don't know what happened, Charlie, but I couldn't help myself. It's just that, sometimes—I hate to tell you this—but, sometimes, you get on my nerves."

"Ditto," I said. Then, I reached over, switched on the air

conditioner, and turned the fan to full blast. The thing kicked on with a nasty growl.

"How about finding some good music on the radio."

I guess that was our way of apologizing back then. Just say something nice and forget the bad stuff.

Seconds later, the Beatles were singing, "Hey Jude," over the airwaves. I got caught up in the music, and it struck me that Jamal had kept the station right where I'd left it. Baffled, I stared at him. One minute the guy had behaved like Darth Vader, the next he was Yoda. I shrugged and flashed him a smile.

"May the Force be with you," I said. Then, bobbing my head, I sang along with Paul McCartney. I pressed my foot to the floor and put more distance between us and Death Valley. Ahead lay San Francisco and the Pacific Ocean. A restored friendship and the thought of all that blue water and fresh sea air had me feeling alive again.

We picked up US 95 heading north/northwest. No sooner had we left Death Valley behind, when Sean started rummaging through the Silver Bullet's food pantry. Two minutes later, I held a slapped-together PB&J sandwich and a fresh bottle of lukewarm water. I placed the bottle in the cup holder in the center consul and bit into my sandwich, surprised to find it tasted a lot better than it looked.

All was well. I hadn't died. My friendship with Jamal had survived a test. And we weren't going to starve. In due time, we'd reach the West Coast, the halfway point of our road trip, San Francisco, our turnaround location, the place where I intended to collect a bottle of ocean water for Heather.

Along the eight-hour drive we passed through or near several national parks, and the landscape was getting more and more lush. I could tell by the electricity in the air that my two buddies shared my excitement. We'd soon reach our destination, and we could head for home. Then, we could get as far away as possible from one another, at least for a little while.

The fact that we'd gotten this far without killing each other was a miracle in itself. What didn't help was that by this time I missed

Heather something awful. A lifetime with her had begun to sound a whole lot easier to take than two weeks with my idiot friends.

I couldn't help but smile. Heather and I had been dating for almost eighteen months, but my attraction to her had started several months before when we both belonged to a young adult group at our church. Even in that crowd of young co-eds, I liked her right away, but I didn't know if she also liked me.

One day, out of the blue, she asked me if I'd go jogging with her. She wasn't asking me to go with a group of joggers, just the two of us. I was stunned.

Jogging? I had no interest in jogging. The most energy I expended in those days involved short sprints around the basketball court. I couldn't imagine myself getting up at 6 a.m. to jog along a park trail.

Still, I said, yes. And that was the beginning. Needless to say, I became an avid jogger after that. It paid off, because, when the time came for me to race Jamal up that steep grade at the Grand Canyon, I tackled it like a pro.

Now, I was on my way to San Francisco, and I just wanted to get that bottle of ocean water for my favorite jogging buddy—the one with the blonde hair and the heart-melting blue eyes.

As we traveled along the highway, the passing landscape continued to turn from brown to green, and then to many different colors, as more flowers, trees, and other types of vegetation popped up along the roadside. Soon, a whole field of orange trees spread out on both sides of the highway. Then came big houses with landscaped lawns, then city streets with stores and schools and malls and restaurants, plus billboards hyping all the wonderful things a person can see and do in San Francisco, including the Golden Gate Bridge, Fisherman's Wharf, and helicopter rides over Alcatraz. I already wanted to go to the bridge and the wharf, and now I started thinking about maybe taking one of those helicopter rides. Most of all, I couldn't wait to inhale the fresh sea air, which promised a welcome relief after slogging through the desert in stifling heat without a bottle of Gatorade to sip. Just the thought of standing in front of the Pacific Ocean got me breathing a whole lot easier.

Chapter Fifteen

It was nearing 7 p.m. Tired of eating junk food, we decided to spend our three bucks apiece on a decent meal. I still had the $30 I'd won on the slot machine. Las Vegas had spoiled us, and we longed for more of the same. I threw caution to the wind and headed for Fisherman's Wharf. Located on the northern waterfront, it teemed with tourists. Decked out in blue jeans and T-shirts, baseball caps on our heads, and aviation sunglasses, we blended in with the visiting crowd.

The departing sun bathed the entire Bay in orange streaks. From the wharf we could see the Golden Gate Bridge. It looked like a giant metallic spider web spanning the mile-long strait connecting the Bay with the Pacific Ocean. As far as I could see, the bridge had earned its name—Golden—because it glowed like pure gold in the wake of the setting sun.

For the first half-hour, we strolled past souvenir shops, kiosks, and a variety of dining places that looked far too expensive for our pathetic budget. I had chosen to take part of my slot machine money and treat my friends to a decent meal, though we still had to choose wisely.

"Don't you dare say the words, *peanut butter*," I commanded. "It's shrimp, tonight. It's crab salad. It's mahi mahi."

"What if I don't like seafood?" Jamal challenged, but I caught the silly grin on his face and the twinkle in his eye.

I cocked my head and narrowed my eyes. "You're kidding, right?"

"Big time," said Jamal. "C'mon. Let's check out the prices at some of these places."

We stopped inside the door of a couple nice restaurants, checked the menus, balked at the prices, then headed for what looked to be a modest eatery away from those with higher priced fare. We followed a young family inside. The hostess seated us at a table by a huge picture window overlooking the Bay. The setting sun painted gold streaks on the blue-green expanse, and I was reminded again of the bottle Heather had given me.

"*Get me some Pacific Ocean water,*" she'd said, or something like that.

"Hey, guys, do you know what became of that Zephyr Hills water bottle Heather gave me? I left it in the back of the car."

"I filled it from a fountain at the last gas station we stopped at and drank from it," Sean confessed.

I cringed at the image of Sean drinking from Heather's bottle. "You didn't throw it away, did you?"

He scratched his temple, then brightened. "No. I'm pretty sure I put it back in the car. It's probably still lying there."

"Well, don't drink out of it again. I need to fill it with Pacific Ocean water for Heather."

"Can't you use one of our bottles from the cooler?"

"No, they don't say Zephyr Hills. They're Walmart specials. I have to use the bottle Heather gave me."

They both looked at me with a mix of puzzlement and sympathy written on their faces.

Jamal shook his head. "You're not serious."

"Yeah, I'm serious. She made a simple request. I think I can do that much for her."

They started chuckling, like they were sharing a sick joke, and I could feel the heat creeping up my neck. I was about to give them a piece of my mind, when a male server stepped up and placed menus and ice water in front of us.

My ire cooled a little when I looked at the prices. Practically every meal in the Specials column was $15 or less. The list included *Baked cod, Seafood medley, Clam strips, Fish and Chips,* and on and on, and every main dish came with clam chowder, baked potato, and a salad. I figured it out. If I drank water with my meal, I'd have enough left over for a decent tip.

"I'm gettin' the seafood medley," I announced.

Sean made a face. "That's got oysters on it. I hate oysters. Too slimy."

"They are not," I contended. "The frying takes the sliminess out of them."

"I can't wait to sink my teeth in the fish and chips," said Jamal. "It'll feel like home. My mama makes the best batter-fried fish and French fries in the world."

Sean counted his money and found he had an extra ten bucks.

"Where'd you get that?" I said, scowling.

He blushed. "Before you guys pulled me away from the roulette wheel, I had a couple wins. Must have tucked it away in my pocket." He checked the menu again. "With my share of your thirty bucks, Charlie, it means lobster tail for me." Then he looked back and forth at us and grinned like a spoiled kid. "Eat your hearts out, boys."

Jamal frowned at him. "Wait a minute. Charlie's sharing *his* win, why aren't you sharing *yours*?"

Sean shook his head, and looked at me for help.

I sighed with resolve. "Go ahead," I said. "Get your lobster tail, but it's $27." I pointed at the menu. "After tax, you won't have enough left for a tip."

He shrugged. "Oh, well. You only live once, right?"

I stared wide-eyed at my friend, a member of a morally upstanding Irish-Catholic family, and he was about to stiff our waiter.

I grunted. "You're too much, Sean. Why don't you move to another table so Jamal and I won't be embarrassed?"

Sean stuck his tongue out at me at the exact moment when our waiter walked up to take our order.

Twenty minutes later, I forgot all about it, when the waiter returned and placed our food on the table. I savored every bite of my meal, right down to the house salad. The dressing, however, left a foul taste in my mouth. For some reason, it didn't taste anything like the blue cheese I'd eaten back home.

After dinner, we took a long walk along the pier, breathed deeply of the balmy air wafting off the bay, and stared into the distance across the water, now being enveloped by darkness.

We found a decent room several blocks away from the wharf. It had a queen size bed and a couple of sofas. I no longer wanted to share a bed with Jamal. Sometimes, he lost control of his long legs and flung them on my side. Instead, I chose to scrunch up in the fetal position on a loveseat. At least I had it all to myself. We slept with the window open, inhaled the fresh sea air, and filled the room with loud snores that must have sounded like feeding time at the San Diego Zoo. Sometime during the night, I rolled onto my other side—although rolled is probably not the right word. The truth is, I unfolded my limbs, shifted my body, and refolded everything again.

In the morning, I awoke with a stiff neck, an achy back, and sore arms and legs. It brought back painful memories of staying at Sean's cousins' house during the first night of our trip.

Meanwhile, Jamal awoke with a yawn and stretched like he was preparing to run a marathon. At that moment, I hated the guy. He'd had the comfortable bed, while I'd lain scrunched up all night. But, I couldn't blame him. It had been *my* idea to sleep on the tiny sofa.

The hotel offered free breakfast items in a room off the lobby. The three of us filled our stomachs with cereal that came in little tiny boxes, plus fruit, toast, coffee, and orange juice. Sean had grabbed another laundry bag from our room and proceeded to stuff it full of nonperishable items, while keeping one eye on the desk clerk beyond the open door.

Jamal and I stared at Sean, embarrassed.

"The sign said, 'free,'" Sean insisted.

Pretending we didn't know him, we walked five steps ahead of him through the lobby and out the door. Then, with Jamal driving the get-away car, we sped off with our loot.

I turned around in the passenger seat and looked at Sean. "I'll bet you also walked away with all the soap and shampoo samples in our bathroom."

"And two clean towels," Sean said, beaming.

I looked at Jamal and caught his attention. He nodded with understanding. With the proficiency of a trained counselor, Jamal flashed a quick glance at Sean in the rearview mirror and addressed the problem up front.

"Hey, pal, don't you feel guilty about some of the things you do?"

Sean perked up. "Like what?"

"Like underage drinking, gambling away money you don't have, stealing hotel bath towels, stiffing waiters out of their tip..."

"Oh, so you guys are saints?" Sean snarled. "How about what you did to Charlie, Jamal, drinking all the Gatorade? You promised to share, but then you didn't." He poked me on the shoulder. "And, what about you, Charlie? Making us suffer in a hot car for almost an hour."

Jamal looked at me and raised his eyebrows. I shrugged and made a screwed up face that said, *He's right.*

Jamal released a sigh. "Sorry, Sean," he said. "You're right, buddy, Charlie and I mess up sometimes. But, you've probably heard the saying, Christians aren't perfect, they're just forgiven, right?"

"Yeah, I heard it somewhere," Sean said, dragging out the words like he was bored to tears. "So what's that? A copout?"

"Not at all," said Jamal. "It's reality. A true Christian, when he knows he's sinned, will repent and try to do better next time."

Sean slumped back in his seat. I ventured a glance at him and found him frowning in thought. He caught me staring at him and glared back, like he didn't want to discuss it anymore.

A noticeable silence filled the Bullet. The tension was so thick you could cut it with a knife. My mind scrambled for something positive to say.

"Let's drive over to the ocean so I can fill Heather's water bottle," I said, changing the subject.

"You're kidding!" Sean straightened and shook his head.

Jamal burst out laughing. "You're really gonna do this?"

I remained firm. "Heather asked me for one thing—Pacific Ocean water—and I'm gonna make sure she gets some."

"Why don't you just scoop it out of the Bay," Sean said. "She'll never know the difference."

"Nope." I shook my head. "I'm gonna do what she asked. Heather's gettin' the real thing." I turned and raised my eyebrows at Sean, then at Jamal. "Anyway, don't you guys want to see the ocean?"

They greeted my question with silence. I took it as approval.

A half-hour later, we took our shoes off and dug our toes into a sandy beach on the ocean side of the bridge. With Heather's

Zephyr Hills bottle in hand, I sloshed into the water. Ripples of chilly surf splashed up against my ankles, rose higher, and skimmed the bottom of my cut-offs.

"This is for you, Heather," I murmured, and I dipped the bottle into the surf and came up with a suitable amount of ocean water, plus a wrapping of seaweed, and a sand crab that had dug its claws into my thumb. After pulling the debris off the bottle and wrenching my thumb out of the crab's needlepoint grip, I tightened the cap and held the bottle high in the air. Sunlight illuminated the bottle like a lantern. I turned to smile at Jamal and Sean. My buddies observed the entire episode with smirks on their lips. I didn't care. It didn't matter what they thought. I had done something special for the girl I loved.

Then, the truth struck me like a bullet. *I loved Heather.* I *loved* her. And, I couldn't wait to get home and tell her.

By the time we got back in the car, I came up with another idea. We couldn't leave this part of the USA without doing something fun.

"Why don't we drive over to the Hayward Airport and take a helicopter ride? Did you guys notice that billboard advertising it? Sure looks awesome."

"Is it free?" Jamal asked with his usual forethought.

I shrugged. "I don't know. The ad didn't list any prices. Let's hope it's cheap." I looked at them and raised my eyebrows. "Whaddaya say, guys? Should we try it?"

The other two nodded, but frowned with skepticism. Scoffing under his breath, Jamal turned south on the highway and headed for the flying field. Sure enough, a helicopter sat idle on the ramp, its rotors still, the door open to a line of tourists—Hawaiian shirts on the men, flowered sun dresses on the women, who also wore wide-brimmed hats and carried straw totes. And every one of them had a camera.

We exited the Bullet and started toward the chopper.

"Hold it guys," Jamal said, stopping. Then, he pointed at a sign that said, *30-minute helicopter rides over Golden Gate Bridge and Alcatraz, $159 per person.*

We stood there, three feet from the pilot who was ushering

the people inside. The guy was built like a Marine, tall, and broad-shouldered, suntanned, and grinning. His crisp uniform had gold epaulettes on the shoulders. I clenched my teeth. He looked like a tall version of Tom Cruise. If Heather had been there with us I'd have steered her away in another direction.

"Hi, fellas. You gonna join us?" the pilot said, his welcoming smile revealing a row of perfect, white teeth.

I gestured toward the sign, then I pulled my linty pockets inside out and showed him how empty they were.

"Where are you from?" He continued to smile, his teeth glinting in the bright sunlight.

I answered for the three of us. "We're from Florida, on spring break from college."

He chuckled. "This is a long way to go on spring break, isn't it?"

"We wanted to take a little drive."

That made him laugh, louder this time. "Listen," he said. "My bird could use a little ballast. Did you see that large woman who boarded a minute ago?"

We all three nodded.

"You guys can help balance things out a little. How about I let you go up with us for free—if you don't tell anybody?"

Don't tell anybody? I couldn't wait to get home and announce it to Heather and her entire family and anyone else who came across my path—even Hank.

"Mum's the word," I said to the pilot.

I suspected he didn't need ballast at all but maybe had a soft heart for three guys on a cross-country trip during spring break, probably even brought to mind some great adventure from his own college days.

"Okay, then." He eyed Sean. "You sit up front. That'll give me the balance I need." Then he looked Jamal and me up and down. "You two grab the last row. There's plenty of leg room back there."

We jostled against each other trying to be the first one aboard. Jamal won. I came in second, and as always, Sean brought up the rear. The pilot gave everyone headsets, so we could listen to his spiel. I felt like a real pilot with those things on.

The high-powered whirring of the rotors sent a thrill into my core. During the liftoff, we experienced a new sensation—back end first—then a heart-stopping rise of the front, and we swept away over the bay. I don't know if it was the upward surge of our aircraft, the tilt of the cabin, or the dip over the water, but I knew I'd left my stomach somewhere back on the deck.

As a distraction, I stared out the window at the diminishing view of the wharf and the bright sun casting sparkles of light on the water. The shadow of our craft rippled on the blue-green expanse below. Moments later, we soared over Alcatraz.

The massive island of rock looked like it had risen up from beneath the water, groomed and ready for habitation. There were several well-fortified buildings, a water tower, and an aircraft landing pad. All around grew patches of lawn, several trees, and a cluster of well-groomed shrubbery. They made a vibrant contrast to what once served as a high security prison.

I couldn't imagine anyone being able to escape from something that secure out there in the middle of the bay. But, I'd read somewhere that several inmates had tried and a couple had made it to freedom. I whipped out my pocket camera and started shooting.

Our pilot filled us in on the island's history, which dated back to 1775 when a Spanish lieutenant gave it its name, *La Isla de los Alcatraces*, The Isle of Pelicans.

"I don't see any pelicans," Sean spouted over the noise of the rotors.

"The brown pelicans have been diminishing since 1960," our pilot responded on cue. "Today, several species of birds roost there. If you look closely, you can see some of them fluttering around the outer edges."

He returned to his memorized spiel. "The United States purchased the island in 1849 as an ideal location for a lighthouse. In 1850, they turned it into a military base. Alcatraz didn't become a high-security, federal penitentiary until 1934. Also known as *The Rock*, Alcatraz is known for once housing some notorious criminals—Al Capone, also known as Scarface; George *Machine Gun* Kelly; and Robert Straud, who became known as the *Birdman*, to name a few. But, the producers of the *Birdman of Alcatraz* movie made at least one mistake. Although Straud was the subject of the film, he didn't take care of birds until he transferred to Leavenworth."

Being a movie buff, I said, "Wasn't Alcatraz also the setting for *The Rock*?"

"Absolutely," said our pilot. "Also *Point Blank, Escape to Alcatraz,* and a few others."

"Is it still used as a prison?" one of the other tourists asked.

"Nope," our combination pilot/tour guide replied. "They closed it in March of 1963."

Seconds later, Alcatraz became a speck on the ocean, and our pilot turned our attention to the Golden Gate Bridge. From our altitude, it looked like a giant kid had built the thing out of a monstrous erector set. The steel glowed red in the sunlight, almost giving it an other-world quality. I shot more pictures.

Next, we breezed over Fisherman's Wharf, where we'd walked the night before. We must have looked an awful lot like those other colorfully clothed ants swarming around, looking for bread crumbs. I wondered if that's how God saw us—like hungry insects, wandering aimlessly through life. How amazing that He hears every prayer, that He knows every thought, that He has a plan for every person. At that moment, I felt extremely small.

Our craft dipped a little, sending a twinge of nausea to my gut. I turned my attention to the sky. *Please, God, get us safely on the ground. And make it fast.*

Chapter Sixteen

As soon as we settled on the helicopter pad, I lunged for the door, and made it outside before everyone else. After I left my breakfast in some nearby bushes, the three of us thanked our pilot for the free ride. We piled into the Silver Bullet with me at the wheel, and I pointed her in the direction of Florida.

"Time to go home," I said, with relief.

We didn't travel more than a couple miles, however, when my stomach knotted up again, and the road appeared to be swirling. I broke into a cold sweat, swallowed hard, and slowed the Bullet to a crawl.

"Guys," I moaned. "I need to find a bathroom. And fast!"

"Go back to the wharf," Jamal suggested, concerned creases on his forehead.

I didn't argue. I turned us around and headed in the opposite direction. As soon as we arrived at the wharf, I parked in a handicapped vehicle spot and started hitting the restaurants, asking for a bathroom. For some crazy reason, all of the hostesses gave me the same snot-nosed answer.

"Our facilities are reserved for our patrons."

They obviously didn't notice the perspiration on my forehead, the flush of my skin, or the trembling of my hands. Or maybe, they just didn't care if I was about to collapse.

At last, I reached the place where we'd dined the night before. Surely, a nice family style establishment wouldn't turn me away.

Wrong.

The hostess shook her head.

"We ate here last night," I reminded her. "I was the good looking one in the blue shirt. I ordered a seafood platter. Don't you remember me?"

"Sorry, I don't."

I finally figured out the unwritten code. A person had to first *buy* something in order to use a restroom in San Francisco. In my opinion, all restrooms should be free to the public.

I didn't know how long I could hold off from exploding right there on Fisherman's Wharf and leave enough scraps for the gulls to dine on for the rest of the day. Now wild-eyed, I zeroed in on a drug store, ran inside and bought a pack of mints, which gave me free access to the restroom in the back of the store. I rushed past the toy and novelty section where several smiling people stood around browsing with their children.

I stayed in there for maybe fifteen minutes. Didn't think about how much noise I was making. Didn't wonder if someone was waiting outside. When I came out, the same folks were still standing there, browsing, but no one smiled.

I made it back to the car, grateful that Jamal and Sean had remained with the Bullet. I didn't want to get another ticket, this time for parking in a handicapped spot.

"Let's get out of here," I said. "Listen, you guys. If you ever come back to Fisherman's Wharf, don't, under any circumstances, order your salad with blue cheese dressing."

We left San Francisco with me popping mints in my mouth every fifteen minutes or so. Somehow, I had to get my stomach back to feeling normal.

Our departure hadn't come fast enough to suit me. Not only was I tired of sharing my car and my bed with those two, but my desire to get home to Heather had intensified. With the impatience that had been growing inside me, I'd gone through some strange kind of metamorphosis. Somewhere along the way, I'd become a different person, leaving me with one question running around in my head. How could one week on the road have that kind of effect on a twenty-one-year-old college student?

All I knew was, I'd started out fairly confident about my plans for the rest of my life. Now, they all centered around Heather.

We rode in silence for a good hour, each of us lost in our own thoughts. I assumed Jamal wanted to find out if any news had come from the Kentucky scout. Perhaps Sean was thinking about Erin Hagelmeyer and their next class together. As for me, I had to admit that Heather had turned from a girl I'd merely been dating into someone I couldn't live without. It troubled me that she might leave Gainesville to start another life in Chicago.

I swallowed hard, and a nervous chill ran through me. This time it didn't come from bad food. I'd been thinking about *marriage*—with an exceptionally long engagement period, mind you—but in the end, such a decision still involved a lifelong commitment.

What if she said, "No thanks, jerk. I have a life."

I'd drop dead, right there on the spot.

But, the way she looked at me before I left told me she'd never brush me off.

I pictured her smiling with tears in her eyes as I knelt on the front porch beneath her father's floodlight and held out a little velvet box with a diamond ring inside—a regrettably small ring on my part-time Walmart salary. I imagined slipping the ring on her finger and finding out it was too large and having it fall off to the floor and disappear inside a crack in the wooden slats. I shook that thought out of my head. I teetered between making a lifelong commitment and forgetting about the whole thing. Though my mother had gone through two husbands and now was dating someone else, I didn't believe in divorce. Marriage, to me, meant forever.

An image of Alcatraz flashed inside my brain. I dismissed the thought, and pictured Heather, dressed in a white gown and gliding toward me down a long, candle-lit aisle in our church. I smiled, and my heart began to throb.

A ball and chain came to mind, and I lost my smile. So did the clank of a steel door shutting me in forever. I shook that off too and forced myself to imagine coming home from work and finding Heather in the kitchen fixing dinner and humming her favorite songs, like my mother used to do.

Two forces were at war inside my brain. One in favor of married life. The other adamantly against it. I spent the next hour of our drive shifting back and forth between the two thoughts. Finally, I gave up trying to figure out the rest of my life.

"It is what it is," I mumbled.

All of a sudden, Sean came up with a question that surprised both me and apparently Jamal, who opened his mouth and couldn't shut it.

"Guys," Sean said, his voice meek. "That stuff you said about my behavior—you know, the drinking and gambling and stealing part. Do you think God sees everything I do? Do you think He's upset with me?"

I nudged Jamal's arm, as if to say, "Take it, pal."

I'd lost count of the number of students Jamal had introduced to the Savior. I could have been jealous, but instead, I was proud to be his friend. Now, he was about to give the same kind of message to Sean.

I kept driving and held my eyes on the road, but my ears and my mind stayed focused on their conversation.

Jamal turned halfway around in his seat and faced Sean. "Let me ask you this," he said. "Have you ever thought of yourself as a sinner?"

"Yeah," Sean admitted. "Sometimes I've felt like a real lowlife."

"Do you think a perfect God wants to spend eternity with a bunch of lowlifes?"

"Well," said Sean. "I suppose I'd remind God that my sins were small ones. Never killed anybody. Never stole anything more expensive than a couple of towels."

Jamal shook his head. "Sorry, buddy, but *all* sins, even the little ones, separate us from God."

I had to hand it to my friend. He knew exactly what to say. If it had been me, I might have sent Sean pressing his hands to his ears and running away. Instead, he appeared to be captivated by Jamal's God-given gift of elocution.

A thought struck me then that my best friend sounded an awful lot like some of the preachers I'd listened to on the radio. He spoke with the confidence of someone who possessed an unwavering faith in God.

"What about all the good things I've done?" Sean pressed. "They must count for *something*."

By this time, I was chewing the fingernails on my left hand and steering the car with my right. I'd been praying for Sean for the past nine months, hoping somehow he would come to know God and not merely follow the rituals he'd grown up with. While I was still trying to think of a way to help him understand the difference, Jamal plunged ahead.

"None of the good any of us have done can get us into heaven," Jamal said, his voice soft. "We need to confess our sins and truly be sorry for them."

"I already know that," Sean said. "As a kid, I must have gone to confession a hundred thousand times. Isn't that enough?"

"I'm afraid there's more to it," Jamal insisted. "You would still need to turn from your sinful life—it's called repentance—and believe Jesus paid for your sins by His death on the cross. It's called salvation."

Sean fell back against his seat. While traffic blared and rumbled all around us on the outside of the car, the inside was as quiet as a tomb.

"That's an awful lot of information," Sean said at last, his voice almost indiscernible. "I'd like to think about it for a while."

"Fine," said, Jamal, and he turned away from Sean and settled down in the passenger seat.

Had Jamal given up? I doubted it. I glanced at him, resting peacefully against the passenger window.

Like myself, Jamal wasn't *born* a Christian. And like myself, he must have lived for himself at times, too, as evidenced by the Gatorade incident. But he knew he could ask for forgiveness, not only from me but from God. Moments ago, he'd presented the Gospel to Sean, while I'd silently prayed. In a way, we were doing what Jesus' disciples did when they went out two-by-two. Perhaps one spoke while the other one prayed. That's teamwork.

A swell of emotion surged into my heart. At that moment, I could look past the road trip, past the time we had left on earth, and I envisioned an afterlife in which the three of us had embarked on a different road trip, one that traveled the streets of gold. And, I smiled.

Our next stop, Winnemucca, lay nestled in a valley in north central Nevada, at the foot of the mauve colored Santa Rosa Mountains. Along the way, still feeling a bit nauseous, I made three pit stops at rural gas stations, and I even broke into a Porta-Potty at a construction site and left them a souvenir, too.

My stomach, now empty, I could have plunged a fork into half a steer, if a grilled one happened to come along. I was still thinking about steak and potatoes when we reached the outskirts of Winnemucca.

The town looked like a set from a wild west movie—broad main street running through the middle, with shops, saloons, and hotels on either side, and at the far end, a view of the mountains looming in the distance. Best of all, the restaurant signs boasted a good supply of griddle cakes, cheese grits, home fries, and grilled T-bone steaks. I didn't care if I had to sleep in the car that night. I was gonna eat whatever I wanted.

As it turned out, after counting our remaining cash, we settled for sharing a thick, juicy hamburger and a pile of golden fries between the three of us. We drank water, then doled out more cash to fill up the Bullet. At least my car had been properly fed.

Most of the establishments in town had casinos and gaming rooms of one sort or another. Jamal and I steered Sean away from the tables and slot machines. Our stomachs still registering on empty, we strolled through town. It looked like everyone drove either a pickup truck or a classic car. Except for an occasional spout of laughter that poured from one of the establishments, the place appeared to be a quiet, sleepy little town, with a population of about 7,000 according to the sign at the city gate. The streets were close to empty. No gunfights. No rustlers riding into town. No posses saddling up and riding out. Jamal's mother would have been thrilled to know the one danger was a mangy dog growling at the end of a long chain, but that could happen anywhere, even in Jamal's own neighborhood.

We ended up stopping at a combination emporium and feed store, where we browsed the shelves and talked about what might suffice for tomorrow's meals, having shamelessly spent our entire daily allotment, plus extra cash, on yesterday's supper.

A middle-aged woman in a western frock stood behind the counter with her head barely showing above the cash register. She greeted us with a grin. "Welcome to Winnemucca, the friendliest town in Nevada."

I didn't doubt her claim. The waitress at the restaurant had smiled at us like we were long-lost relatives, and several men on the street had tipped their ten-gallon hats at us.

Though concerned about our dwindling budget, I asked the clerk the question that promised to bring more disappointment. "Where can we find a night's lodging for a low price?"

She snickered, which sounded odd coming from a woman with snow white hair and a wrinkled face. Other people in the shop turned their cowboy-hatted heads to look at us.

The woman leaned over the counter toward me. "Son," she said, her voice oozing with sympathy. "You ain't gonna find nothin' for less than sixty bucks."

I swallowed hard and turned to my friends. "What are we gonna do?"

They both shrugged.

"Let's talk about it outside," Jamal suggested.

We started for the door about the same time a frail little woman dressed like a cowgirl strode up to the counter and requested her *usual* supply of feed.

"Is Bert here?" she asked the clerk.

"He's out delivering an order," the clerk said. "Should be back in about two hours."

"Who's gonna load the supplies in my truck?"

"No one, unless you wanna wait for Bert," the heartless woman behind the counter said.

The little old cowgirl sounded so helpless, I spun back toward the counter. "We'll do it," I said, to her obvious surprise. "My buddies and I will load your truck."

She accepted with a big smile, and her glass-like blue eyes shone with appreciation.

"Meet me around back," she said.

The three of us left the store. Jamal didn't say anything, but Sean's face had screwed up with annoyance. He poked my arm. "What were you thinking, Charlie? We're supposed to be finding a place to stay for the night, and you signed us up for day labor."

"Come on, Sean," Jamal spoke up in my defense. "Charlie just wants to help the poor woman. It won't hurt us to take a few minutes of our time and put a couple sacks of grain in her truck."

When we got around back, all three of us stood stock still. Instead of a couple sacks of grain, the dock had disappeared beneath more than two dozen huge burlap sacks that looked to weigh at least fifty pounds each.

I took a deep breath, then moved forward. So did Jamal. With some reluctance, Sean joined us on the dock, and we loaded the bags on the bed of the little woman's pickup truck.

When we finished, we stood there, sweat dripping off our foreheads and our underarms bearing dark stains. She approached us. "My name's Annie," she said, and I pictured a famous female gunslinger from the old west.

We gave her our names, and she shook hands with each of us. "I can't thank you enough for helpin' me out," she went on. "I needed to get back to the ranch, and I didn't want to wait for Bert to come back and make up his mind when and if he could help me."

Then she looked us up and down as though evaluating us for more work. "I couldn't help but overhear your conversation with the desk clerk," she said. "And my goodness, the disappointed looks on your faces when she told you how much a room in this town might cost. It just broke my heart."

I gave her one of my most pathetic looks, which I usually reserved for hard-nosed professors and mommies with cookie jars.

She raised her eyebrows, two furry little caterpillars, and her blue eyes sparkled, like she was about to reward us with cold, hard cash. Instead, she said something that lit up my eyes.

"Have you young men ever slept in a bunkhouse?"

Chapter Seventeen

The lady's invitation hung in the air for a few seconds. We looked at each other, eyes wide, then all three of us broke into huge grins, which served as answer enough for the little woman. She invited us to follow her to the ranch, which turned out to be a forty-five minute drive over unadulterated territory. Sagebrush and tumbleweeds blew across the open fields, and broad stretches of dry and dusty wasteland sprawled on both sides of the road. The dismal landscape lay beneath a cloudless blue sky that seemed to go on forever. The contrast between the dull beige of the land, the distant purple mountains, and the stark blue sky was staggering.

A good fifteen miles outside of town, Annie's black pickup turned off the paved highway and onto a dirt road, and so did my Silver Bullet, close behind. At that point, we moved away from a literal dust bowl and entered a verdant stretch of farmland. As we continued along the country road, the vegetation became more dense. Huge oak trees lined the drive, and well-watered gardens revealed rows of corn, lettuce and cabbages, tomato plants, bean stalks, and low-lying bushes that produced everything from cucumbers to yellow squash. Tall poles held grape vines and something that looked like the wisteria my mother grew on a trellis behind our house.

We'd entered a western version of the Garden of Eden, a literal oasis in the middle of a vast wilderness. The drive ran past a huge, three-story mansion with a wrap-around porch. Annie pulled up to a stop in front of a gigantic barn. Beyond was a fenced area separating the main property from acres of grazing land. By this time, I'd begun to feel more like a westerner and less like a Floridian.

I hopped out of the Silver Bullet, expecting to unload the pickup and further earn our night's lodging, but Annie waved us away.

"My stable hands will take care of it," she said. "Let's get you guys settled in the bunkhouse. Then we'll meet at the big house for a cookout."

We looked at each other again, eyes wide. Sean stepped close beside me and gave me another poke in the arm. This time, his tone had softened.

"Sorry, Charlie," he said. "I guess I should have trusted you."

I smiled and kept walking.

The bunkhouse stood about twenty yards behind the barn. Except for the six wagon wheels adorning the front and sides, plus a wraparound porch with wooden benches scattered there, the structure could have been another barn. A broad overhang provided shade from the hot sun and shelter from the rain—that is, whenever precipitation decided to fall on that parched section of the west.

We mounted four wooden steps and passed through a screen door into the coolness of a well-insulated longhouse. Inside, cedar paneling put out an amazing aroma. There was a sitting area and a small kitchen, and then a long, narrow room that resembled an Army barracks, but cozier with all the colorful quilts and pillows strewn over the bunk beds. Paintings of cowboys and wild horses covered the walls, and two bathrooms stood at the far end of the room.

A young cowpoke moved about laying out stacks of laundered towels at the foot of each bed. He offered us a welcoming nod. Annie introduced him as Jimmy. He set aside his work to shake hands with each of us. Annie matched each name to the right person, which totally amazed me. I had college professors who couldn't get my name right after having me in class all semester. For some reason, they called me everything but Charlie.

Jimmy dressed like a real cowboy—tailored plaid shirt with a fitted waist, tight jeans, belted with a huge metal buckle, and pointy-toed leather boots with two-inch heels. He'd pulled his hair back in a low ponytail at the nape of his neck, and he gave us a quaint, lopsided smile. For a young guy, he had an unreal amount of crows feet, most likely from squinting into the sun while herding cattle or riding the range, I presumed.

"Get these three greenhorns settled and let them get cleaned up,"

Annie told him. "Then bring them to the big house. We'll have company for dinner tonight."

She said it as though having guests for dinner was the highlight of her day, or maybe even her life. It had to be pretty lonely out there on the ranch with nobody to talk to for long stretches of time. I felt drawn to the sweet, little thing, in a grandmotherly way. My own grandparents had passed away long ago, so I suppose this was as close as I'd ever come to having a grandmother in my life, if only for a couple days.

You can imagine my surprise when I got to the big house and found out why they called it *big*. I gawked for a minute at the huge, three-story mansion with its front porch the size of Toledo and four pillars gracing the entry. Annie must have had a dozen grandchildren of all sizes and ages running about, from a dark-haired girl in a fringed skirt, down to a freckle-faced toddler in a Roy Rogers outfit. Mature women in flowered dresses wandered about, setting up the dining room and carrying bowls of corn, potatoes, beans, and salads to the table. On the back patio, several young men had fired up two grills and a large roasting oven. As quick as they plated the steaks and slabs of ham, teenage helpers bore them inside and then went back for more.

I stood there with my mouth watering and my eyes glued to the parade of organized workers. Annie directed us where to sit. I took a deep breath, settled into a high-backed wooden chair, then acknowledged her family members as they gathered around the table and announced their names, most of which I forgot about two seconds later. We all held hands and Annie's son, Jeff, thanked God for the food and the company. I had to smile. Little did they know, I'd been yearning for a nice, thick slab of beef.

God had answered my prayer. After having to share a burger with the other two that same afternoon, I now looked down at a huge, medium-rare steak, so big it spilled over the sides of my plate. The strip of fat had been singed to perfection, and the juices oozed out and dripped onto the tablecloth.

I glanced at Jamal and Sean. They looked down at their over-loaded plates and grinned like they'd died and gone to heaven.

I ate in silence, answered a question or two, but preferred to fill my stomach and just listen to the chatter that went on around the table. The guys talked about calving and foaling, and barbed wire fences, and new crops coming in. The ladies chatted about samplers and quilting bees, and trips to the mall for new clothes. The dark-haired girl, who's name was Maribelle—one of the few names that stayed with me—let everyone know she had won a barrel racing competition the day before. She got a couple pats on the back over that one, and she blushed when her brother mentioned her collection of first-place ribbons.

I came away from the table feeling like I had experienced the west the way it was meant to be experienced. Simply driving through this part of the country didn't do it justice. A person had to stop and smell the cactus, or something like that. People could never know anything about the west until they settled in with a real family on a real ranch and ate a steak from a real steer that had been butchered that very morning.

Then Annie said something that made my day.

"Maribelle, why don't you and Jimmy take these three city slickers on a trail ride in the morning?"

"I'd be glad to," she said with authentic western charm.

She smiled at me and held my gaze, which made me a little nervous. I'd met a brown-haired beauty in a cowgirl outfit, and she'd set her dark eyes on me. At that moment, I pictured myself as the star of a blockbuster western, with a beautiful blonde waiting for me at home, and a dark-haired saloon girl beckoning me to stay. Then I imagined the final scene. Me, sitting tall on my silver horse, riding off in the sunset, leaving behind the saloon girl, sobbing her heart out.

"And get them something decent to wear," Annie said, frowning at the three of us. "They look a sad sight in those miserable clothes they're wearing. Not only that, but we need to get them out in the fresh air and sunshine. They're as sickly looking as a cow in labor."

At that moment, my western movie bubble popped, and I became the real me again. Sickly, pale, poorly dressed, and ready to deliver a calf.

"The two tall ones should fit in Roy's clothes," Annie went on torturing us. "And Buster's pants and shirt should be just right for the short fella."

The evening didn't end there. Annie invited us to go to the bunkhouse and relax, while the family cleaned up the dinner dishes, took care of ranch business, and prepared the grounds for an evening campfire meeting.

We didn't argue. The three of us were tired from the long drive. Plus, we had drunk the sweetest milk I've ever tasted, and it had come straight from Annie's own cows, raised right there on the farm where they fed on a rich, unadulterated field of alfalfa. The tryptophan did its job. I needed to take a nap, and I think Jamal and Sean did too, from the way their eyelids drooped. We slunk back to the bunkhouse and fell on our cots, snoring away almost before our heads hit our pillows.

I didn't wake up until the sun had dropped to oblivion, leaving it pitch black outside. The sound of distant singing drew me back to the real world. I checked my watch—9:30 p.m. Jamal and Sean also began to stir.

"Sounds like the campfire meeting has started," I said.

"Good call, Einstein," said Sean. He reached for a wall switch and shed a yellow glow on our section of the bunkhouse.

I ignored his sarcasm and said, "We should join them."

"Why?" Sean sneered. "So you can hit on Maribelle?"

I sat up in bed and stared at him. "Do I detect a tone of jealousy?"

He snorted. "Get real. I didn't make googly eyes at the girl."

"Neither did I," I said defensively.

"Come on, Charlie. She liked you, and you led her on."

"I swear, I didn't."

"Oooh, did you hear him, Jamal? Charlie swore."

Instead of adding fuel to Sean's fire, Jamal came to my rescue. "Quit it, Sean. Why don't you get off his back?"

"Okay," Sean conceded. "But somethin' was cookin' at the table tonight, and it wasn't black-eyed peas."

"Look," I said, tired of his barbs. "I already have a girlfriend. Got it?"

"Sure you do," he persisted.

"You know," I said. "So far, during our road trip, I've seen plenty of pretty girls, but that's all they were, lovely to look at. Nothing more. I had no desire to get to know them better. Maribelle included. And do you know why? Heather is the only girl for me, and my interest in her goes far deeper than her outer beauty. She's beautiful on the inside too. I've gotten to know her, and I like her. Not only that, I *love* her."

It struck me then that I had said the word, *love*, out loud to my two friends. I'd given Sean something else to ride me about.

Instead, the two of them stared at me, kind of stunned.

"Now," I said, rising from my cot. "What do you say we join the campfire crowd?"

A half-hour later, we sat on logs laid out in a circle around a huge bonfire. Several of Annie's children and grandchildren sang "Kumbaya, my Lord." Some of the little ones extended marshmallows on sticks over the coals. Maribelle and a couple of the older girls were making S'mores and passing them out to the others. One of the teenage girls handed me one. I savored the gooey sweetness and begged for another.

Maribelle squeezed onto the log between Jamal and me. I scooted farther away. She slid closer and closed the gap between us. She leaned toward my ear and whispered something I couldn't hear.

I faced her. "Huh?"

"Wanna take a walk?" she murmured, loud enough for me to hear, but no one else.

I shook my head no.

"Why not?" she cooed.

I caught my breath. Shocked by her boldness, I couldn't think of anything to say. I ran through a dozen excuses, then settled on my newly coined mantra.

"It is what it is," I said, staring her in the eye.

She frowned in puzzlement. "Huh?"

I repeated the same thing, this time a little weaker and a little less sure of myself. I may have even put a question mark on the end.

It is what it is so far had succeeded in silencing other people, probably because they didn't know what I meant. I got a different reaction from Maribelle, who now glowered at me.

Huffing, she scrambled to her feet, a look of disgust marring her beautiful face.

"You're nuts!" she said, and she walked around the fire pit and joined the girls on the other side. After that, they kept giggling and casting amused glances at me.

Later, when the gathering dispersed and the three of us guys lay on our bunks, I told my two buddies what had happened with Maribelle. They started laughing and couldn't stop for a good twenty minutes. I snickered, softly at first, then I put aside my embarrassment and gave in to the fun. I think we laughed ourselves to sleep that night.

I slept well with the window open and a gentle breeze stirring the bunkhouse curtains. The aroma of cow dung and leather saddles wafted on the air, sending me straight to a dream about the wild west.

The next morning I arose refreshed and ready for pancakes and eggs at Annie's table. Maribelle had vanished. About the time breakfast ended, young Jimmy came to the big house to take the three of us on the promised trail ride. I couldn't believe our good fortune. This wasn't going to be one of those pony rides going around in a circle inside a pen like the one I rode on when I was a kid. This was the real thing, and I was hyped up for it. So what if I'd never ridden on a *real* horse before?

Chapter Eighteen

Sometime during the night, Jimmy must have laid out authentic western attire for us to wear during our trail ride.

As I slid into a pair of leather chaps, I asked Jamal and Sean if they'd ever ridden a horse before.

Jamal said he took a trail ride last year at a horse farm in northwest Ocala.

"They call Ocala the Horse Capital of the World," he said, like he was bragging about a city he didn't even live in. "And I can see why. I took a tour of the county, amazed at how much of the land is used for horse farms. There's a ton of fenced paddocks, huge, state-of-the-art barns, and acres and acres of rich grazing land. Somebody said the county has more than a thousand horse farms. More race horses are bred there than anywhere in the nation. Something about the rich soil and all the minerals in the grass they eat, which strengthens their bones."

"How did you like it? Your trail ride, I mean," Sean wanted to know. "It might help me to know something about horseback riding before we head out on the range."

Jamal peered with amusement at Sean, who was struggling to close the gigantic buckle on his belt. "Are you telling us you've never ridden before?" Jamal said, his voice a little patronizing.

"Nah! Does it matter?" Sean held his breath and sucked in his waist.

"I think you'd better let Jimmy know," Jamal cautioned.

"Right," Sean said with a grunt, as he got the thing closed with a loud snap.

"Well," said Jamal. "They say once you've ridden a horse, you never forget, that it's kind of like riding a bicycle."

"Sure," Sean came back. "Like you're Butch Cassidy now."

"No, really," Jamal persisted. "The guy leading our trail ride in

Ocala gave us plenty of instruction. He taught us how to post and how to signal the horse with the slightest movement, sometimes with just a flick of the reins or with an oral command. I'll tell you, those animals are well-trained. Riding is a breeze. It's exhilarating. Man and beast, moving as one. You're gonna love it, guys."

Sean and I looked at each other, then at the ceiling. One trail ride and Jamal was ready for rodeo competition.

"Anyway," Jamal went on as if he hadn't picked up on our silent exchange. "You're gonna find your first trail ride a thrill you'll never forget."

Then he turned his attention on me as I huffed and puffed while trying to shove my foot inside a boot that looked way too narrow and had no zipper or buckle. I looked at the pointy toes and thought about the pain.

"Let me help you," Jamal offered.

I still thought he sounded a little arrogant, but I stuck out my foot and invited him to kneel in front of me.

With Jamal pushing on the bottom and me pulling on the top, we finally got the impossible looking piece of leather around my foot. What a surprise that my toes never reached the pointy part. Apparently, it was only for show.

Then he asked me the question I'd been trying to avoid—the same one he'd asked Sean only a minute ago.

"What about you, Charlie? Have you ever ridden before?"

I wasn't about to tell him about the time when I was ten and, though terrified, held onto a Shetland pony that was plodding around a sand-filled pen.

"No," I said with a shrug. "But how hard can it be?"

"Well, you don't just hang on," Jamal said with a grunt. "You have to let the horse know who's boss."

"Yeah," piped up Sean. "The *horse* is."

We shared a nervous laugh, then grabbed our Stetson hats and sauntered out of the bunkhouse, our two-inch heels thumping against the hardwood floor. Something about wearing those boots and that hat had me feeling tall in the saddle, and I hadn't even gotten on a horse yet.

Jimmy stood waiting for us in front of the barn with four of the biggest animals I'd ever seen. I swallowed the lump of fear in my throat.

Three of the horses were brown with black manes and tails. They could have been triplets, except there were some noticeable differences.

Jimmy handed me the reins to one that had a white star on its forehead. "This is Prince," he said. "You'll want to bond with him."

I looked my horse in the eye and established contact. "Howdy, Prince." There. Was that bonding enough? Even more important, did he know I was boss? I couldn't say for sure, especially when he looked away and bobbed his head toward the other horses, then whinnied, like he'd already made fun of me in horse talk.

Jamal got one of the bigger animals, named Junior. He didn't look like a junior to me. He looked more like the master of the house. Sean got a gentle looking horse called Misty. She was gray and looked a little like an equine version of Annie.

Standing next to our animals was one thing. Getting on board was something else. Jamal had no trouble mounting his horse. He inserted one foot in the stirrup and easily flung the other leg over the saddle. When he looked down at the rest of us, I wanted to punch his arrogant face.

Sean needed a little assistance from Jimmy. Though Misty looked smaller than the other two, Sean's legs were shorter than ours and he had to contend with that round stomach of his. Jimmy struggled to get under Sean so he could boost him into the saddle. Sean straddled the leather seat, teetered a little, then gripped the horn for dear life, and at last settled onto the saddle, though he had a brief argument with Jimmy about the length of his stirrups.

"Shouldn't they be longer, like Jamal's?" Sean whined.

"Your legs are shorter than his," Jimmy reasoned.

"I don't think my knees should be bent like they are."

"Yes, they should. That's how you can grip the withers."

"The what?! I don't want to grip the withers. I want to sit here, not gripping, just holding on."

Exhaling an exasperated huff, Jimmy complied and lengthened

Sean's stirrup straps until it looked like he was riding standing up instead of sitting down.

I shook my head along with Jimmy. Not to be outdone by Jamal, I tackled mounting my own saddle with feigned confidence. First my foot slipped out of the stirrup. My second try succeeded. Then, wildly grabbing whatever was within reach—the horn, the halter, tufts of the horse's mane, even his tale—I finally made it up. I wobbled a little, took a deep breath, smiled, and tried to give the impression that I always mounted a horse that way.

Before climbing onto his own horse, which he called Captain, Jimmy went through a list of instructions, probably much like what Jamal had heard on *his* first ride. Although I wanted to enjoy the experience, nervous jitters ran through me, and I missed a lot of what Jimmy said. I did catch certain words, like *post,* and *canter,* and *balk,* but they meant little to me. I had a bunch of my own words cantering around in my head. Words like, *big mistake,* and *not too late to change your mind.*

The next thing I knew, we started out on one of those dirt trails that led away from the barn and into a wasteland of rocks and sand. It was reminiscent of when I was ten years old, helpless up there in the saddle. The thrill of getting close to a horse of any size had melted away as soon as I *did* get close to one.

"How long a ride will it be?" I asked Jimmy.

"Oh, about an hour," he drawled. "Once we git started, the time will fly by."

Sure, I thought.

He told us to follow him single file, and I trusted my horse also knew how to do that. Weren't they trained to follow the leader? I'd seen a similar grouping in a documentary about trail riding in Montana. The photos showed a whole line of horses and riders traveling single file along a grassy plain.

But this wasn't Montana. It was Nevada. Maybe the Nevada horses had a different kind of training. Maybe they were like the people who came there to gamble, having a sort of devil-may-care attitude, doing whatever they wanted and taking risks with their hard-earned money, or even hard-earned lives in this case. Before we started out, I said a silent prayer and asked God to bring us back to the big house in one piece.

The ride began with an easy walk. Jimmy took the lead, then Jamal, followed by Sean, and finally me. If that's all we did, a slow and lazy walk, I could handle it. I made up my mind to relax and enjoy the scenery.

We plodded along for a while, past patches of scrub grass and clusters of spindly trees. With every step, I evolved into a real cowboy. As I rode on, in the middle of cowpoke country, to the sound of creaking saddles and clopping horses' hooves, it was easy to dream a little. I could even picture myself roping calves, herding cattle, and taming a bucking bronco.

After a while, we picked up our pace to a gentle trot. I kept my eyes out for Sean, who, until that moment rode smoothly along. But as soon as Misty began to trot, he started bouncing in the saddle like a bloated, oversized beach ball. I winced with every slam of his butt against the hard leather. Still, he didn't complain. He must have gritted his teeth and borne the humiliation, too embarrassed to admit he'd been wrong about the length of his stirrup straps.

I enjoyed the new pace and even thought it might be fun to gallop, like the movie cowboys did, whipping the reins from side to side and goading their horses forward with a kick of their spurs. Although I imagined such a ride, I didn't have the nerve to try it. I simply trusted Prince to stay in line like he was supposed to do. For a few seconds, I released my death grip on the reins and patted his neck. It felt soft and furry beneath my hand. He let out a snort. I frowned, unsure of what he was trying to tell me.

Close to town we came to a couple areas where more trails crossed the one we'd been following. I caught sight of a sign that said, **Bloody Shins Trail,** and while I nervously wondered whose shins they meant, two dirt bikers bounced into view, the roar of their engines piercing the air. They disappeared into the woods about as fast as they'd appeared. The distant revving of the engines and the hooting of the riders hovered in the air behind them. I moved on, grateful the sign hadn't meant *my* shins.

The trail ahead spread out a little, and pretty soon we didn't travel single file anymore. In fact, Prince and I moved a little past bouncing Sean and came up beside Jamal. When we got close enough for me to start a conversation, Jamal's horse bucked and flung his back hoof at my horse. Jamal nearly flew off the saddle.

After that, every time Prince got within kicking distance of Junior, Jamal's horse put his ears back and started bucking and flinging his back leg at us.

"Hey, Jimmy!" Jamal called out. "What's going on with this horse?"

The three of us had pulled back on the reins the way we'd been taught and, wonder of wonders, all three of our steeds came to a complete stop in a group.

Jimmy had been traveling ahead, like he had drifted off in his own little world. Hearing our commotion, he turned back and wanted to know what had happened.

Jamal and I tried to respond, but with both of us describing Junior's actions in animated voices, the explanation came out a little garbled.

Jimmy smiled and figured it out for himself.

"Junior doesn't like other horses coming too close," he said.

Jamal frowned with puzzlement. "What's the matter with him? Does he have social anxiety or something?"

Jimmy chuckled, then told Jamal what to do. "When Junior puts his ears back, you need to tap him gently on the top of his head and get his attention forward where it should be." Then he turned to me. "Charlie, it's best if ya keep your distance. You don't want to spook someone else's horse."

As Jimmy moved on, I mumbled at his back, *Thanks for telling us before we started out, Big Shot.*

I looked at Sean. His face had flushed bright red, and his forehead wrinkled like he was suffering intense pain. "Why don't you ask Jimmy to shorten your stirrups?" I offered.

He shook his head. "We've been out here for almost an hour. Ride's nearly over."

I breathed a sympathetic sigh and moved on, happy with the way my own ride had been going. Prince had been behaving quite well. I hardly had to do any steering at all.

Meanwhile, Jamal's horse moved away from the rest of us and headed for some low-hanging trees. I stared with interest as Junior entered the thicket and appeared to be trying to brush Jamal off his back with the branches. By this time, Jamal lay fully back with his head on the horse's rump and his feet sticking straight out in front. Amazingly, he stayed astride—how, I'll never know. When Junior emerged from the copse of trees, Jamal lunged upright. A bunch of twigs and leaves had gotten caught in his dreadlocks. I let out a chuckle. Mister Expert Rider now looked like Medusa, the Greek mythological creature whose hair had turned into snakes.

Unable to restrain myself, I started laughing out loud and nearly fell off my horse.

Sean came up beside me, took one look at Jamal, and started laughing too. I fumbled for my camera, shot as many pictures as I dared until Jamal ordered me to stop. As we moved on, he pulled twigs and leaves out of his dreadlocks and tossed them at Sean and me.

I rode along comfortably for a while, quite pleased with the horse I'd been given. Then, all of a sudden, Prince decided he wanted to go back to the barn. He took off like a shot. At that moment, my dream of galloping across the range became a reality. I tugged on the reins. Nothing happened. I flailed about, my arms and legs flying in all directions. I grabbed the horn and cried, "Whoa! Whoa!" to no avail. Prince barreled down the grassy slope like he'd been stung by a bee. He didn't slow down until he screeched to a halt in front of the water trough, and nearly propelled me off the saddle.

Several minutes later, the others came trotting up. This time, *I* was the one being laughed at, and *they* were doing the laughing. I shook so hard, I had trouble dismounting and ended up getting my boot stuck in the stirrup. As soon as I was able to extricate my foot, I gave Jimmy and my two *friends*, a nasty look, but that didn't stop their joking.

I stood there and took the ribbing for a while. Prince let out a loud whinny that sounded an awful lot like he was laughing at me too. Disgusted, I started to limp off to the big house when Jimmy called me back.

"You're not done, cowboy," he drawled. "It's time to cool down our horses. We need to get the saddles off and groom the animals, then put them in their stalls. *And*," he added with emphasis, "before we get our own lunch, we have to make sure they're fed and watered."

To be honest, I resented Prince and didn't want to do anything for him. He appeared to be gloating as I followed Jimmy's instructions and pampered the spoiled animal. But I discovered that brushing Prince had a calming affect on me. Anyone who's ever groomed a horse must know how soothing it feels to run a brush over the animal's luxurious coat and then follow with a stroke of your hand. I found it surprisingly therapeutic.

Jamal and Sean also took care of their horses. In between running the brush over Junior's coat, Jamal kept pulling leaves out of his hair. And Sean paused now and then to rub his bottom and release an indiscernible stream of curses.

By the time I finished grooming Prince, the horse and I had become old buddies. As I led him to his stall and filled his feed bin, I looked straight into those chocolate brown eyes, and I confessed the truth. "Okay, you're the boss," I said. He whinnied back, and I thought I saw him smile.

The three of us joined the family in the dining room. Three cast iron pots of beef stew stood on the table along with several platters of cornbread and a huge salad. After being out on the trail for over an hour, I was ready for a stick-to-your-ribs kind of lunch.

As before, Annie sat at the head of the table, and it occurred to me that I knew little about the woman who'd been our host for two days. I took the seat beside her and started asking questions, subtly at first and then with enthusiasm.

I learned she'd been widowed for twenty-two years and had kept the ranch going with the help of her three sons and two daughters. Her children had blessed her with a dozen grandchildren. Most of them still lived in the big house, but two of the sons had built their own homes on the property, which, by the way, covered 110 acres of prime land in Humboldt County.

Maribelle sauntered in at some point, leaned over my shoulder and apologized for having been so forward. "Jamal told me you have a girlfriend," she whispered. "Lucky girl." She smiled and took a seat on the other side of the table.

I could have stayed there forever amidst a family that loved and cared for each other. I could have ridden Prince every day—now that we both knew who was boss—could have slept in the bunkhouse and done chores around the ranch like the other guys, could even have been friends with Jimmy.

But we needed to get back on the road. Jamal and Sean had already packed. After all, they had similar homes to go back to, where love prevailed and good food always graced the table. I had an apartment with a near empty refrigerator and a roommate who left dirty socks on the bathroom floor. But one thought made everything worthwhile. Heather had promised to wait for me. In another week, she'd be back in my arms. Lucky girl? Hardly. By that time, I had come to realize, *I* was the lucky one.

Chapter Nineteen

W e drove away from the homestead with a sack of roast beef sandwiches and fruit, compliments of Annie and her crew. They also filled our cooler with water bottles and ice, and a good number of them stood on the front lawn and waved good-bye to us—Maribelle included.

The scene behind my car gave me a warm feeling. The family atmosphere had gotten to me, and it was something I wanted in my own life someday.

We didn't get far, when Jamal mentioned it was Sunday.

"We don't have to go searching for a church," he quickly added. "How about we pull over somewhere and have a little prayer meeting of our own?"

I shrugged. An outdoor church meeting, and we didn't have to lose any time stopping at another friendly little country church with a three-hour service followed by an hour of food and fellowship. Sean didn't say anything, so I assumed his silence meant he agreed. Anyway, the majority ruled. I pulled over to the side of the road and got out of the car.

Jamal grabbed his Bible and we gathered on a rocky ledge in the middle of a wasteland. My friend must have already been pondering a sermon, because he flipped to John Chapter 15, verses 12 and 13 and began to read the passage aloud.

"This is my commandment, that you love one another, just as I have loved you. Greater love has no one than this, that a man will lay down his life for his friends."

I had to admit, the message hit home. Several times over the course of our journey we'd gotten a little irritated with each other. I listened to Jamal's spiel, eager to hear what else my friend had to say. He hadn't used his, "Know what I'm sayin'?" phrase since

I insulted him with it on the desert. Nor had he tried to get even by saying, "It is what it is," or by pushing any of my other buttons, and Jamal knew exactly what they were.

Without stopping to take a breath, Jamal began to expound.

"You know," he said. "This is a time of life when friendships are either cemented or broken, a time when we walk together or go our separate ways. College can make a difference. You make friends. You lose friends. Some relationships can last a lifetime."

"Amen to that," I said.

"I'd like to think of our road trip as a kind of bonding experience," Jamal went on. "These past few days, we've been getting to know each other. For instance, I now know that Sean gargles with mouthwash every morning. Loudly."

I snickered, and Sean grunted.

"And I never saw Charlie pluck the hairs out of his ears before," Jamal added. "I guess, there's a huge difference between an overnight camping trip and two full weeks cooped up in the same car, sleeping in the same room, and eating the same food, sometimes off each other's plates."

I thought about the many times during our road trip when I'd wanted to punch one of them. Then, another passage of scripture came to mind. Didn't the Bible say something about thinking you want to kill someone being the same thing as doing it? The verse convicted me, but let me be clear, I didn't *really* want to take a knife or a piece of piano wire and do them in. It had only been a passing thought, something to satisfy the hostility I'd felt toward them at times.

But at that moment, on that little patch of sterile ground, Jamal's mini sermon gripped my heart, and I began to regret some of the angry remarks I'd made.

Though Jamal kept talking, I didn't hear anything else he said. His voice buzzed in my brain like a distant weather system. What stood out in my mind was the verse of scripture he'd read from John's gospel, the one about loving one another so much a person would lay down his life for him.

I looked at Sean and then at Jamal. They'd become like brothers to me. Though many times over the last few days I'd thought about driving off without them, the truth was, if they were in trouble, I *would* risk my life for either one of them. And I believed they would have done the same for me.

I waited, filled with interest, while Jamal wrapped things up. He truly had a gift, and I tried to imagine what he might do with it someday. With a resounding "Amen," the three of us drew together in a group hug, then we piled back in the Silver Bullet. We didn't speak at first, didn't even look at each other, just drove off, each of us lost in our own thoughts for the next half-hour.

The landscape drifted by and turned more and more dismal, with nothing but sand dunes and sage brush and the land in muted shades of gray and brown. Everything was way too quiet to my liking.

Jamal must have sensed it too, because he turned on the radio, fiddled with the dial, and caught Johnny Cash singing about the dirty, dusty road to Winnemucca.

Sean came alive. "We just came from there!" he called out.

Johnny sang about having been everywhere and glibly listed the names of about a hundred different cities without missing a beat.

"Yeah," I shouted. "Not only Winnemucca. We've been *everywhere!*" I looked at Jamal and then in the rearview mirror at Sean. "This could be our theme song, right?"

We laughed, and all three of us began singing along, stumbling over the lyrics and missing some of the locations, but who cared? Johnny kept on without our help.

We let the music play out. It stayed in my head for a long time after, and I couldn't help but reminisce over some of the highlights of our road trip—good and bad. Best of all, I was glad I had experienced them with my two best friends.

We crossed the Utah border. As we drew closer to Salt Lake City, we caught sight of snow-capped mountains in the distance. We'd been riding for the last couple of hours with the windows down and without the air conditioner droning. The mountain breezes drifted through our open windows and brought a breath of fresh air to the inside of the Bullet.

Besides clean air, a whole new pallet of color greeted us in Utah. More of those snowcapped mountains rose up in the distance. Brown turned to green, and trees and flowering plants popped up out of the ground. The sky had turned a dusty purple, and with the setting of the sun, streaks of orange trailed across the horizon.

The highway ran past Salt Lake City, but we didn't stop, just kept on going, with a goal to reach Green River before nightfall.

"We're staying at your Aunt Lucy's place, tonight, aren't we?" I said to Jamal.

"That's right. She lives on the other side of Green River. If we stop once to eat the lunch Annie gave us and once for fuel, and if we don't need to hit every bathroom on the way, we should be there in about three or four hours."

"She's your mama's sister, isn't she?" I wondered.

Jamal nodded.

"Is she a good cook, too, like your mama?" I ventured to ask.

Jamal beamed. "She's prize-winnin'."

My mouth had already begun to water. If Aunt Lucy was anything like Jamal's mama, we could expect another terrific supper that night. I couldn't believe we had almost $50 apiece left.

We breezed past Salt Lake City. Sean said he was hungry, so I pulled the Silver Bullet onto a soft shoulder, and we sat on the grass where we could take in the distant scenery while we ate. After finishing off Annie's sandwiches and fruit, we took off again, this time with Jamal driving.

I settled into the passenger seat with the charts and maps spread open on my lap. With my index finger, I followed the route we'd already traced with a black, felt-tipped marker. My heart surged with anticipation. I allowed my eyes to stray to the right side of the map where we'd marked a red star over Gainesville, Florida. I was on my way home, and I'd be seeing Heather soon. I pictured her angelic face smiling up at me, like I was the next best thing to a pair of new shoes. Believe me, I know how girls think. Besides a boyfriend, clothes topped the list, particularly shoes. Many Saturday mornings, my older sister and her girlfriends planned many a shopping spree to the mall. Becky's closets already looked like she had a store of her own. I assumed Heather did the same thing.

Jamal looked pensive.

"What's the matter?" I said.

"I'm thinking that our time together is drawing to a close."

"Yeah," I mused. "It's been a real trip, hasn't it?"

"We're gonna keep hangin' out, aren't we?"

"Well, there were times I wanted to get as far away as possible from the two of you, but I can't imagine never seeing you again. You're my best friends."

He smiled at me, then turned his attention to the road ahead, and I went back to my maps.

Meanwhile, Sean had quieted down. Maybe he was thinking about Erin Hagelmeyer. Better yet, maybe he was mulling over the conversation he'd had with Jamal. Maybe he was reading the religious tract the trucker had given him. I could only hope.

We traveled on in silence, each of us lost in our own thoughts. A kind of peace settled on the Bullet, and I liked the feel of it.

Aunt Lucy lived about fifty miles past Green River. We reached her place at dusk. Having been there before, Jamal knew the address. He maneuvered the Silver Bullet around the side streets and eventually stopped in front of a quaint little brick cottage.

Aunt Lucy was waiting for us on the front porch. She'd wedged her round body into one of the wicker chairs, and when we drove up, she struggled to get to her feet. She stood there, grinning from ear to ear. In her white apron and fluff of graying hair, she looked like the Pillsbury dough boy, only with darker skin—oh yeah, and female.

Jamal flew from the car and bounded up the front steps. "Aunt Lucy, Aunt Lucy," he cried out.

"Jamal, my dear boy," she responded, a split second before they collided. "You're a sight for sore eyes."

She gasped for breath, then laughed aloud and carried on like her long-lost son had come home to stay.

Sean and I mounted the stairs behind Jamal and stood waiting until the two of them separated.

Then, Aunt Lucy turned her attention on Sean and me. "I've got an oven full of good food waitin' for you boys. Now, go collect your bags and come inside." She waved us on, then she disappeared through the screen door, allowing it to bang shut behind her.

By the time we disposed of our baggage in the front room, the most pleasant aromas lured us into Aunt Lucy's dining room. An attractive young girl flitted around the table, setting out bowls of sweet potatoes and black-eyed peas, a large platter of sliced ham, and a basket of hot rolls. All I could think was, *God sure is taking care of us.*

I was halfway into a chair, when Aunt Lucy raised a hand. "You boys go wash up first. I won't have dirty hands at my table." She sounded exactly like Jamal's mother.

Jamal led the way to the bathroom, but I beat him back to the table. As always, Sean lagged behind us. As we settled in high-backed chairs, Aunt Lucy introduced us to her daughter, Penelope. With her bronze skin and short haircut, she looked an awful lot like Halle Berry. Besides having a stunningly beautiful face, Penelope had a soft-spoken way of rolling words off her tongue. It wasn't *what* she said that held my attention, but the way she said it. To this day, I don't recall a single word that poured from that girl's mouth, but I do remember the musical sound that accompanied what she said.

Aunt Lucy drew my attention away from Penelope when she asked God to bless the food and to protect the three of us on our journey. As bowls made their way around the table, I loaded up my plate, still aware of the super model sitting across from me. I was reminded that I had an equally fantastic beauty waiting for me at home, so I made up my mind to behave myself. Nobody had to stand over me with a whip. I wanted to be good, partly out of loyalty to Heather, but also out of faithfulness to my Father in heaven. I didn't want to disappoint Him.

At one point, I looked at Sean and found him drooling, his eyes on the girl instead of on the heap of vittles in front of him. For the first time since we started our trip, he picked at his food and tried to make intelligent conversation. I chuckled to myself. While Sean rambled on about geologic formations, the ice age, and global warming, a dribble of brown gravy dripped from his chin and onto the map of Ireland on his shirt.

By the time dinner ended, I was having a hard time keeping my eyelids open. Aunt Lucy stopped clearing the table and ushered us downstairs to her finished basement. I gazed in awe at the furnishings, which included three single-size cots lined up in a row and a night stand with a TV against the opposite wall, like she'd redecorated the place for our one-night visit.

I lay there in the dark, quiet basement, while overhead the sound of running water and the clank of pots and pans told me the two women had started cleaning up our dinner dishes. I didn't have the strength to hop out of bed and rush upstairs to help them, so I lay there with a black-and-white western flickering on the TV screen. I didn't even have the energy to turn the thing off—I just lay there, staring at the screen. One of the actors removed his ten-gallon hat and leaned forward to kiss the schoolmarm good-bye.

Right about then, my eyes began to sting. "I miss Heather," I said aloud.

Jamal sat up. "You're kidding."

"No, I'm not. I miss her."

Sean broke into such hysterical laughter, he almost fell out of bed. "Come on, Charlie. There's a beautiful girl moving around one story above our heads, and you're missing *Heather*?"

"Yes, Sean. I am." My voice had a serious tone that caused his eyes to widen and his jaw to drop. "And, what about you, smarty?" I challenged him. "I thought you'd set your heart on Erin. What's happened? Have you changed your mind about her? Is she no longer the *only* girl for you?"

"I'm not blind," he said with a shrug. "I like hot girls. So, sue me."

I shook my head with disgust. "It's okay to look," I cautioned him. "I couldn't help but notice, either. But really, I have something more permanent waiting for me back home. And so do you."

Jamal joined the debate. "Charlie's right, Sean. You should get your priorities straight."

"Oh? You didn't notice how gorgeous Penelope is?" Sean teased. "Oh, wait. She's your *cousin*. She's off limits to you. But not to us."

Jamal picked one of his sneakers off the floor and let it fly, striking Sean in the right shoulder. Sean grabbed it and sent it sailing back at Jamal, and moments later, all three of us were tossing shoes and dirty socks and pillows back and forth. Then, exhausted from laughing and throwing things, we all settled down, and at some point stopped laughing at ourselves and fell asleep.

I awoke the next morning to the aroma of bacon frying in an iron skillet and coffee brewing in a pot. I couldn't dress fast enough. I got to the kitchen in time for Penelope to slide a loaded plate and a cup of coffee in front of me. A few days before, when we reached San Francisco, my belt had gotten loose around my waist, but with all the satisfying meals I'd had since then, the same belt had grown tighter, and I knew I'd turned into the fatted calf. I suppose I should have cut back a little, but the bacon smelled and tasted great, and the coffee went down real easy.

The three of us visited with Aunt Lucy and Penelope for a while. We talked about our long-distance trip, and through some unwritten code, each of us mentioned the bright points of our journey and avoided all the stupid mistakes we'd made, like almost falling to our death in the Grand Canyon and my embarrassing bout with food poisoning.

When the time came to say goodbye, Aunt Lucy lunged at me with such force, she almost knocked me off the front porch. Her show of affection left me feeling all warm and fuzzy, like someone cared about me and wasn't afraid to show it.

Jamal hugged her for the longest time and even wept a little. Sean's goodbye hug was the funniest of the three. Between Aunt Lucy's dough boy tummy and Sean's well-fed gut, they had a difficult time getting close to each other. They ended up backing off and blowing kisses in the air, giggling the whole time.

Choking back unexpected emotions, I settled in the pilot's seat, grabbed the wheel, and pretended to adjust the controls. We drove away in silence, and I followed Jamal's directions to the highway, then turned the Silver Bullet in the direction of Kansas, with the ultimate target for the day being Missouri.

"If all three of us take a turn driving, we can make it to St. Louis tonight," I told the other two. I flashed a look at Sean through the rear view mirror.

He pursed his lips and gave a half-hearted nod. I didn't push it. I figured we'd give Sean a small block of time, and Jamal and I could share the bulk of the driving, like we'd been doing. For now, I owned the driver's seat, kind of like a long-haul truck driver, with my eyes, hands, and feet operating mechanically, and my brain focused on the road ahead.

Chapter Twenty

By mid-afternoon we had driven all the way through Colorado and were flying through Kansas with miles and miles of corn stalks on both sides of the road. It looked like we'd been trapped inside one of those never-ending corn mazes. To say it felt claustrophobic is an understatement. There I was, traveling through Kansas in a Honda Accord with two cell mates, and nothing but corn on either side of us.

More than ever, I wanted to get home to Heather. Her face kept coming up before me, and driving gave me plenty of time to think, especially when the other two nodded off.

The alone time also gave me the liberty to evaluate my two friends. I'd had my fill of Jamal's holier-than-thou attitude. The guy should be able to skip church once in a while without whining about it. And I'd reached my limit with Sean making body noises in the backseat.

I wanted somebody soft in my arms, somebody who smelled a whole lot better than the two of them. Not that I gave off an aroma of fresh-cut roses. We all had bathed spontaneously and only when we had a hotel room. Plus, I'd soiled my clothes during my bout with Montezuma's Revenge. Though I'd rinsed everything out and stuffed it all in a plastic bag, the residual scent still hung in the air.

Truthfully, though, I wasn't a quitter. I'd begun this journey with the two of them, and I'd made up my mind to finish it with the two of them. No matter what. We still had a few more days and hundreds of miles ahead of us. I kept reminding myself we were friends, not enemies. I had to also admit that they must have grown as tired of me as I was of them.

The rotation of drivers worked well. Sean even took the wheel a couple of times. Whenever we stopped to switch drivers, we stretched our legs and sometimes bought gas and snacks. On rare occasions, I also checked the oil and water. We were like a well-oiled machine—rarely had to discuss or plan anything.

I thought a lot more about the money than the other two did. Jamal had this attitude that God would take care of us, and Sean imagined a pot of gold waited around every bend in the road. Their nonchalance about our budget had me stressing all the more. I didn't want to run out of funds before reaching the Florida state line. To be stuck that close to home and not be able to see Heather again...

Jamal had the wheel on the way to St. Louis. I rode shotgun and Sean was snoring in the backseat. It was near midnight when we finally approached the outskirts of St. Louis. Like a welcoming committee, the city lights rose up to greet us. Jamal and I both caught sight of the Arch at the same time. It was lit up like Christmas. Red, blue, and green streaks fell across the Mississippi River. After escaping desert sands and then plowing through corn fields, the place looked magical.

Jamal and I erupted with a loud cheer, awakening Sean who sprang from the backseat as if we'd yelled, "Fire!"

He sat up straight and rubbed his eyes, then, catching sight of the spectacular array of colors, he started shouting and screaming along with us.

"We gotta see that thing up close tomorrow," Sean squealed. "We gotta see it."

I was wired by this time. Though exhausted from the drive, I doubted I'd be able to get to sleep anytime soon. As the Arch vanished behind us, I turned my attention to the road signs.

"We need to find a place to stay," I reminded my friends.

Jamal took the next exit. Following the *lodging* signs, he made a few turns and took us into a part of town that looked a little run down, but, oh well, it was only for one night. Might as well end our road trip the way it began, sleeping in another bug-ridden motel room.

We found a motel that charged $24, and all three of us agreed we didn't want to waste anymore time driving around in the dark. The higher class hotels would have closed their doors by now. Anyway, they would have cost us a lot more than $24.

Our room appeared clean, no roaches that I could see, no bedbugs either. And there was a pool right outside our room. Not the kind of pool we'd want to swim in. Someone had forgotten to buy pool cleaning chemicals. It smelled like a sewer, and algae floated around on top.

Jamal said he wanted to hit the sack. I went outside and dropped into a lawn chair, soaked up the night sky and sipped on a Sprite I'd purchased in a soda machine. Then, big surprise—Sean sauntered out and pulled up a lawn chair next to mine. He sipped on his own can of Sprite, tossed a bag of pretzels on my lap, and dug into another one exactly like it.

We sat there, side-by-side, munching and sipping and staring at the sky so we didn't have to look at the dirty swimming pool water. Then Sean broke the silence with a question that threw me for a loop.

"That stuff Jamal told me—you know, about sinners and heaven and hell—" Sean said, his voice soft.

I turned my upper body toward him. His eyebrows had gathered in a frightened way that touched my heart.

"What about it?" I said.

"Well, I don't understand why our good deeds can't make up for the bad we've done. I think I've done enough good to balance out the bad."

As I sat there for a little while trying to come up with the right answer, I recalled a youth minister's message from back in the day that made a lot of sense to me. I heaved a sigh and tried to tell it to Sean the way the minister had said it.

"Imagine somebody ends up in court for robbing a convenience store and beating up the clerk," I said, and Sean raised his eyebrows with interest. "His defense attorney admits this wasn't the first time," I went on. "But the guy has been volunteering in a soup kitchen all year, and he takes care of his widowed grandmother. Do you think the judge should say the good he's done outweighs the bad? Should he forgive him, ignore the crime, let him go free?"

Sean shook his head. "Not a chance. The guy's good deeds have nothing to do with the trial. He needs to pay for his crimes."

A sudden silence settled between us. It was as if a light bulb had gone off in Sean's brain, and a deep truth had settle there. He stared off in the distance for a long moment, then his shoulders slumped, and he turned to face me.

"That means I'm guilty," he confessed, his voice weak. "I'm as guilty as sin." He swallowed. "If God sees everything I do, then He knows I'm guilty of all sorts of bad things. I mean, even things I've never told anyone—not even you—right?"

"Right."

"So, if that's true, then the good things I've done can never erase the bad things I've done."

I nodded. "That's what we've been trying to tell you, buddy. But, listen. You're not alone. We're all guilty. Everybody is a sinner. Jamal. Me. Everybody."

Sean gripped the arms of his lawn chair, his eyes filled with panic. "From what you're saying, if everybody's guilty, then God should punish everybody. I'm guilty, so He should punish *me*."

I nodded. "We've all sinned," I told him. "And, the cost of sin is death. Spiritual death. No matter how hard we try, we can't pay the price."

Sean looked at his hands, still gripping the arms of the lawn chair. He released his grip and narrowed his eyes at me.

"If that's true, then why do you and Jamal think you're going to heaven? You just told me you also sin and deserve to be punished."

"Yes, but here's the cool part," I said. "God knew we couldn't be good enough to make up for the bad we've done. So He sent His Son, Jesus, to take the punishment in our place. All we have to do is repent of our sins, commit to doing better, and believe that Jesus took our punishment. It's kind of like going to court, the judge finds you guilty, but your best friend steps up and pays your fine."

Sean's eyes grew as wide as tennis balls. "Is that why Jesus died? To pay for our sins?"

"Bingo!"

It was like a blindfold had been removed from Sean's eyes. In that moment, he understood scriptural truths he'd never grasped before.

"So—what do I have to do?" he wanted to know.

"It's simple. Accept Jesus' gift of salvation."

He shook his head and stared at me, the blank expression returning.

I breathed a long sigh and sent up a silent prayer for help. Immediately, an idea came to me. I pulled my wallet out of my pocket and held it out to him.

"Here, Sean. Take this."

He did.

"You know what just happened?" I said. "I offered you a gift. But it didn't belong to you until you received it. It's the same thing with Jesus' gift of salvation. God has offered it to you, but you still need to accept it."

He kept blinking, like he had awakened from a dream. "All my life I've known about Jesus and the cross and how He suffered for the whole world." He stared at me as moisture filled his eyes. "Now, I know the truth," he whispered. "He did it for *me*." Turning his eyes upward, he added. "Thank you, Jesus."

He inhaled a deep breath and let it out slowly. "Now I understand why you guys go to church and read the Bible and pray a lot," he said, nodding. "Now I know why you prefer to order a cheaper meal, so you can leave a tip. Why Jamal doesn't worry about where his next meal is coming from. Why he talks to God like he's talkin' to a member of his family."

I patted his arm. "It's called a relationship, Sean. You can talk to God, too. You don't have to wait for me or Jamal to pray for you. The line of communication is open. You can use it anytime."

"Thanks, Charlie. Thanks for being a good enough friend to tell me all this."

He stood, smiled, and started toward our room.

"Hey, Sean," I called after him. "My wallet."

Chuckling, he came back and released the wallet into my open hand. I smiled up at him.

"You *had* to give *this* back to me," I said. "But God's gift is yours forever. There's no giving it back."

As Sean turned and walked away, a tenderness filled my heart. It came to me that our friendship had grown into something deeper. Sean was more than a college buddy now. He was a spiritual brother. While many friendships fade away after time, a spiritual connection can last forever. What a great feeling, to know I had that kind of relationship with my two best friends.

After Sean disappeared inside our sliding glass door, I continued to sit there, smiling, profoundly aware that I may have had a hand in bringing my friend to faith in God. It struck me then that Jamal had planted the seeds, and I had helped to water them. But the truth was, like the scripture says, *Some plant, some water, but God brings the increase.*

I sighed with contentment and was about to sigh again, when something crashed into the side of my head. I tumbled off the lawn chair to the pavement.

Groaning, I tried to get up but another blow came, this time to the other side of my face. I peered through swollen eyelids and caught a glimpse of two guys in dark hoodies hovering over me. One of them kicked me in the ribs.

When people tell you they saw stars after getting beat up, believe them, because that's what happened to me. And my stars had nothing to do with the diamond-studded sky overhead.

I turned toward my hotel room a few yards away. Jamal and Sean were on the other side of that sliding glass door. I hoped they hadn't turned up the TV so loud they couldn't hear the commotion going on outside our room.

I tried to cry out, but something wet and sticky lodged in my throat. The two strangers continued to pound me. I managed to flail about with my arms and caught one of them on the cheek, but I missed hitting anything after that.

One of my eyes had completely shut. My cheek burned and something warm trickled down the side of my face. My side hurt so bad I knew they'd broken a couple ribs.

For the first time in my life, I was helpless. Couldn't fight back. Couldn't even yell.

The beating finally stopped, but the pain didn't. Before I blacked out, I sensed that someone was going through my pockets. I thought about my wallet. My cash. Heather's picture. Then all went still.

Chapter Twenty-One

When I came to, I found myself on a bed beneath clean, cool sheets in a dimly lit room. Something hissed beside my bed, and something else kept up a steady pinging noise. I tried to open my eyes, but my left eye had sealed shut, and my right eye opened only a slit, enough for me to know I was not in a dingy hotel room. From the sterile white walls and the antiseptic smell, I figured I'd ended up in a hospital.

I drifted off, not sure for how long. When I opened my one eye again, two indistinct figures stood beside my bed—one tall and thin, the other short and dumpy. The tall, thin one was praying. The short, dumpy one was moaning and whining.

"I shouldn't have left you," the short guy whimpered. "I should have stayed until we went back inside together."

I mumbled something incoherent and tried to focus. Everything faded to a blur.

Someone else entered the room. I turned my head and froze, certain an angel had come in. But instead of a white robe and wings, she had on light blue scrubs and a stethoscope around her neck. She had sky blue eyes, like Heather's, and her honey blonde hair had been cut short in a pixie. She smiled. I didn't have the strength to smile back. I hurt almost everywhere—my face, my shoulder, my side, my left leg, even my lips.

I stared at the enchanting blue eyes. "Heather?" I murmured.

"No," a sweet voice replied. "I'm Janice. Your nurse."

I liked her. Don't ask me why. Maybe she'd come here to get rid of the pain.

She stuck something sharp in my arm, and I didn't like her anymore. Mercifully, I drifted off again.

I awoke sometime later to bright sunlight streaming through

the one window in my small hospital room. High on the opposite wall a TV flickered to life. The *Dr. Phil Show* was on, and people were screaming at each other. I could see a little better now. My one good eye had opened fully, but my other eyelid remained at half-mast.

Jamal stood by the window looking out at my view of a brick wall. Sean sat in a chair, his attention on the TV.

"Wa happen?" I mumbled. "Why'm I in this bed?"

They both spun around and gaped at me.

"He's awake!" Sean blurted out. "He's awake!"

Jamal rushed to my bedside. "Hey, buddy. You've had quite an ordeal."

Sean came up next to him. "Yeah, you got mugged last night, pal. Don't you remember?"

I started to shake my head, but stopped when a sharp pain pierced my temples.

"No," I managed to say. "I rember prezzles by the pool, that's all."

"Somebody beat you to a pulp and took your wallet," was Sean's graphic description. "They took all your money—what was left of it."

"The point is, they didn't kill you," Jamal quickly interjected, his voice sympathetic. "They roughed you up a little, but you're gonna get better. And soon."

"You were all alone out there," Sean said. "A sitting duck."

Jamal frowned at Sean as if to say, "Shut up!" Then he leaned closer. "I heard a lot of commotion. I ran outside in time to see two shadows disappearing down the alley. I thought about running after them, but I saw how bad you were hurt, and I wanted to get you to a hospital." He paused and swallowed, like he was trying to keep his emotions in check. "We called the police. So far, they haven't arrested anyone."

I groaned. The pain had begun to intensify. My left eye throbbed. My jaw felt like it was in a vise. And the ache in my right side took my breath away with the slightest movement.

"We went to the Arch this morning," Sean said, making me feel even worse.

"I wanted to go, too," I mumbled.

"It was awesome," Sean went on, like he could care less for my feelings. "We rode the tram to the top. That thing is six hundred and thirty feet high. The car was small, and it shook a little on the way up. It's tiny windows gave a partial view of the St. Louis skyline and the Mississippi River. We got the weekday rate, twelve bucks." He chuckled. "We made up the cost by sleeping in the car last night. No way did we want to spend even one night in that motel—not with muggers on the loose outside."

I gave them a sorrowful look. "Slept in the car?" I murmured. "Muss-a been awful, 'specially for you, Jamal. Whaddja do, hang your feet out the window?" I released a pathetic version of a laugh, then gripped my side again.

Jamal nodded. "It was a little cramped, but I slept fine. Now, we just want you to get well, so we can finish our road trip together."

Right then, a young girl came in with a tray of food. Jamal slowly raised the head of my bed, and the two of them fussed over me, plumping my pillow, swinging the tray table in front of me, and pulling the lids off the plastic dishes on the tray. My one eye stared at a bowl of thick oatmeal, a hard-cooked egg, and dry toast.

"We ate downstairs in the cafeteria," Sean announced. "Not bad for hospital food. And it was cheap."

Jamal sprinkled some kind of artificial salt on my oatmeal, and he spread imitation butter on my toast. My first bite confirmed what I already suspected. Everything tasted like yesterday's newspaper.

I'd no sooner finished eating my breakfast when I had to go to the bathroom. Sean went out in the hall and flagged down a male nurse. I hated that I needed help to do something that only yesterday morning I did all by myself.

The rest of the day went pretty much the same. Me feeling helpless, and everyone else fussing over me. If I didn't have so much pain, I might have enjoyed all the attention, especially when the pretty blue-eyed nurse came back, this time without the needle.

I drifted off a couple more times, then awoke to another TV talk show and a drink of water. As far as I knew, my two best friends never left my side.

Late in the afternoon, I fell into a deep sleep. This time, when

I awakened, I could see out of both eyes, except my left one was still a little blurry, but not so much that I didn't recognize my two friends standing side-by-side at the foot of my hospital bed. They didn't smile. The two of them stared at me with genuine concern in their eyes, which troubled me. Had I been hurt that bad?

I tried to open my mouth to speak, but my jaw ached, and before too long, I drifted off again. I awoke to someone holding my hand and weeping. At first, I thought Sean had fallen to pieces. But his hands weren't that soft. Nor did he smell like Elizabeth Taylor's White Diamonds perfume. But my mother did.

The voice was my mother's too, and she'd started praying. I lay there in disbelief. It couldn't be her. My mother didn't pray much anymore. Nor had I seen her weep in a long time.

I frowned and strained to hear her words.

"Dear God, please heal my son. And please, help him to love me again."

I couldn't believe my ears. My mom had prayed for me. I began to think that maybe this wasn't the first time. Maybe she'd prayed for me lots of times, though I couldn't be sure.

I shifted my frame to a more comfortable position. My movement brought my mom's head up. She leaned closer and searched my face for some sign of life. Then she changed her plea to something more personal. "Charlie. Charlie, my boy. I'm here. I'm not gonna leave until I know you're okay. Please, Charlie, speak to me. Let me know you're all right."

She buried her face against my chest and began to sob.

It took every ounce of strength for me to raise my hand and place it on my mother's head. Her hair felt thick and curly, like it used to feel when I was five years old and sitting on her lap. I used to hang onto her curls while she read me a Dr. Seuss story. Strange, but I'd forgotten those times until that moment when I lay flat on my back in a hospital bed. Now the memories came flooding back as if they'd happened yesterday.

The next recollection that came to mind, I was six, gripping the ropes of a swing, with my mom pushing me from behind and singing "Row, Row, Row Your Boat," to the rhythm of the swing going back and forth. Then I was ten, coming home from school to a kitchen that smelled like fresh-baked cookies. Then, twelve, and Mom's gentle arms surrounded me as I wept over losing my father to another woman and another family.

After that, the images became muddled. Mom changed, and so did I. Instead of drawing closer, we grew farther apart until we didn't know each other anymore. Two strangers, living in the same house, with different plans and different ideas about the rest of my life. It didn't work. I continued to go my way, and she continued to go hers. We communicated through Post-it notes stuck to the refrigerator door.

Last year, another man came into her life. That's when she and I grew even farther apart. Then, in this, my final year of college, she'd kicked me out of the house by paying nine months rent on an apartment I now shared with a stranger named Hank. I didn't even get to choose my own roommate. From the day I moved out, I didn't see or hear from my mom again.

She had appeared out of nowhere and flung herself on my corpse, weeping and wailing like she'd lost everything she owned. Fully conscious now, I gazed at the thick mass of brown curls beneath my hand.

Along with consciousness, intense pain returned, and I began to groan. Mom's head came up again.

"He's awake! Charlie! My son's awake!"

At that instant the tiny room filled with people, a couple of them in scrubs in different colors. The pretty, blue-eyed angel came in, so did another nurse, a grandmother type.

Two men walked in. One appeared to be a doctor. He had graying hair and wore a white jacket with a stethoscope sticking out of his pocket. The other one looked an awful lot like Mom's boyfriend, Jack. Ruggedly handsome, dark hair, gray eyes, and a head taller than Mom. What surprised me most was the look of concern on his face. I didn't think the guy cared.

My two best friends hovered in a corner of the room. Jamal's lips moved in silent prayer, and Sean gnawed away at his fingernails.

A lot of conversation went between the doctor and my mom. I

lay there, pretty much ignored, like an audience of one. I started to voice my complaints, when the room began to clear. Everyone left, except for my visitors and the one angel nurse, who raised the top of my bed again, causing my head to swim for a second. Then she fluffed my pillow, gave me a drink of water, and swept out of the room like a phantom.

My mom continued to squeeze my hand. But she'd stopped crying.

She leaned close. "Did you hear what the doctor said?"

"No. What happened to me? Did I get hit by a car?"

Sean stepped closer to the bed. "No, man. Did you forget already? You got mugged."

Jamal frowned and pulled him back to the corner.

Mom frowned in Sean's direction, then she leaned closer to me. "The doctor said except for some bad bruises, you have no concussion, and no broken bones." Her crying jag over, she was practically singing now. "They want to keep you in the hospital one more night for observation, and then maybe you'll be able to leave."

"Great," I grunted. "I'm ready to leave *now*." And I started to push away the sheets.

Mom pulled them back up to my neck. "No, you're not. You're gonna stay right here and listen to your doctor."

She placed both hands on my shoulders and held me fast. For some reason, I couldn't budge. My 125-pound mother was stronger than I was.

Little flashes of the attack started coming back to me. A fist to my face, a boot to my rib cage, another fist, pounding, slapping, punching.

"Tell me the truth. How bad are my injuries?" I wanted to know.

Sean stepped closer to the bed. He shook his head and frowned. "Oh, you're a mess."

Jamal nudged him aside. "You have a black eye, a bruised jaw, and they said your right side is also bruised, but, like your mom said, you have no broken bones. You're banged up a little, that's all. You could have gotten the same injuries falling off a bike."

"What else did those guys do to me?" All kinds of sick thoughts ran around in my head.

"Nothing else," said Jamal, his brow wrinkled in sympathy. "They scattered when I came out of our room."

"For one thing, you got robbed," Sean interjected. "Whoever did this to you dropped your wallet, but they took your cash and your one credit card."

"What about my picture of Heather?" I tried to lift my head off the pillow, but fell back, exhausted.

"It's still there," said Sean. "Look." He handed me my wallet, open to Heather's photo.

I sighed with relief and pressed it to my heart.

Then I had another thought. "What if they max out my credit card?"

"Don't worry," Jamal said. "I called your bank this morning and reported your card stolen." He frowned with sympathy. "But you have no money now."

"It's time you came home," Mom said. "You can fly back with Jack and me."

I shook my head, then moaned from the pain of it. "No, thanks. I'm gonna finish this trip."

Mom let out a long sigh. "I figured you'd say that." She pulled an envelope from her purse and pressed it to my chest. "Here's a little something to help you get home. The boys told me how the three of you have been living—or I should say, barely existing. And then this terrible mugging." She shook her head like she used to do when I came home past curfew. "Jack wants you to take this gift and enjoy the rest of your trip. He understands about the guy thing, although it escapes me."

I looked at Jack. He smiled with compassion. All of a sudden, there was something warm and likeable about him.

"We want you to get well," Jack said. "No more staying in run-down motels. You have a few more days of travel left and a couple nights. Have a terrific time, and come home safely."

Mom bent close and planted a kiss on the one part of my face that didn't hurt.

I searched her face. At that moment, I was able to see her the way she used to be, when I was six and then when I was ten. She hadn't changed much at all. *I* must have been the one who'd changed. Without a father's hand to keep me in line, I'd become difficult and rebellious over the years. The truth struck me like I was getting beat up all over again. Mom hadn't put the wedge between us. *I'd* done it.

Tears trickled down the side of my face and fell onto my pillow. I hated that I was lying there helpless and crying. "I'm sorry, Mom," was all I could say with my throat choked up like it was.

She placed a cool hand on my forehead and leaned close, then kissed my cheek again, salty tears and all. "It's okay, Charlie. I love you, son."

I blinked up at her, kind of like I did the day my Dad left us. Teary eyed and sniffling, I'd promised to look after her, like any twelve-year-old kid might do. She'd fallen to pieces when he left. Now *I* was hurting, and she'd come to comfort me.

She smiled and stroked the part of my face that wasn't bruised. "Jamal gave me Heather's phone number," she said. "I called and told her what happened. She started crying when she learned you'd gotten hurt. She wanted to come here, too, but her father said no."

Heather cried for me? Hearing that touched me most of all. Funny how, even while I lay there in extreme pain, I cared more about someone else's hurt than my own. I wanted to comfort Heather, wanted to tell her not to worry about me, that I was going to be okay.

I still had one phone call left. I figured I'd better wait until I sounded like a normal human being. Not someone who couldn't talk for all the pain I had. I didn't want her bawling through our entire lousy ten minutes.

"Tell her I'll call," I said to Mom. She smiled and nodded.

After Mom and Jack left, I tore open the envelope and found $1,000 inside. I showed the cash to Jamal and Sean. "Look at this! We're gonna travel in style from here on out. No more canned tuna and peanut butter. No more staying in fleabags."

The two of them burst out cheering. They grabbed the bills out of my hand and counted them, then strewed them over my bed. Beaming and laughing like I'd gotten straight A's and a scholarship to my chosen school, I gathered up the money and stuffed it back in the envelope.

"Get well," Jamal said. "Show that doctor you're well enough to leave this joint, and we'll get on the road again, like before—only better."

They left to get some lunch, and I waited for someone to bring whatever the doctor had ordered for me. It turned out to be a bland meatloaf, apple sauce, and a glass of milk. I complained to the aide who delivered it, told her it tasted like they'd scraped it up off the highway. I made up my mind, I was gonna break out of that place tomorrow. I longed to dig my teeth into a thick, juicy hamburger, French fries, and a chocolate milkshake with whipped cream and a cherry on top. With that on my mind, I could feel myself getting better already.

I relaxed against my pillow and thought about all that had transpired. Somehow, God had taken something bad and had given it a better outcome. First of all, the mugging incident had brought my mom to my bedside, and second, instead of a few lousy bucks, I now had enough cash for us to finish the road trip like kings. I had to chuckle as I thought about the piddly bit of cash those two thugs got away with.

I began to count my blessings. Heather, of course. But also, school. Do you believe it? I couldn't wait to get back to Gainesville, to the shops and the cafes and the people, even the classes, even Professor Stevens, who'd gotten on my case about my lab work. I vowed at that moment to surprise him—no, to *shock* him. When I got back in class, I wanted to cover his desk with grade A papers. It isn't that I hadn't known the lessons. I'd been slacking off. Well, things were about to change in that area too.

I even missed my boring job at Walmart, putting things on the shelf and having them disappear into the hands of shoppers, then doing the same thing all over again. That, too, needed to change. I determined to be more responsible, to go the extra mile and impress my supervisor, maybe set myself up for a raise or one of those Employee of the Month awards they hand out.

Believe it or not, I even thought about Hank, the big oaf, and I vowed to be nicer to the guy, maybe even lead him to Christ, like Jamal and I had done with Sean. It's amazing how facing death can affect a guy's thinking.

I wasn't a broken up drifter who'd stupidly gotten himself mugged behind a rundown motel on a dark night. At that moment, I was Rocky Balboa, struggling to lift my battered body from the floor of the ring, charging up the stairs of the Philadelphia Museum of Art, reaching the top with both hands extended overhead, the theme song from *Rocky* playing over and over again. And I knew without a doubt, I was going to make it. I raised my hands, like Stallone did at the top of those stairs, and—*Ouch!*—the pain in my side took my breath away, and I lowered my arms ever so slowly.

Catching my breath, I reached for the phone beside my bed and called Heather. This time it would be on *my* dime. This time we could talk for an hour, if we wanted to.

Chapter Twenty-Two

Since I awakened from my stupor, I'd been complaining about the food, the cold air, and the terrible view out my window. I kept telling the nurses, and the aides, and anyone else within earshot, that I was well enough to leave the hospital. I threatened to walk out the door if someone didn't release me soon. They must have passed my complaints to the doctor, because he showed up like a spirit from Hades, fire in his eyes and his lips pinched together in a straight line. He didn't say a word to me, just signed my release papers, and walked out the door. I was certain I heard him sigh with relief.

Thankfully, Jamal and Sean walked in just as the doctor left, and they brought my duffel with a fresh set of clothes jammed inside. They were wrinkled, but they looked and smelled a whole lot better than the bloodied and torn jeans and shirt I'd come into the hospital wearing. I left them hanging in the miniature closet they give you, then I rode off in a wheelchair with Jamal pushing like a Formula One racecar driver. Ten feet from the exit, I sprang from the seat and called out, "*Adios, amigas*," to the shocked volunteers at the information desk.

My head throbbed, and I walked like a drunk, but I made it to the car. I dropped into the passenger seat and let out a contented sigh. I was so happy to be out of there, I might have kissed the dashboard, if it hadn't disappeared under a coating of road dust. I made a mental note to give the Bullet a good cleaning when we got home.

Though I didn't complain to my buddies, fastening my seatbelt hurt like the dickens and brought back a painful memory of the guy's boot plowing into my side.

I held onto the $1,000 my mom's boyfriend had given me,

181

determined to control how we'd spend it. One thing was certain. No more living like a pauper—at least, not until I got back in school.

Jamal drove us away from the hospital and made a few turns like he knew where he was going. Next thing I knew, he pulled into the parking lot of a little cafe.

He smiled at me. "While you lay there unconscious, Sean and I took a tour around town, and we stumbled onto this place. Hope you don't mind."

"No," I said with some hesitation. "Not if you filled up the Silver Bullet while doing all that driving."

"We did," Jamal assured me. "We're all set for the drive. But first, let's fill up our own tanks. Take it from me, the food's great in here."

Like always, when it came to mealtime, Sean was the first one out of the car. Jamal trotted along behind him, and I dragged myself off the seat and hobbled up the long walk, moaning and groaning and questioning whether I'd left the hospital too soon.

Sean burst inside and picked out a booth. Jamal paused at the door, then he stepped aside and held it open for me. With one hand pressed against my rib cage and the other rubbing the back of my neck, I limped past him, thinking, *This must be how old people feel when they have one foot in the grave.*

A breakfast of ham and eggs, fried potatoes and orange juice had me thinking I might live after all.

Before we left the cafe, Sean ordered a biscuit and a strawberry milkshake to go. Astounded, I shook my head. Wasn't a four-course breakfast enough for him?

"It's *your* stomach," I said aloud.

Our next scheduled overnight was Nashville, Tennessee, about six hours away. We no sooner got on the road, when Sean complained that his biscuit was too dry.

Jamal glanced at him in the rearview mirror. "Dip it in the milkshake," he suggested, his eyebrows forming an amused triangle.

"No way," Sean whined. "It'll leave crumbs in my drink."

Personally, I hate to hear anyone whine, especially a guy. "Eat it and shut up," I snapped, then pressed my hand against my side and took a breath.

"I've got an idea," Sean said.

Suspicious, I tried to ignore the excruciating pain in my side, and I slowly turned around in my seat and set my eyes on Sean. In one hand he held the biscuit. In the other, he tilted his milkshake and was about to pour that thick, pink liquid on the biscuit.

"Don't!" I shouted. "You'll make a mess in my car."

He frowned at me. Then, raising his eyebrows like he'd gotten an idea, he rolled down his window, and with both hands extended outside, he again started pouring the milkshake on the biscuit.

By that time, we were doing fifty-five on the highway. I guess Sean hadn't done well in physics class, or maybe he hadn't paid attention to the laws of aerodynamics and wind velocity.

"Sean, don't—" I yelled, too late.

The strawberry shake flew past the biscuit and bathed the Silver Bullet's side from the window to the rear bumper. At the same time, the force of the wind hurled a spray inside the car. Let me tell you, the last thing a guy needs is a car with pink upholstery. Sean had dropped the biscuit somewhere over the last half-mile of highway, but the milkshake covered the entire interior of my car. The headliner, the rear seat cushions, the back of my seat—even the radio got hit. While I was screaming at Sean, I also caught a mouthful. And, Jamal's dreadlocks glistened with pink highlights. Nor did Sean escape. His face was bathed in strawberry freckles.

Speechless, I glared at Sean. That one strawberry milkshake episode released a whole slew of pent up hostilities that had been festering inside my brain. It was the frosting on the cake, the straw that broke the camel's back, the extreme end of my patience. By this time, I was tired of both of those guys.

For one thing, Jamal kept teasing me about the number of times I talked about Heather. I admit, nearly every blonde we came across reminded me of her. But he'd been keeping a record of "Heather sightings" in a little notebook he carried in his pocket. To top that off, I hadn't completely gotten over the Gatorade incident. Whenever Jamal irritated me, the memory resurfaced like a corpse that wouldn't stay buried.

And Sean? He'd been whining ever since we left Gainesville. He didn't want to do anything fun. We almost had to drag him up the Grand Canyon pillar. And what about all those times he'd bored me to tears spouting scientific nonsense about the different sites we visited? Couldn't he just enjoy the trip?

At this point, I just wanted to head straight for Gainesville. No stops, except to buy gas. No restaurants, strictly carry-out. No motels, just drive straight through. I even found myself wishing we had taken Sean's truck, so we could take turns driving and sleeping in the back.

Dripping in strawberry milkshake, Sean bit his lower lip. "Sorry, Charlie. I promise, I'll clean your car at the next pit stop."

"You bet you will," I growled.

As he'd promised, at the very next gas station, Sean grabbed a hose and a handful of paper towels and cleaned the Silver Bullet, inside and out. I washed my face in the restroom, and I helped Jamal rinse the pink streaks out of his dreadlocks. Unfortunately, I couldn't get them all out. He sure looked a sorry sight. It took all of my strength to keep from laughing out loud. I didn't want to end up back in the hospital.

Sean, who'd been closest to the blast, pretty much needed a full bath. He settled for the gas station's restroom sink. All three of us, and the Bullet, emerged refreshed enough to finish our journey.

After another two hours passed, I started thinking about lunch. We came upon a diner, and settled down over a meal of chili burgers and fries. No one ordered a milkshake of any kind.

As we left the restaurant, Sean ignored the to-go menu, slunk past the register and made his way to the car, didn't even look twice at the huge banana split some guy was enjoying at the counter.

The tension inside the Bullet had gotten so thick you could cut it with a knife. When you've been injured the way I had been, every part of your body screams, "Unfair!" I didn't have to utter a word. They both knew by the scowl on my face, the clenching of my fists, and the rigid posture of my body, that I needed time to cool down. One wrong word from them, and I'd be driving home alone, and they'd be standing by the side of the road with their thumbs out—and they knew it.

We rode in silence and reached the outskirts of Nashville around five o'clock. I'd had plenty of time to think, and with several hours of together time ahead of us, it had fallen on me to break the ice. I had to admit, a lot of what had happened was nobody's fault. Not theirs and not mine. We were tired is all, and we were taking it out on each other. I also conceded that my two friends had gotten me to the hospital and then had stayed by my side much of the time.

Sure, they did a few things I didn't like. They went to the Arch without me. So what? I'd gotten to see it lit up at night. I doubt I could have ridden in that claustrophobic little car all the way to the top. I had to admit, I'd been mulling over too many negatives over the last couple of days, and I hadn't dwelt on the positives. Like the stroll in New Orleans and the great time we had playing cowboy in Winnemucca.

I took a deep breath. "Hey guys, whaddaya say we let bygones be bygones and try to enjoy the rest of our trip?"

To their mumbled acceptance, I added. "How about we check into a swanky hotel and eat in the dining room? Jack's treat." I waved the stack of $50s at them.

The cloud of hostility dissolved like magic. By 6:15 we checked into a high rise hotel in the middle of Nashville and took the elevator to our suite on the seventh floor. We took turns using the bathroom, and a half-hour later we sat in the hotel's rustic dining room with its hardwood floors, wagon wheel light fixtures, subdued lighting, and Dolly Parton's mellow voice pouring out of a speaker on the ceiling.

"Doesn't she sound like she just ate a big bowl of tapioca pudding?" Sean sighed, his green eyes dancing with delight.

Jamal and I looked at each other and shook our heads. Of the three of us, Sean was the most star-struck over celebrities, especially country western entertainers. He went nuts whenever a performer came to the college. A couple of times, he shelled out a small fortune for concerts we never bothered to attend.

While Sean gazed at photos of Dolly Parton and Shania Twain plastered on the wall by our table, Jamal and I pored over the menu.

"I've never been a fan of country music," I mumbled.

Jamal nodded. "Same here."

Sean frowned at us like he wasn't about to defend his taste in music.

"Come on, you guys," I said. "Let's order."

We drank root beer out of frosty mugs, speared prime rib with three-pronged silver forks, and slathered real butter on steamy baked potatoes. Between the room fee and the dinner for three, I spent $190 of Jack's money.

I slept well that night. We'd gotten a suite with two queen-size beds and a hideaway sofa, so we each had a place to sprawl in comfort. Once again, Sean didn't mind getting stuck with the sofa.

The next morning, I opened the balcony door and breathed deeply of the fresh air. Below and to the far left stood a row of shops—antique stores, western apparel outlets, and a real old fashioned emporium—all of them constructed of faded barn wood and lined up in one long, rustic wall of marketing.

Jamal stepped up beside me. "I say we spend a little time in this berg. We can hit some of those shops, maybe do something fun. There might be a zip-line attraction out there.

It took only a couple seconds for me to ponder this idea. Zip-line? Sounded great to me. I'd always wanted to try it. Somehow, I'd forgotten about my injuries.

I glanced at Sean. He appeared to be shuddering.

We *had* planned to stick together on that trip. And I *did* still hurt from the assault.

"I suppose I can put off zip-lining for another day," I conceded.

"Let's hit some of the stores," Jamal suggested.

I nodded. "Maybe I can find a little trinket for Heather. After all, a lousy bottle of water might not be romantic enough of a souvenir. I'm thinking some nice jewelry. Maybe a locket to hang around her neck, something she can put my picture in so she'll think of me every time she wears it."

Jamal and Sean shook their heads and left the room, with me trailing behind them. By the time we hit the restaurant, my mind had segued onto breakfast. No shopping trip, no locket, not a single thought of Heather. Just a stack of pancakes with plenty of maple syrup and a side of crisp bacon.

Afterward, we strolled through town like we owned the place. We'd arrived there about ten days after a devastating tornado had ripped through the city. They'd cleaned up the downtown area so well, it looked like the twister never touched it.

My wad of bills had all three of us feeling like wealthy tourists. I soaked up the rustic atmosphere, and the fresh country air had me deep breathing with less pain in my side. I was on the mend and ready to go zip-lining if the suggestion came up again.

Nor had I given up the idea of buying a piece of jewelry for Heather. Certainly, I could spend a little of Jack's money on a gift for my girlfriend.

I started to enter a gift shop when a poster in the window caught my eye.

"Hey, look at this," I called out to the other two. "White water raft trips." I turned to face them. "Ever done it?"

They both shook their heads. Jamal grinned from ear to ear. Sean froze with terror in his eyes.

"We should do it," I urged. Sean backed away. Jamal checked the price. "We'll be using a sizeable chunk of your money," he warned. "That's $45 apiece for a half-day."

"Yeah, but there's a coupon. See? They're offering $20 off per person, good only on weekdays," I noted. "It's Thursday, guys. It's a weekday. When else will we get an opportunity like this?"

Sean took another step back. "I say we save your money for hotels and food."

I laughed. "I say we throw caution to the wind. Come on, they're selling tickets inside."

Sean looked about to panic. "What about your injuries, Charlie? You just got out of the hospital."

I touched my side and winced. "Pain's almost gone," I said, trying to convince myself. Then, I released a long, frustrated sigh. "You don't have to go, Sean. Jamal and I can enjoy the ride, and you can go somewhere else and listen to country music."

"Look," Jamal said. "Either we all go or none of us goes. We have to stick together. That's been the plan since the beginning, right?"

By then, Sean had started shaking like the spin cycle on a broken washing machine.

I placed a hand on his shoulder. "Here's the deal, Sean. We go for a white water raft trip this afternoon, then we stay another night in that great hotel and we take in the Opry."

I didn't have to say another word. Sean's face lit up and his green eyes sparkled like Christmas lights. "Really? The Grand Ole Opry?"

I nodded. "Jack's treat." I patted my pocket that held the cash.

I glanced at Jamal. He eyeballed the ceiling and gave a little shrug. "The Grand Ole Opry?" he said. "All right. Anything to be able to go on the raft trip."

Before Sean had a chance to change his mind, Jamal and I hurried inside the shop and signed up for the afternoon trip. The shopkeeper frowned at my battered face and black eye.

"You sure you want to do this?" he said. "Looks like you already came through some serious rapids."

I shrugged and gave a little chuckle. "I had a minor run-in with a man's fist."

His eyes wary, he slid a disclaimer form in front of me and eyed me while I filled it out. A wrinkle of concern remained on his face, but he issued us the tickets.

I watched another $75 of Jack's money disappear, but I figured it was money well spent. Didn't he say we should have a good time?

A half-hour later we rode in a van toward the Ocoee River. It took another hour to get to the dock. Our guide handed us life vests and helmets, then we boarded a big, blue raft along with two other guys and a burly guide who said his name was Phil.

Our guide eyed my facial bruises with concern. "Are you sure you're ready to make this trip?"

I nodded and forced a smile. Little did he know my rib cage felt like it had been run over by a semi, and the bruises on my face hadn't stopped throbbing for even a minute. But, I wasn't about to tell him that, not with a couple hours of high energy fun ahead of me.

I found a place on the rim of our shiny, blue inflatable raft, and sat through Phil's safety rules for the next ten minutes. The five of us grabbed a paddle each, and Sean settled down on the floor of the raft.

Our guide looked at Sean and shook his head. "Let him be," he said. "This ain't the first time. Trust me. We'll be able to maneuver this thing better without him."

Curled up in a ball on the bottom of the raft, Sean had no interest in the scenery. But I took it all in, like an artist's painting—moss-covered banks, rocky shorelines, towering pines, colorful foliage, all set against a deep blue sky and a river that reflected everything.

We started out easy, just drifted along with the gentle movement of the water. I began to think that's all there was to it, just a leisurely cruise down the river. Did the brochures and TV ads lie about the *wild* adventure? Had the photos been shot somewhere else? Maybe out west on the Colorado or some other raging river? Did anyone ever hit rapids or plunge over waterfalls on this peaceful little stream?

Soon, however, the flow picked up a little speed, and the river shifted into overdrive and carried our raft along with it. No longer were we on a leisurely cruise in nature. Now, nature had grabbed hold of our raft and was flinging it about. We sailed over foaming waves, narrowly missing huge, jagged rocks. With the movement of the river came a harsh rumble of water. No longer could I hear our guide hollering commands. The exultant cries of our traveling companions blended with the deafening roar of the river. As for me, I aimlessly wielded my paddle, used my other hand to hold on for dear life, and tried to keep from plunging over the side.

In the midst of all that activity, I clean forgot about my injuries. A spray of river water stung my face like tiny pellets. My stomach dropped a couple times when we plunged over a series of small waterfalls. I thought my heart might jump out of my chest.

It was terrific!

When I wasn't busy paddling—or pretending to—I looked at Jamal. He looked back at me, wide-eyed and laughing. He looked terrified and happy all at the same time.

As for Sean, I couldn't even see his face with his backside raised like a protective shelter over the rest of him.

Meanwhile, our party of five met the challenge, dipped our paddles simultaneously, leaned first one way, then the other. Once we cleared the rapids, we returned to smooth sailing for a while, until we hit another set of roller-coaster waterfalls.

At the end of the ride, I started to take a deep breath, then caught it midway when the pain in my right side returned with a vengeance. Jamal looked at me with concern.

"You okay?" he mouthed.

I nodded, but couldn't speak. I kept holding my side and smiling through clenched teeth.

When we reached the dock, Sean unfolded himself, stumbled out of the raft, then fell to his knees on the wooden deck. Jamal and I helped him up, and we staggered together, arm-in-arm, back to the van.

Later, when we were in our hotel room getting ready to go to the Opry, we relived our afternoon on the river. I described our raft trip as *exhilarating* and *fun*. Jamal called it *da bomb*. Sean couldn't speak at all.

Chapter Twenty-Three

We were going to the Grand Ole Opry, something I hadn't planned on doing, but I wanted to go for Sean. Since my friend had agreed to the raft trip, I supposed I could sit in a concert hall for an hour and listen to twanging guitars and nasal whining about lost loves and dead people. The thing was, Sean loved it, and so did about 100 million other Americans.

I searched my bag for something to wear. None of my jeans and shirts looked like anything a real cowboy might show up in at the Opry. I found myself wishing I still had my ten-gallon hat and pointy-toed boots, which I'd left behind with Jimmy in the bunkhouse.

In the end, I settled for a pair of blue jeans and a plaid shirt I reserved for church services, and topped it off with a baseball cap.

Jamal rummaged through his bag and came up with a T-shirt that said, *Cowboys love Jesus too!* He slipped it over his head and faced me, then caught my look of surprise.

"I bought it before we left Gainesville," he said. "I hoped I'd get a chance to wear it *somewhere.*"

Meanwhile, Sean put on a psychedelic emerald green T-shirt emblazoned with the words, *I'm Irish, and proud of it!* It looked like it would glow in the dark, but I didn't want to dampen his enthusiasm, so I didn't say anything. I doubted there'd be any Irish cowboys milling about the Opry. But, stranger things had happened to us during our road trip. Somebody might saunter up to Sean and offer him a Guinness.

I looked the three of us over and shook my head. We were gonna stand out like sore thumbs in that crowd of country music lovers. But not being fashion conscious, I didn't care. We weren't the ones on stage performing. We'd be sitting in the audience, in the dark.

Jamal didn't make a fuss about it either. After all, his shirt carried a message. Someone was bound to see it sometime during the night.

Meanwhile, Sean checked his outfit in the mirror and wrinkled his brow.

"We should at least have cowboy hats," he moaned. "This is a once-in-a-lifetime opportunity. We need to blend in with the crowd."

"They don't have a dress code," I grumbled. "You just have to wear clothes. It doesn't matter what kind. C'mon. Let's go. The main performance starts at seven."

The desk clerk gave us half-price coupons for sleeping in his hotel. Like the raft trip tickets, it was another stroke of luck. I paid at the gate, and there went another $135 of Jack's money. Jamal and Sean still had about thirty bucks apiece remaining from their original funds, so they combined their money and bought dinner for all three of us at the Opry Mills Mall.

"We won't need much cash once we leave Nashville," Jamal reasoned.

He spoke the truth. My sister, Becky, had invited us to spend our last night on the road at her place near Atlanta, Georgia. Then it was just a hop, skip, and a jump across the state line to Gainesville, Florida.

Gainesville. The word sent an electrical charge through me. In two days, I'd see Heather again. By this time, I knew without a doubt I wanted to spend the rest of my life with her. Two brief phone calls and a photo in my wallet didn't satisfy me. I wanted to hold her hand. I wanted to stroke her golden hair. I wanted to say the words I'd been holding back for way too long.

Loud music drowned out my daydreaming the instant we walked into the concert hall. We blended in with the other visitors and tried to find seats on one of the padded benches. Entertainers I'd never heard of took the stage. I didn't recognize them as anybody famous, but they'd decked themselves out in spangles and bangles as if they were headliners.

Instead of distracting me from thinking about Heather, the Opry stars and their lovesick lyrics had me mourning for her all the more. Mel Tillis served as the emcee that night, and some of the more well-known entertainers included Diamond Rio and Tim McGraw. Even the lesser known singers got my foot tapping with their catchy rhythms, and I found myself enjoying the show.

Jamal also started clapping his hands and bobbing his head. My friend, the gospel music lover, had gotten caught up in the country music scene like he'd grown up with it. But I knew the truth. He was putting on a good act for Sean. I had to respect him for his sensitivity.

Meanwhile, Sean was in his element. When the raft trip ended, he'd looked a little numb, but now he'd come alive, smiling and moving every part of his body. He even started singing along with the performers, loud and off-key, mind you, and drawing annoyed stares from people sitting nearby, but he kept up with the lyrics like he'd been born in a barn.

After the torture he'd endured on the raft trip, I wasn't about to shut him up. *Let him have his moment,* I reasoned to myself. *He's earned it.*

By the time we sauntered back to our hotel, I'd heard enough country music to last me at least another five years. Sean, however, belted out the lyrics of Jo Dee's "I'm Alright," and kicked up his heels like he wasn't even tired.

Minutes later, he ran out of steam, flopped down, fully clothed, on his sofa bed, and within two minutes he was snoring like a buzz saw.

We spent that night in the comfort of the five-star hotel and took advantage of the free breakfast bar in the morning. My sister lived about four hours away. By this time, Jamal and I had tired of the twangy country renditions that poured out of every cafe, bar, nightclub, and shop in town. Thankfully, Sean never sat in the passenger seat up front, so he didn't get the opportunity to select his favorite music.

While Jamal and I were itching to get back on the road, Sean was behaving like a kid in a toy store. He didn't want to leave Nashville. I expected him to break into a tantrum at any moment, maybe fall on the floor wailing and pounding his fists like I'd seen one of Jamal's little brothers do. Of course, Mama didn't let him get away with it. She turned her back on the screaming five-year-old and pretended he didn't exist. His tantrum was short lived.

Perhaps I should have done the same with Sean, but being the kind, considerate guy I am, I didn't want to spoil the rest of our trip.

"Okay. What else do you want to do?" I said, releasing a sigh.

"Well, we could spend some time out at the pool," Sean suggested. "Maybe swim a few laps, get a little exercise."

Before I had a chance to say I agreed with him, Sean stomped into the bathroom and slammed the door, the closest thing to a tantrum for an adult.

Jamal drew me aside and lowered his voice. "I feel bad that we forced Sean to go white water rafting. It was fun for you and me, but it sent our friend into a panic. Did you see how pale his face got? I swear, all the blood must have drained down to his feet. And how can we expect him to forget the Grand Canyon disaster that nearly got all three of us killed? Poor guy's been putting up with an awful lot."

I didn't respond right away, but Jamal's comments got to me. Since I'd been sitting in the car for most of two weeks, I hadn't gotten in my usual workout at the gym. No wonder I was grumpy. An hour by the pool might help us wind down and get us ready for another 250 miles of highway.

I puffed out another sigh, then I opened my bag and dug out a pair of swim shorts. "Let's go down to the pool."

I banged on the bathroom door. "You win, Sean. I'll see you downstairs."

In five minutes, I was in my suit and out the door. Jamal was still searching through his suitcase for his bathing trunks, and Sean hadn't come out of the bathroom yet.

I hurried down to the pool, shed my T-shirt and sandals, and plunged into the crystal clear water—a far cry from the dirty, algae ridden cesspool behind the motel where I'd gotten mugged. Amazingly, I had it all to myself—not a single tourist in sight.

I did six laps, then came out of the water and collapsed on a lounge chair. Jamal and Sean came down and headed for the edge of the pool. Sean stuck his toes in the water at the shallow end—testing the temperature, I guessed—then grabbed the handrail and tiptoed down the stairs.

Jamal hurried around to the other end and went off the kiddie slide. I had to smile. The three of us were as different as—well—chocolate, vanilla, and strawberry ice cream. I couldn't help but think what an amazing God we have to design so many different people, and animals, and species. My buddies and I didn't grow up in the same neighborhood, nor did we take the same courses of study. Our parents didn't know one another. Nor did we share the same taste in music, food, or religious practices. Yet, somehow along the way, we had bonded. We understood each other. We had fun together. In a sense, we were like the Three Musketeers.

Jamal was D'Artagnan—young, quick-tempered, fast on his feet, and maybe a little impulsive. Wasn't he the one who instigated the most dangerous feat of our entire road trip when he led the way up a pillar of rock and had us hanging over the Grand Canyon?

I likened myself to Athos, a heroic leader with a quiet, imposing strength. Yep, that sounded like me. Hadn't I brought peace when things got a little testy between us? Hadn't I managed our finances well—at least in the beginning?

Since Porthos was less agile than the other two and had a much bigger appetite, it stood to reason he matched my friend Sean.

Yes, sir, we were the Three Musketeers on a mission. One for all, and all for one. I leaned back on the lounge chair and released a contented sigh. Though at times I'd found myself wishing I'd never met the two of them, I had to admit, we hadn't come as close to a breakup as I'd expected. If anything, the road trip had brought us closer together. We'd bonded in a way I never thought possible

A new thought crossed my mind. After we finished college, went on to our respective careers, and headed off in different directions, was it possible we'd never see each other again?

I shook my head.

Not possible, I thought. This isn't the end of a friendship. *It's the beginning.*

With that thought in mind, I leapt from my lounge chair, ran to the side of the pool, and did a cannonball right between them.

As soon as the water settled, we started after each other, grabbing arms and legs, pulling each other underwater, striking the surface with open palms and sending huge sprays of chlorinated water into each other's nostrils. Jamal raced me to the other end and pulled himself out of the water before I reached his side. Then he plunged back in the pool, and the two of us raced back to the shallow end where Sean stood sunning his upper body. We charged into him, knocking him to the floor of the pool. Seconds later, he came up sputtering, then he grabbed my arm and flipped me on my back. Satisfied, he went after Jamal like a red-haired torpedo, and chased him back to the deep end, where Jamal cried, "Uncle!"

After a while, we grew tired of playing in the pool and returned to the deck chairs to dry off in the sun. As I lay there with my eyes shut, one thought kept running through my head. In another day or two, I'd see Heather again. I wanted to wrap my arms around her and, for the first time, let her know I loved her.

That is, if she hadn't given up on me. But of course she hadn't given up on me. Didn't she weep when she learned I'd been mugged? My mom said she had. And hadn't she sounded genuinely concerned when I called her from my hospital room? I needed to hold onto those thoughts.

Think positive, I told myself. We still had a couple more days of travel left. I didn't want to end the road trip feeling miserable.

As soon as my suit had dried enough to pack, I decided it was time to hit the road. I hurried back to the room and changed into my traveling clothes. Mere seconds later, Jamal and Sean came in.

Sean grabbed the little bottles of shampoo and conditioner, but this time he left the towels. I smiled with satisfaction. Perhaps, God *had* gotten through to him.

We loaded everything in the Silver Bullet, then turned our attention to Atlanta and a free stay at my sister's place—our final overnight before heading for home.

Instead of spending more money on an expensive hotel lunch, we agreed to do the fast food bit for a change. For me, it meant reprogramming my stomach for what I ate while attending classes. As the road trip was coming to an end, I held onto memories of rich hotel cuisine, Annie's cookout, and the Fisherman's Wharf seafood platter. Now, I'd be going back to PB&J, ramen noodles, and Spam.

Jamal and Sean, however, didn't have to worry about where their next fancy meal might come from. They both lived at home, and at the end of each school day they returned to a kitchen that smelled like a Bob Evans Restaurant.

We shared a pizza at a little place on the outskirts of town, then we picked up I-24 and headed southeast. Our water fight in the pool convinced Jamal that I was well enough to drive. I hardly ever complained about my side anymore. And, over the last couple of days, my black eye had faded to purple.

Comfortably settled in the right seat, Jamal surprised me for the second time on our trip when he dialed in a '70s music station with James Taylor singing "You've Got a Friend."

"Hey, that's us," he exclaimed and settled back in his seat with a smile.

The lyrics tugged at my heart. I'd been thinking what a fantastic friendship I had developed with these two guys. Like the song said, if I was in trouble, they'd come runnin' to my aid. And I knew I'd do the same for them. The three of us had been poor together and we'd been briefly rich together. It didn't matter. What *did* matter was that we were together.

As I drove along to one heart-rending song after another, I kept to the speed limit, grateful to have come this far without getting a speeding ticket. Okay, I admit it. Occasionally, I'd pushed the pedal, going five to seven miles over. But except for the parking ticket I got in the French Quarter, I had no other fines—nor had Jamal—an amazing feat after driving almost 6,000 miles, sometimes with tempers flaring. I glanced at Jamal in his usual passenger pose, leaning his head against the side window. This time, however, his eyes were open, and he was grinning, so I knew he wasn't asleep. I figured the Golden Oldies had gotten to him, too.

As usual, Sean relaxed in the backseat and let us do the driving. I glanced in the rearview mirror and caught him laughing about something.

"What's so funny, Sean?" I had to know.

"Oh, I was just thinking about that rafting trip we took. Did you see the height of those waves? How awesome! And the scenery? It was like cruising through the Garden of Eden."

I screwed up my eyebrows in disbelief. Had Sean just called his terrorizing rafting trip *awesome*?

"Come on," I said, frowning. "You were scrunched up in the fetal position at the bottom of the raft, so how could you see anything?"

"Well, I did," he said. "I snuck a few peeks when you two were busy trying to hold onto your paddles."

I had to laugh. Mr. Trepidation himself had ventured a peek from the bottom of the raft.

"So, what do you think?" I asked him.

"I think next time I'll do what you guys did. I'll sit on the edge with a paddle and pretend like I'm steering the thing."

Jamal sat up straight and turned to look at Sean. "Whaddaya mean, *pretending*? We weren't pretending. We *were* steering. For *real*."

Sean shook his head and laughed again. "The guide and those other two guys were steering. You kept flailing about like two fish out of water. It's amazing you didn't run us into the rocks."

"Next time I'm gonna bop you with my paddle," I jeered. "That should get you up off the floor. You have no idea how hard it was to keep paddling and not fall in the water."

The bantering went back and forth like that for a while. Then we settled down, all three of us smiling, and I figured we'd concocted three different versions of the raft trip and everything else we'd experienced on our journey.

Feeling a little spunky, I challenged our backseat driver with an offer he'd surely refuse. "Hey, Sean, wanna drive?"

"No way," he said, and slumped down on the seat. "I already did my share."

I didn't press it. The couple of times Sean drove, I'd found myself holding my breath. He went through two red lights, and once it looked like he might drive off the road into a big ditch. I pictured the Silver Bullet crumpled up in a heap and the three of us trapped beneath twisted metal with smoke rising from under the hood.

Jamal offered to take over, and we never asked Sean to drive again. The guy didn't own a car. He either hitched a ride to work with his dad or rode his bike to school. The truth was, I didn't even know if he had a license.

Chapter Twenty-Four

The drive to Atlanta took about half as long as most of our other legs although we lost an hour when we crossed into the Eastern Time Zone in Chattanooga. We arrived at my sister's place in the country at 5:30 and snaked up the long drive to her rustic cabin in the woods. Becky must have heard us coming. She bounded out the front door and scrambled down the steps into the front yard, smiling and waving her arms as we pulled up.

She hadn't changed much from the last time I visited her. Still had that country living look—blue jeans, barefoot, and hair pulled back in a pony tail. With her dark hair and eyes, and the square shape of her jaw, there was no question she was my sister.

I turned off the engine, and pretty much fell out of the car into her waiting arms. As gentle as she was, I flinched, still a little sore from the beating I had taken, plus the additional punishment inflicted by the raft trip. I should have listened to the doctor and rested up for another week, but then I might have missed out on all the fun.

Becky backed away and checked out the bruises on my face. "You poor boy. Mom called and told me what happened."

I gave an awkward shrug. "So? I survived a little mugging."

"Little? You look like you got hit by a train."

Puckering her lips, she reached up and gently patted the bruise on my cheek, then she stared at my swollen eyelid. "You have a black eye. What else?" She looked me up and down.

"I'm fine," I assured her.

She shook her head in disbelief. Assuming she'd get nothing else out of me, she turned her attention to Jamal and Sean. I introduced them, and Becky gave them each a friendly hug before ushering us into the house.

"The baby's asleep," she whispered as we stepped across the threshold. "And Tom's not home from work yet."

Her husband ran a big tractor parts warehouse in Atlanta. Their home in the country acted as an escape, a gentleman's farm where he could kick back and get out in nature for a few days. They had one horse, two goats, and a huge garden, as evidenced by the pile of vegetables strewn across the kitchen table.

"I've been gettin' things ready for your supper," she said, and my mouth watered for what felt like the hundredth time since we left home.

She began peeling and scraping and chopping. Skins flew everywhere. She laid out the potatoes, carrots, celery, and green beans, gathered up the peelings, and put them in a bowl for the compost pile out back. I'd seen her do this same thing during a previous visit.

For a while, we sat around the kitchen table sipping lemonade while Becky flitted about the kitchen. It had been a year since I last visited my sister. I'd never known my baby nephew, and I'd only seen Tom one other time since the wedding.

Suddenly, Becky stopped chopping and dicing and stared at the three of us. "I hate to see you sitting there with nothing to do. Tom carved out plenty of trails in the woods behind our house. Do you guys want to take our four wheelers out?"

Jamal shot out of his chair. I thought about my injured side for half a second. With the idea of driving a four wheeler pressing on my ego, I chose to ignore the pain.

"We do," I said, struggling to my feet.

"We only have two machines," Becky informed us.

Sean scrambled to my side. "I'll ride with Charlie," he said, excitement building in his voice.

Finally, an activity Sean didn't turn down.

Becky provided three helmets and two sets of keys. She led us outside to the barn and uncovered two hot-looking vehicles with *Polaris* etched on the grillwork. They were painted steel gray with blue accents, kind of like the *Star Wars* hovercraft.

Jamal climbed onto the seat of one, turned the key and took off. I scrambled aboard the other one, revved it up and tore out of the barn with Sean clambering to get into the seat beside me. We hit several ruts, bounced and went airborne, then hit the straight-away and closed in on Jamal. He headed into the woods, weaving along a meandering dirt path, and we followed close behind. Now and then, I got a little too close to the edge of the trail and snagged a few vines. Sean's shrieking got me grinning like a demonic racecar driver. Instead of slowing down, I picked up speed and made even sharper turns.

We broke out of the woods and sailed onto a broad field of grass peppered with dandelions. I scooted to one side and pulled up next to Jamal. We drove side-by-side for a while, then I picked up speed. He did the same, and we got into an all-out race. We yelped and howled like two cowboys in a rodeo. Trouble was, my imaginary bronco nearly bucked my passenger clean off. Out of the corner of my eye, Sean's two legs went flying in the air and he dug his fingernails into whatever he could grab hold of.

"Hold on, buddy," I yelled, "We're gonna teach Jamal a lesson."

I ignored his scream, swerved to the left, and as we flew past Jamal, I gave him a disarming smile, then cut him off. He hit the brakes so hard, he spun around like he'd hit an oil slick. After leaving him in my dust, I turned and caught sight of him waving a fist at me.

I guess I got a little cocky after that. With Jamal trailing far behind, I goosed the engine a couple of times. Then, oblivious to an upcoming rise in the path, I tried goosing it again and ended up flying through the air—ATV, me, and Sean—like one unit, with my passenger wide-eyed and screaming.

We landed with a jolt, the sharp pain in my side telling me what a fool I'd been. Nevertheless, I kept going. Too stunned to apply the brake, I put more distance between us and Jamal. When I finally stopped to catch my breath, Sean was gasping for air and struggling to pull his legs under him. he shifted his weight to a more sturdy place on the seat beside me. Jamal came up behind us, laughing and howling.

"You should have seen that last move from where I was sitting," he yelled over the engine noise. "You took off like a rocket. It was spectacular!"

I broke down and laughed with him. Sean still had a death grip on the dash. He released his fingers and joined our revelry, slapping his knee and shaking his head in disbelief. I was laughing so hard, I had to press one hand against my bruised side. I had never felt so good in the midst of so much agony.

We started back toward the barn in time to hear Becky ring the dinner bell that hung from a post on her front porch. After spraying down the vehicles, we placed them under cover, shut the barn door, and strode toward the house. I should say Jamal and Sean strode. I limped along several steps behind them.

Tom had arrived home looking pretty much like the typical weekend farmer with hands the size of baseball gloves, dirt under his nails, leathery skin, and crow's feet at the sides of his eyes. He turned on a welcoming smile that immediately set me at ease.

I made introductions, and after washing up, we grabbed our chairs at the table.

Becky had laid out a spectacular array of country cookin', similar to what Annie had provided for us, but on a smaller scale. And my sister had made my favorite dessert—a black forest cake with thick, white frosting oozing between three layers and a jumble of cherries on top. Becky noticed my drooling eyes and wisely placed the cake on a sideboard next to the stove, as far away from me as possible. She gave me one of her big sister glares that clearly said, *Don't touch until I say so.*

We held hands while Tom asked God to bless the food. It had been a long time since I'd held hands with anyone at the dinner table, a long time since I was part of a family. Yet, during our road trip, I'd done so three or four times already.

While we ate, my mood changed from solemn and reflective to energized. Jamal raved over the thrill of driving an ATV in the woods. Sean and I got into it, too, as we relived the heart-pounding rush of adrenaline.

What a great way to end a sometimes tedious, sometimes mundane road trip with two buddies. The evening respite at my sister's put a fine finish on what the three of us had started with—a friendship we had assumed could endure anything, even being locked up inside a metal tube together for the better part of two weeks.

The fun we had riding those four wheelers added another memory to our road trip. As we hashed over the experience, even little Tommy, seated in his highchair beside the table, got caught up in our exhilaration, banging his plastic spoon on his tray and shrieking with joy, though he had no idea why we were doing the same.

That night, we slept in the spare bedroom and had a choice of two bunk beds. I gazed at the ladder of one, gripped my aching side, and chose the bottom bunk. Jamal sprinted up to the top. Sean chose the bottom of the bunk across the room.

For a while, before any of us fell asleep, we reflected on our adventures over the last couple of weeks. The changing landscapes we'd encountered, the carjacking, the near death experience over the Grand Canyon, my $30 victory on a slot machine, the helicopter ride over Alcatraz, the food—and the lack of it—the trail ride and cookout at Annie's, the mugging, my mom's unexpected visit, Jack's gift of $1,000, and the exhilaration of driving ATV's in the woods behind my sister's house. By the time I fell asleep, I had a big smile on my face. It turned out to be one of the most satisfying nights of the whole trip.

The next morning, I awoke with mixed feelings. Though I was anxious to get home, see Heather, and get back to my routine, I was overcome by a twinge of sadness, knowing our road trip was about to come to an end.

I looked at Jamal. He returned my smile. Sean sat on the edge of his bed, his hands folded on his lap.

"Whaddaya say we pray together?" he said, to my astonishment.

Though Jamal usually was the one who suggested prayer, and I was the one who followed, this time Sean had taken the lead. Before either of us could say anything, he launched into an awkward but amazingly heartfelt prayer. He talked about friendships and loyalty and dependence on God. He finished by asking the Father to guide us home with grace and mercy. At that moment, I imagined my Irish friend must have had a front row seat directly before the throne.

His prayer was short and sweet, not a long-winded exposition filled with scripture, but his words sent goose bumps up and down my arms, and I sat there transfixed, like someone had zapped me with a laser. It occurred to me that a person didn't have to be a longtime believer to pray from the heart.

The neat thing was, we'd moved past the friend stage. We'd become brothers, united through a shared faith in Jesus Christ. I knew that despite all the aggravation and disagreements, I loved those two guys. It was going to be a tough call deciding which of them I might choose as my best man. Maybe both of them, if such things were done.

Best man? Where did that come from? The term caught me off guard. I guess I'd been missing Heather so much, I had marriage on my mind. Maybe not this year. Maybe not until I finished my master's degree and landed a suitable job. I could handle a long engagement. I could wait for the walk down the aisle. That would be easy. But waiting for the intimacy—that would be difficult. I just needed to know she wasn't about to run off to Chicago or that she hadn't accepted a proposal from that obnoxious playboy Robby Richards.

The wheels of finance began to turn in my head. I counted my cash. Figuring in what I'd been spending on fast food and a couple of stops for gas, I still had about $400—enough to buy Heather a decent promise ring, maybe white gold with one of those little solitaires I'd seen advertised in the newspaper. My face flushed with a sudden burst of heat. That wasn't a promise ring. It was an *engagement ring.* My throat tightened up. Such a move spoke of permanence. There'd be no turning back. Ever.

I didn't believe in divorce. I'd come from a twice divorced home. I knew what the experience did to my mother. Saw the pain of failure written on her face, heard the quiet crying in her bedroom with the door closed, watched her shuffle the bills, trying to decide which ones to pay. No one wins in a divorce. Everyone suffers, emotionally and financially, and in some cases, physically, as well. At twelve years of age, I hurt too. I'd been abandoned by my father and ignored by my mother. I grew up thinking their split was my fault. Mom kept reassuring me that he'd left *her*, not *me*, but in the back of my mind I carried the guilt of their divorce for a long time. No wonder I couldn't help her heal and move on. I couldn't even help myself.

When Jack came along, my mom started singing in the kitchen again. A pink flush colored her cheeks, and a sparkle returned to her dark eyes.

When I didn't accept Jack, she paid my apartment rent and got me out of the house and on my own. Now, after what had happened in St. Louis—their visit to the hospital, the envelope of cash, and Jack's offer to be there for me—I regretted how I'd treated him. Jack could have been the father I'd been missing, if I'd let him. I made up my mind to be nicer to the guy, maybe even let him take me fishing.

Such were the thoughts that swam around in my head while I cleaned up in the bathroom that morning.

I went to the kitchen, smiling like I'd cured world hunger, but, in reality, all I'd done was heal myself.

Chapter Twenty-Five

As I should have expected, Becky had outdone herself. She put so many breakfast foods on the table there was hardly enough room for a glass of orange juice and a cup of coffee. I wasn't about to complain. I like grilled sausages, fried bacon, scrambled eggs, pancakes, sour dough toast, fried potatoes, and oatmeal. I just didn't know what to grab first. As always, I ended up with a little of everything on my plate.

Becky stood there beaming as the three of us made quick work of the feast she'd laid out. Tom filled his own plate with amazing nonchalance. I figured he ate like that every morning, though it escaped me how he'd kept from becoming obese. But then, besides working a job that had him on his feet most of the day, he spent evenings and weekends burning calories on the farm.

I looked at my sister and her husband with a mix of envy and pride. They had already demonstrated to me that a marriage could work, if both parties pitched in and did what they could. Tom worked hard, there was no doubt about it. Becky did her part gathering whatever she could pick from the garden, keeping the house, taking care of little Tommy. And she had a lucrative side gig selling women's clothing on the internet. She acted as a middleman of sorts, handling each transaction without ever having to leave home. She took the orders, arranged for shipping, and kept track of her commissions.

Of course, little Tommy kept her jumping, too, but she loved it. I could tell by the way she doted over him, leaping out of her seat to take care of his needs, whether to pick up a spoon he'd dropped on the floor or for a quick diaper change. Whatever she did for that little one always included a hug and a kiss.

I tried to picture Heather doing the same thing. Heather loved kids. Why else had she applied for that teaching job in Chicago? But imagining her taking care of our own children sent a flurry of jitters through me. One minute, I dreamed of that kind of future with her, the next I feared it. Sure, I could picture her as a mother, but I couldn't yet pictured myself as a father. I still faced four more years of college, for goodness' sake. I didn't know if I could handle more than that.

Little Tommy had finished eating and now sat in a playpen pounding the life out of a wooden carpentry set. He cooed now and then like babies do and turned his big round eyes on his mother. I must have started out that way too, admiring Mom while she puttered around in the kitchen. Meanwhile, I would have been confined to a playpen, waiting for the moment when she'd pick me up and hold me close. Though I didn't remember that time of my life, I imagined it must have happened that way. Why else did my heart soften like it did when she came to the hospital?

When breakfast ended, Becky refused Jamal's offer to help with the dishes. Sean and I got busy tossing our bags in the car. It had always been hard to say goodbye to my sister. Despite the upheavals in our home, the two of us had somehow bonded. Even though she'd moved out when I was young, we never lost touch.

With the Silver Bullet all loaded up, we began our last leg of our road trip, a little over five hours down I-75. Once we filled up the Bullet's gas tank one more time, there'd be no other reason to stop. We had a terrific sack lunch filled with ham and cheese sandwiches, chips, and cookies—enough to keep us well fed until we pulled into Sean's driveway.

The final leg turned out to be the most pleasant of all. Jamal sat straight and tall in the driver's seat, his head bobbing to my selection of golden oldies songs. The air had cleared. No longer did tension permeate the Silver Bullet's inside. It was just like it had always been in the past, whenever the three of us went out somewhere. Our conversation turned light. We now focused on Jamal's raves about the Blue Devils, Sean's upcoming science classes, and, of course, my relationship with Heather. No longer did the guys appear bored with my constant reflections on my girlfriend.

They either had learned to block out my sentimental babble or they secretly enjoyed it.

"I'm sorry I talk about Heather so much," I apologized. "I can't help myself."

Jamal winked at me. "You know, I'd tell you to shut up if I didn't like her so much. You got yourself a real nice catch. Don't mess things up, okay?"

I released a sigh. "I've never known anyone like her."

"Not even Bunny?" Sean joked from the backseat.

"Please," I moaned, then turned the tables on them. "Say, Jamal, what about Caroline, the *question mark* girl? Is she still in the picture? And Sean, how about Erin? You'll be seeing her next week in lab. Gonna pick up where you left off? Come on, you two. I can't be the only lovesick fool in the car."

Over the next twenty miles we teased and chided each other about the girls we were interested in, each of us reciting pros and cons. And when the cons outweighed the pros, it became obvious that my two buddies and their girlfriends had not reached the level of acceptance Heather and I enjoyed. So far, a relationship had taken a backseat to Jamal's dream to play pro ball. And Sean hadn't made up his mind what he wanted to do with his life, which had become more complicated now that faith in God had entered the picture.

Around lunchtime, I passed around Becky's sandwiches and snacks. We ate in silence. My sister sure knew how to put together a sack lunch. She'd piled the ham so high, I couldn't get my mouth around both pieces of bread and had to pick away at the thing.

Meanwhile, I kept track of the big, green signs strung over the highway, noting with each passing mile that we were drawing closer to Gainesville, Florida.

Suddenly, Sean let out a whoop, leaned over the front seat, and pointed through the windshield. "Archer Road!" he cried out. "We're practically in my backyard."

Jamal took the exit and followed Route 26 for a while, then made a couple turns into a residential area where Sean's family lived. We pulled up in front of the huge brick and stucco, two-story monster of a house. Sean's brothers and sisters came tumbling out the front door like a green and white avalanche. Sean obviously wasn't the only member of the family who wore Ireland's colors. Even his mom, the last one out the door, wore a ruffled white apron over a solid green housedress.

Sean's dad came from the garage, his hands covered with grease. "Faith and begorrah!" he shouted. "Look who's back."

Joe Murphy kept his distance and refrained from hugging his son. He pointed at Sean's Ireland-themed T-shirt. "I don't want to dishonor our homeland," he said holding up his hands. "Been workin' on my truck." His lips spread in a big, welcoming smile. "Glad to see you, boys." Then his smile faded as he stared at my battered face. "To be sure, you've got some wild stories to tell."

"Yes, we do," I told him. "But if you don't mind, we'll save it for another time. I have to get Jamal home, and I've got plans." Of course, I was thinking about Heather.

Jamal nudged me and smiled. "Yeah. *Plans*," he said, like he knew.

Sean had all but disappeared inside a huddle of his swarming brothers and sisters. His mother fought her way through the crowd, pulled him close, and smothered him with kisses.

The greeting Sean received stayed with me for a long time after I drove away and chauffeured Jamal to his place in a less affluent part of town. His reception was no less intense. His mama wrapped her arms around him. She blubbered a lot, shed tears all over the place, and held onto her son like he'd been covered in Super Glue.

"I want to know the truth," Mama said, as she backed away. "Did you come across any gunslingers?" Her eyes darted toward my face, and I shrank a little. That woman had a look that could disembowel a hardened criminal.

I took a step back. "No, Ma'am."

Jamal looked like he'd dropped two inches shorter. "No gunslingers, Mama."

"Snakes?"

He shook his head. "No snakes."

"Barroom brawls?" she said, her voice laced with suspicion.

She peered closer at my bruised face. "Glory be!" she cried. "Please, don't tell me you two been in a barroom brawl."

Jamal tried to set her at ease. "No, Mama. Charlie got mugged is all."

Her eyes opened wider. "Mugged?" She placed her balled up fists on her hips. "And where did this here muggin' take place?"

Jamal shrugged. "Behind one of the motels we stayed at. I guess we picked the wrong place."

"You guess? You *guess?*" She shook her head with disgust. "And what about you, Jamal? Did you get mugged too?" She looked him over, poked his arms, smoothed the dreadlocks back from his face. "I don't see no bruises on you, Son. How did you get away and Charlie didn't?"

He let out a troubled sigh. "I'm fine, Mama." He glanced at me. "Look, Mama. Charlie's waiting. I need to get my stuff out of his car and let him go."

She backed off then, but the glare on her face said she wasn't finished.

"I promise, Mama," Jamal said. "I'll tell you everything once we get inside. I'm hungry."

Jamal had said the magic words. If there was one thing that could distract Mama Waters it was finding out her son had come home hungry. That's all it took to get her off the current subject and thinking about what to make for supper.

Jamal grabbed his bag, and as the two of them linked arms and went up the porch steps, a lump came to my throat. Truth is, I was a little envious, having never experienced that kind of care, even if it did come in the form of a grilling. Jamal had jokingly labeled his mother's indulgence as *smothering*. I just called it *mothering*.

While I'd been wishing for a little of the same, my mom's tearful kisses in the hospital had surprised me. For the first time in a long time, I had experienced the taste of a mother's love. But she left too soon, and I didn't know if I'd ever be able to recapture that moment.

It had been years since my mother showed the kind of concern for me that Jamal's mother had for him. The last time, I had fallen off my bike and had skinned my knees and the palms of my hands.

I think I was ten. She kissed my wounds, even though they were caked with blood and gravel. The memory almost brought me to tears.

To rescue my emotions, I turned my thoughts to Heather. I drove away with a smile on my lips. My smile grew wider as I turned toward the Oaks Mall and its lure of stores and kiosks. I parked near the entrance closest to JC Penney and headed straight for the store's jewelry counter. Time to buy that piece of jewelry I'd missed out on in Nashville. But this time, I didn't want to buy a locket. I wanted to find something with a lot more meaning.

With a young salesgirl hovering on the other side of the glass, I shuddered as I peered at the array of rings. I glanced up at her a couple of times, embarrassed to have her witness my indecision. She looked like a teenager. Her pulled-back, frosted hair in a pony tail and overdone makeup made her look like a child playing dress-up. I shuffled my feet, searched the display of diamond rings, and balked at the prices. I drifted over to another part of the case where everything was under $400.

"Could I see that one?" I pointed through the glass.

She followed my gaze and withdrew a velvet box with a white gold band and a diamond that resembled an open rose. The tag said $369. My heart leaped to my throat. I was facing the biggest do-or-die moment of my life.

"That's my favorite," the salesgirl said, and I raised my eyebrows in surprise. Her nose piercing looked bigger than the chip of a diamond I'd picked out.

"I–I'll take it," I stammered, and I dug into my pockets for what remained of Jack's cash. Then, I hesitated. What had Jack told me? *Have a terrific time, and come home safely.* He'd intended for us to use that money for the trip. Hotels, food, fun. He never said, *Buy an expensive ring for your girlfriend and change your life forever.*

But I reasoned that he'd given me that money with no strings attached. If having a *terrific time* included making my girlfriend happy, so be it.

My fingers trembling, I counted out the bills on the counter—$369, plus tax. "I don't need a bag," I said. "I'm gonna use it right away."

Use It? Use it?! What an idiot. I wasn't surprised when the sales-girl started laughing. In fact, she lost control and dropped some of my bills on the floor, bent over to retrieve them, and came up giggling.

"Good luck," she called after me as I skulked away, the velvet box in my hand, my pockets nearly empty, and a hot flush on my cheeks.

In any case, I had to make another decision. Do I go straight to Heather's and kneel on the front porch like in my daydream? Do I check for cracks in the floorboards to make sure the ring won't disappear through one of them while I'm in the midst of my speech, like what happened in my nightmare? Or do I go home first, take a shower, brush my teeth and gargle, then put on some decent, unwrinkled clothes? Do I call her and ask her to go out to dinner? Oops! Not a good idea. I'd just spent the last of my money on the ring. No cash for eating out. Not even McDonald's.

I reached the Silver Bullet and was about to open the door, when I paused and took a step back. *What am I doing?* I had no money, I worked a part-time job stocking shelves at Walmart, and I was look-ing at four years of graduate school. I stared at the box in my hand. Had I acted impulsively? I needed to talk to someone. But who?

Not Jamal. Not Sean. They wouldn't understand.

Jack came to mind. He had given me the money. Didn't he have a right to know what I did with it? I shoved the box in my pocket, saddled up the Silver Bullet, and took off for the house Mom and Jack had bought in the Ocala National Forest. For the first time in my young life, I admitted I needed advice from someone older and wiser.

Chapter Twenty-Six

I found Mom and Jack sitting in rocking chairs on the front porch. They were sipping something hot and steamy and tossing bread crusts on the lawn for the birds and squirrels.

A memory surfaced. Mom and me, tearing up bread ends and tossing the pieces to ducks on a city pond. It faded as Mom rose from the rocker.

"Do you want some tea?" she offered. At my refusal she sat back in her chair and resumed rocking. She looked me over. "Looks like you healed well, Charlie."

A moment of silence settled on the front porch. Jack gestured toward a wicker chair on the other side of my mom. I took it and settled back. My mind scrambled for the right words.

"You took your friends home?" Jack said, rocking.

I nodded.

Concern washed over Mom's face. "Is something wrong, son?"

I shook my head, then I let out a sigh and nodded.

"Did something happen on your trip, I mean, besides the mugging?" Mom scooted to the edge of her seat. "Did something go bad between you and your friends?"

"No, Mom. Please, just give me a minute."

More silence, only the *squeak, squeak,* of two rocking chairs in motion.

Mom looked back and forth at me and Jack. Then her eyes widened. She stopped rocking and rose from her chair. "Be right back," she said. "I'm going inside to freshen up my tea."

She passed through the screen door and let it close with a gentle *click*.

Alone with Jack, I looked into his eyes and found acceptance there. He didn't frown at me. In fact, he had a calm expression that

I found comforting. Before I knew it, I had moved into Mom's chair and was spilling my guts—how I'd gone on the road trip caring little about my relationship with Heather, then finding out I missed her more than ever. I told him I'd tried to imagine what my life might be like without her, that I'd come up empty and lonely. How I'd pictured a future with Heather and a family of our own, and how I'd impulsively stopped and bought an engagement ring with the rest of Jack's money.

"Did I have the right to do that?" I said. "Shouldn't I have given you the change?"

He chuckled, and his eyes sparkled with mirth. "Of course not, Charlie. That was yours to keep. Yours to do whatever you chose to with it. If it meant buying your girlfriend a nice ring, then so be it."

"Was I being impulsive? I mean, who does that?"

I held my breath. Maybe he'd tell me to return the ring and get my money back.

Instead, Jack's smile stretched from one ear to the other. Crinkle lines appeared at the corners of his eyes, which flashed with amusement.

"Who does that?" he repeated my comment. "I'd say someone who's in love."

The mirthful lines vanished, and he stared with intensity at me. "I went through a similar upheaval the day I proposed to your mom."

I widened my eyes and dropped my jaw. "You did? But you guys are"—I almost said, *over the hill*. "You're almost *fifty*," I managed.

Jack shook his head. "Age doesn't matter, Charlie. We all experience cold feet and a mix of emotions. You're no different from me or the next guy."

"So, the two of you are gonna get married?"

"Do you object?" Jack said, raising his eyebrows.

"No, not at all," I assured him. "For the first time in a long time, my mom is happy. I think you have a lot to do with that."

He patted my knee. "Look, Son."

He called me, Son.

I liked the sound of it. I didn't draw back from him. I hung my head, then raised it and dared to look into his face.

"You can tell me anything," he said softly.

I gave a little shrug. "I don't have a decent job. I've got another year of college, I'm still facing grad school. And I can't promise Heather anything, except this tiny ring," I withdrew the box and opened it, "and a very long engagement."

Jack took a long look at the ring and smiled. "She's gonna love it," he said. "And I'll bet she won't mind waiting. I don't really know Heather—just met her that one time—but if she's the kind of girl I think she is, I'm guessing she'll be thrilled to wear this ring, knowing what's at the end of that long engagement period. Think about it, Charlie. Four years isn't all that long. It'll give her time to plan the kind of wedding every girl wants."

Mom came back out to the porch at that moment, but I suspected she'd been standing behind the screen door the whole time.

She smiled like the cat that ate the canary, didn't say anything, just sat in the other chair, steamy cup in her hands, and resumed rocking. She didn't try to stop me when I rose to leave. Didn't invite me to stay for supper. Didn't even ask where I was going.

I had no doubt, she already knew.

An hour later, I emerged from my apartment, showered and doused with Cool Water. I'd put on my one pair of designer jeans and a cobalt blue button-down shirt—Heather's favorite. I drove up to her parents' house and entered the part of my daydream that had me standing on the front porch with Heather before me, a look of anticipation on her face.

First thing, I handed her the Zephyr Hills water bottle. Her smile of joy changed into a frown of disappointment as she raised the bottle and looked closer. I figured out what had happened. The heat inside my car had gradually reduced the level of clear Pacific Ocean water to a few inches of pale liquid, riddled with specks of debris. It looked like trash.

I frowned at the bottle. "It was full when we started out from the coast," I said, shaking my head. "And the water was a lot clearer, too."

She accepted the bottle. "Thank you, Charlie. I love it." She pressed the bottle to her heart and smiled sweetly. I wavered a little, then went down on one knee.

My combination daydream/nightmare faded away and everything went smoothly, from the drawing of the little box from my pocket to the sliding of the ring on Heather's finger. There were no gaping cracks in the floorboards, nowhere for the ring to fall through, never to be seen again. No angry father hovering over my shoulder, no mother weeping on the other side of the front door. Even the front porch spotlight had been shut off for the night and only the full moon cast its glow on the two of us.

As I proposed marriage to the girl of my dreams, my voice didn't falter or shake as I had expected. I didn't lose my balance and topple off the porch. I didn't lose my courage, didn't mess up one bit. Nor did I hesitate or change my mind. I'd finally made a decision that would affect the rest of my life.

Best of all, Heather didn't respond with, "No way, loser." In fact, she couldn't speak at all. She could only nod, tears streaming down her face, her eyes closed as I planted a kiss on her lips.

The deed was done. I'd made a commitment to the one person who meant the world to me. And you know what? It felt good.

Could I have grown up that much over the past two weeks? Had I started out on the road trip an irresponsible college student with self-centered plans for my own life and no room for anyone else in it? Had I returned a man with a purpose and a future that appeared to be built on rock instead of sand? Had I, in two weeks time, turned into someone who cared more about someone else's happiness, and by doing so had experienced enormous joy himself?

I am here to tell you, I did. I really did.

Epilogue

Twenty-five years later, April, 2023

I don't want to leave you hanging, so here's the rest of the story.

That initial conversation I had with Jack was the first of many more *father-son* talks. He took me fishing on several occasions, and even at my age I had the chance to know what it meant to have male guidance in my life.

I went on to earn my master's degree in architecture. About midway through my four years of study, Heather and I chose not to wait any longer. She wanted to plan a wedding, and I wanted—well, you know. We were married in a church ceremony with my mom and Jack present and Heather's mother and father both weeping like they'd lost their daughter forever. Her younger brother served as ring bearer, looking super fine in his little tux.

Jamal and Sean both served as my best men. They made a unique pair at the altar. Jamal, six-foot-four, looking debonair in his black tux, and Sean, ten inches shorter, but also looking quite stylish in formal attire, having lost thirty pounds over the last two years.

For our honeymoon, Heather and I flew to San Francisco and refilled her Zephyr Hills bottle. I secretly prayed that this time the water would last longer than the first one had.

Heather took a teaching job in our church's Christian school, and we rented an apartment near the college. She made a far better roommate than Hank Schwartz. For one thing, she knew how to cook. And she didn't snore. Or smell bad.

Speaking of Hank, I followed up on my personal commitment to be kinder to the guy by listening when he talked and by encouraging him in his efforts to become a lawyer instead of a garbage collector as I had presumed. After the success Jamal and I had in evangelizing Sean, I returned to my apartment with enough confidence to share the gospel with Hank and found him equally receptive. Two weeks after graduation, I attended Hank's baptism. I recently visited him and learned he'd continued attending church and now taught a Sunday school class for teenage boys. I also found out he no longer leaves his dirty socks on the bathroom floor. His wife won't let him.

As for Sean, he also had taken his profession of faith seriously. He went on to Bible school and studied biblical archaeology. He married Erin Hagelmeyer, and together they joined a Christian archaeological study team. As I write this, they're conducting a major dig in Samaria. In his last email, Sean said he'd already unearthed some pottery and a human skull.

Jamal broke up with Caroline. He also loosened his mama's apron strings and went off to make a new life for himself with her blessing. She figured anybody who could survive two weeks in the western badlands with us two crazy guys could probably take care of himself wherever he went. Anyway, Jamal's siblings and a few grandbabies have provided Mama with enough worries to keep her busy for a while.

After graduation, Jamal pursued his initial dream and played pro ball for a year. But he abandoned that life and signed up with a missions group headquartered in Central Florida. After completing four years of training, he shipped off to Brazil and moved into a thatch roofed hut.

I'd seen him deliver the gospel message to Sean and a lot of other young people. Now he's got a whole nation to preach to.

My buddies and I still keep in touch. Sean texts me often about the artifacts he's been finding beneath the desert sand. Jamal tries to visit every time he comes home on furlough, but I detect an anxious restlessness to get back to his work in the rain forest.

We recently had a reunion when the two of them came to town at the same time. We went to a high-priced, Italian restaurant and ordered almost everything on the menu—my treat. Being a well-paid, in-demand architect these days, I could afford to splurge a little.

Now that all three of us had gotten together again, we couldn't help but reminisce about our unforgettable road trip. We laughed out loud over the crazy things we did, cringed over the near-death fiascos, and smiled over memories that stirred our hearts.

"I still can't believe you suggested we pick up that hitchhiker, Charlie," Jamal said, shaking his head.

"And, I can't believe you had us dangling over the Grand Canyon," I countered.

I turned to Sean who had raised a ball of spaghetti to his mouth. "What about you, Sean?" I said. "Anything stand out to you?"

"Let's see," he said, lowering the fork to his plate. His green eyes sparked with a memory. "The main thing that jumps out at me as far as our road trip—you two never gave up on me. Gradually, but persistently, you led me into the presence of Jesus. You changed my life."

Speechless, Jamal and I looked at each other and shared a message of satisfied elation. While the two of us had been reveling in our moments of insanity, Sean had hit on one of the most important events of our entire road trip.

What had started out as a fun escapade for three guys had ended up being a whole lot more. During those two weeks on the road, we'd stepped away from our childhood diversions and moved into adulthood. For Jamal, it meant buckling down and racking up grades to earn a scholarship, whether or not the pro scouts offered him a deal. For me, it meant dropping my inhibitions and making an honest commitment to Heather. And for Sean it meant a new direction in life, this time dependent on the leading of his Savior.

To this day, I still think about all the amazing things that happened to us on our cross-country road trip, and I'm in awe of how God had His protective hand on us, guiding us and handing us new values in the end.

Many more changes happened after we got home. Some of them took years. For one thing, the three of us buckled down, got serious about our studies, and focused on substantial goals in life.

Sad to say, I had to put the Silver Bullet to rest. But not *too* sad.

I am after all a successful architect now. I drive a Mercedes. But I made sure I bought one that is silver gray.

Heather's Zephyr Hills water bottle sits on my desk. I fill it with tap water every now and then so she won't know the Pacific Ocean water keeps evaporating. Oh well, it is what it is.

Heather and I have three kids. Two teenage girls, and a boy, Charlie Jr., who's ten years old and is showing signs of restlessness. He keeps checking out faraway places on the computer, and his eyes light up, like he's already planning a road trip somewhere. It makes me a little nervous, but also a little proud. Maybe in ten years, he'll buy an old car and head off into the sunset with two of his buddies. Maybe my boy will have an adventure of his own to write about.

A wise man once said, "Regardless of how well you prepare, when the real time of testing comes, you will be challenged—and you will be changed. That's how you'll know it was a real test."

What I know for sure is, that road trip tested me in ways I'd never been tested before. In the end, I came home a different person. Maybe that will happen to young Charlie too.

A Word From The Authors

What fun to write a book with so many hilarious happenings interwoven with heartwarming moments. This novel was inspired by actual events. But, we'll leave it to the reader to figure out which of those events belonged to Mario, which to Marian, and which were simply made up.

And now, dear reader, *Thank you!*

Thank you for giving your time to read this book. It means a lot that you trusted us as authors to entertain and hopefully inspire you with this story. Stories need an audience, and we appreciate you being our audience for just a little while. Thank you.

Now we'd like to ask a favor—and we know this is a big request—if you enjoyed the story of Charlie, Jamal, and Sean and the events of their epic Road Trip, would you consider leaving a review wherever you bought this book or on your favorite social media platform? We'd love for as many readers as possible to discover this story, and your voice can help do that. Leave a review and tell a friend! Word-of-mouth is still the best way to introduce this story to other readers.

Just like it takes a village to raise a child, it also takes a lot of hands and eyes to raise up a novel worth reading. We owe much gratitude to our beta readers: my daughter Joanna Jones, whose eagle eye catches typos and passages that don't make sense; and Laurie Rabold, an avid reader and dear friend, whose suggestions made the finished work so much better.

Thanks to Judy Berthelot, who once lived in New Orleans and fed us the details about the French Quarter and the landscape and atmosphere surrounding the city. Judy also permitted us to use her late husband Elmo, a true Cajun, as a model for the lemonade street vendor.

Thanks to popular entertainer Bobby Goldsboro wrote a glowing endorsement. His song, "I'm a Drifter," fit nicely within the rambling escapades of our three main characters.

Thanks also to Dave Schlenker, an author and columnist in his own right, who took time away from his humor writing to give us a thumbs up endorsement.

Credit for the final work goes to our editor/publisher, Mike Parker of WordCrafts Press, who easily guides his writers over the hills and valleys and twists and turns of novel writing. He was also the "wise man" who provided the adage about "testing time" at the end of the epilogue.

Finally, thanks would not be complete without acknowledging the gifting and guidance of our Lord and Savior Jesus Christ, our Heavenly Father, and the Holy Spirit who leads us.

To God be the glory!

About Mario Villella

Mario Villella grew up in Ocala, Florida. He spent his early adult years as a youth minister in Rockwall, Texas, and Leesburg, Florida. A graduate of the University of Texas at Dallas with a degree in arts and performance, Mario has been involved in educational and community theater, teaching acting to students, and performing in plays like *The Comedy of Errors*, *The Sound of Music*, *Oliver!*, and *Beauty and the Beast*.

In 2011, he moved back to Ocala and started Good News Church with his wife, Heidi. They have three children and twenty-four chickens. He has written two other books titled, *Working Our Way Through Life* and *It Takes Two to Tangle*. Many—but not all—of the things that happen to the characters in this book, happened to him.

Mario's sermons can be viewed at Good News Church Ocala on YouTube.

About Marian Rizzo

A Pulitzer Prize nominee in the field of journalism, Marian Rizzo has won numerous awards, including the *New York Times Chairman's Award* and first place in the 2014 *Amy Foundation Writing Awards*. She worked for the *Ocala Star-Banner Newspaper* for thirty years and also wrote articles for the *Ocala Gazette, Ocala Style Magazine*, and Billy Graham's *Decision Magazine*.

Several of Marian's novels have won awards at Florida Christian Writers Conferences and Word Weavers International retreats. In 2018, her suspense novel, *Muldovah*, was a finalist in the Genesis competition at the American Christian Fiction Writers Conference. Two of her novels earned Amazon Best Seller status. Through interaction with other members of Word Weavers International, she's been able to hone her craft.

Marian lives in Ocala, Florida, has two daughters, three grand-children, and a dog named Buddy.

Also Available From

Wordcrafts Press

Land that I Love
by Gail Kittleson

Paint Me Fearless
by Hallie Lee

Little Reminders of Who I Am
by Jeff S. Bray

Oh, to Grace
by Abby Rosser

Maggie's Song
by Marcia Ware-Wilder

You've Got It, Baby!
Mike Carmichael

www.WordCrafts.net

Made in the USA
Columbia, SC
22 February 2024

31824160R00143